KENNEDY SUTTON

THE SNEAKY LASS

THE SILVER LOCKET, BOOK 1

NEVER MISS A RELEASE

The Silver Locket Series
    The Sneaky Lass
    Feathers at Sea (Coming August 2022)

NEVER MISS A RELEASE

If you're interested in delving deeper into these characters and the world of Goran through short stories, character interviews, deleted chapters, and a free gift upon sign up, please subscribe to my monthly newsletter at:
    www.kennedysutton.com

THE SNEAKY LASS

THE SILVER LOCKET, BOOK 1

KENNEDY SUTTON

Cover Artwork by Fruzsina Szanyó https://www.facebook.com/ChromesDesign

Copy and line editing by Lynne Blance, lynneblanceeditor@gmail.com

ISBN (ebook): 978-1-958453-00-1

ISBN (paperback): 978-1-958453-01-8

 Created with Vellum

Westley, my beautiful boy.
Rosalyn, my clever girl.
These characters came to me when we were up all night together in the early months of your lives. Thank you for listening to me sing shanties to you. I hope they gave you dreams of the sea.

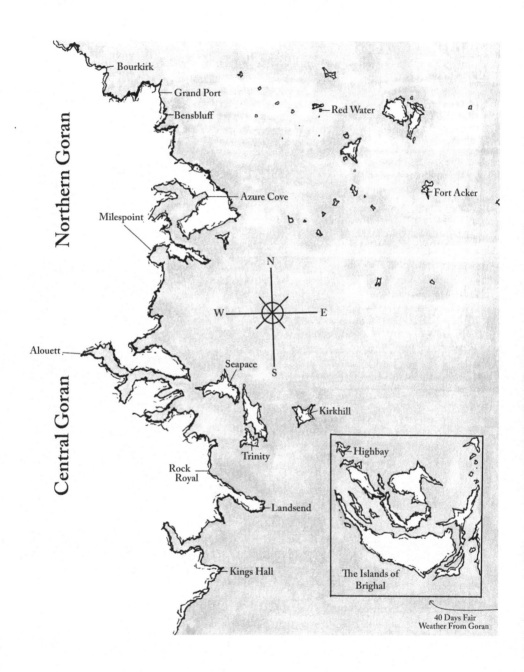

Northern Goran

Central Goran

Bourkirk

Grand Port

Bensbluff

Red Water

Fort Acker

Azure Cove

Milespoint

N

W — E

S

Alouett

Seapace

Kirkhill

Trinity

Rock
Royal

Highbay

Landsend

Kings Hall

The Islands of
Brighal

40 Days Fair
Weather From Goran

CHAPTER 1

My assailant is right beside me, but his words are hardly a murmur above the ringing in my brain.

Tham!

My head hits the wooden floor again. He thinks I deserve this. I did bite the most precious thing the man owns, after all. He should have paid me properly for his pleasure. It was not as we agreed.

He lifts me with one hand on my bicep and the other beneath my chin. My head hits the brick wall behind me. For a moment, I see nothing at all with my eyes wide open.

1

Blood trickles down the back of my neck and the dark room comes back into focus. The shadows on the man's face make him look like devils from a children's book my brother used to read to frighten me. White lights pop and fade in and out of existence before my vision. This thirty-something sailor with a beard and bad breath is going to kill me. A second ago, I might have let him.

I jam my knee between his legs and the moment his hands loosen on my neck, I duck beneath him and run out into the hall, flying down the stairs. Stars are still assailing me from all sides, but no one in this building is going to help me if I am caught. No one in all Grand Port would stop to help the likes of me. Probably no one in Goran.

I can hear the man shouting behind me, his voice coarse from my blow. I do not pause to look over my shoulder. I run through the frozen streets only slowing to avoid the ice that has reformed in the night, making the cobblestones slick. It would be a shame to escape death at the hands of a rough customer only to die from slipping in the street.

My chest is tight. With each throb of my heart, my skull is cleaved with pain. Eventually, I will run right into the sea if I do not stop, but like a frightened mouse I might run until death takes me.

Slowing my frantic pace, my heart threatens to beat clean out of my chest. I lean against a salt-eaten building near the docks. It supports my weight while I tuck my head between my knees. Holding the back of my head, sticky with drying blood, I try to catch my breath.

Awash with less acute panic now, my only problem is I cannot get enough air. At least it is only my own body that I must conquer.

I force myself to count breaths.

In. One. Two. Three.

Out. One. Two. Three.

With time, the space between heartbeats lengthens and my breathing returns less labored. I sink to the filth of Grand Port's gutters and alleyways, feeling nothing at all. I do not even feel relieved to have lived.

The hour is such that even the roughest Grand Port has to offer have found places to sleep in the little time remaining before dawn. Everything is silent save for one ship anchored. A ship that flies no colors. The ship arrived nearly two weeks ago to make a great deal of repairs. The men aboard have frequented the brothels. I have listened to them only as much as I listen to customers speak of anything. They have told harrowing tales of what happened to bring them to the northern tip of the empire in such a state.

The vessel is nearly ready to sail again, and the men aboard are singing a common drinking song on its deck. I cannot make out the words, but the tune is clear enough. Their low voices waft across the still night air.

On the ground with my knees pulled tight against my chest and music in the air, I am almost able to forget the way I came to be here. How he had taken me in ways in which we had not agreed. He did not even pay me for his pleasure.

My fingers rise to my bruised neck. Maybe it would have been better to just let him kill me. It is not as though tomorrow night will be any better. The rest of the nights for what promises to be a short life will look precisely like this. Someday, the night will end and me with it.

I lift my hand higher to my right eye, which is still sore to the touch from a customer who got rough last week. Countless other wounds litter the rest of me, invisible to anyone unless their gaze falls heavy upon my body. No one ever looks so closely at a whore. Is this not the same life I was running away from when I came to Grand Port?

With my nerves frayed to tatters, my mind returns to the two masts, silhouetted against the stars. A couple of the men were in the streets tonight soliciting for new crew between their drinking and whoring. They are struggling to find anyone who wishes to join them.

If only I could. Mine are the injuries every prostitute in this port town share. I would see us all saved, but I would accept saving only myself. I would damn all these wretched women to a lifetime of this if I was saved. My own soul is beyond redemption anyway.

I do not care if those sailors are pirates or if monsters chase their ship as some whisper. If I were a man, I would jump on their offer. I would sail with them for free if it got me out of here.

As the deep baritone of the sailor's song trails off into silence, I watch the lanterns get blown out on the mysterious ship save the one of the men on watch. I envy those men, and all men. No matter how dire their situations, they will never sink so low as me. Perhaps I should be more grateful. At least I always have something to sell.

Every muscle in my legs rebels when I drag my exhausted body upright, straighten my skirts, and run my fingers through the hair that has fallen from its braid. I must get back to the madam and her brothel before they give my cot to some other poor girl. I am in for it when I get there, too. The madam will not care that I might have been killed, but she absolutely will care that I did not stick around to make him pay me for it. Pay *her*.

I am certain I look like a frightful mess and the streets are only populated by the occasional staggering drunk, but maybe I can make the money I have lost before I make it back to my bed. The thought of one more set of hands on me feels like an impossible task. Bile rises in my throat even imagining it. Thankfully, sex is not the only way to make money in town full of drunk sailors.

Farther from the docks I pass the stumbling stragglers from the night's reveling. I scan each man in much the same way that they scan me. I look for loose purses where they look for swaying hips. Most appear as though they have already spent their coin for the night, but not all of them.

Ahead a man with short dark curls, with a beard trimmed close to his jaw and a crooked nose like it has been broken badly before, stumbles. He is not too tall, but sturdy like an oak, or he would be sturdy like an oak if he were not stumbling drunk. He holds his hat in one hand and a nearby wall with the other.

I have found my prey.

I approach with purpose and try to look like I have not had the life beaten out of me. Discreetly, I lick the blood away from my lips.

He does not even notice me until I have one hand on his shoulder and another on his belt, carefully feeling for purse strings.

Smiling with what I hope is not a busted lip, I purr by his ear, "You look like you could use some company, sailor."

His eyes take longer than they should to focus on me. When they do, they land on my bruised neck and his brow furrows. He shakes his head and attempts to weave away from me, but falters. I feign catching him out of concern but mean only to keep his belt in reach.

The drunken man nods in thanks for my aid and then sees the lustful look I have leveled at him. He once again notices how my hand rubs circles on his chest. His eyes shadow with disgust and he corrects the notion I am working so hard to give him.

He slurs, "You're not my type. I'll be on my way."

Running my hand along his belt, I brush his heavy coin purse near his back. I push my bottom lip out in a pout. "Not into blondes?"

He responds flatly, "Not into desperate."

I finish untying his purse from his belt with deft and sober fingers just as he pushes me aside. I move demurely from beneath the press of his hands and rush away, playing the part of rejected strumpet, smirking.

I only make it six steps.

Arms wrap around me and lift me off the ground. I do not even have time to shout or bite before the purse is out of my cold hands. In an instant, my prey has sobered up. I keep struggling in his grip as he growls at me, "Don't steal from a thief, girl."

The stranger throws me down onto the frozen pebbled path and lifts his arm to strike me. I felt the pistols on his belt just as surely as I felt his purse. My muscles go still with fear. I would beg him for mercy, but I cannot find any words. It has been too long and too terrible a night.

His eyes shift between fury and pity, but his mouth remains set in a scowl. I cover my face with my hands and wait for a beating that never comes.

Three silver coins land on the ground beside me, more than three times what I am worth.

The man saunters away into the night muttering like he must remind himself why he has not killed me.

I only catch a few words. The last of them sounds more pitying than anything else. "She's only desperate."

I do not stick around to give him a chance to change his mind. I collect the silver from the dirt and run again, my soreness and exhaustion forgotten. I do not have a home to return to, but I have a cot and a few walls that promise some protection from the chill air that blows in from the sea tonight. I do not want to give fates and gods any more chances to keep me from them.

CHAPTER 2

I WAKE FROM A NIGHTMARE DRENCHED IN SWEAT. IT IS ONE OF THE SAME dreams I have often. I hear what I think is a crying lamb and go searching for it only to find the lamb has been torn apart by some foul beast. I have had the dream countless times, but it startles me just the same. This evening, there is no time to be distraught over it.

The madam shouts loudly enough that anyone on the block would hear her through the thin walls. "Wake up, ladies. I do not let you sleep here for free."

Unlike when she first brought me here under the guise of safety, in this she speaks the truth.

She takes nearly every cent we earn in exchange for handling everything else. The shift I am wearing, the shoes tucked under my blankets, the small room I share with fourteen other women above the tavern below, even the ribbons in my hair, all belong to her and the house.

Some were up before the madam's bellow to get an early start with the men who have come to port by day. I do not see much point in rushing, though maybe if I did, I would not have to botch robberies to make up for lost coins. As though the madam can hear my thoughts, she comes up behind me and pinches my thigh hard enough to bruise through my shift.

Yelping, I pull away from her.

The madam glowers at me and reminds me of the same threat she gave last night when I arrived short for the night. "Remember what I said, Jane Polk. Do better or you will sleep on the streets."

I scowl at her turned back as she stomps out of the room. Her ire is worth the three silver pieces I still have tucked in my bodice. I am not sure why I wanted to keep them. The three coins fill me with shame. That man had clearly been a good enough sort. I tried to rob him blind. He could have killed me and did not.

They also fill me with hope. Hope that there is one man in all the world who would not kill a whore for being precisely what she is: desperate.

After tying my skirts up high around my thighs, I re-tie my long, blonde braid, and pinch some color into my pale cheeks. Another woman is tying my corset without me having to ask. I return the favor by lacing hers when she finishes with mine.

I check my reflection quickly, having only one mirror for a room full of women. My husband would often tell me that my hair was too lovely for my face. He would say the rest of me was stretched too thin. Looking at my pointed face and boyish figure, I cannot help thinking he was right. Cruel, but right.

Last night only added more evidence to the mountain of proof that I would be better off almost anywhere but here, but this is better than the marriage I left behind. I know what rock bottom looks like. This resembles it but so long as my name remains one of my own choosing, this is a step above.

I follow the others into the hall below. The tables downstairs are beginning to fill with men eager for the comforts of land. Some look my way, but none call me over. One man stands out from the rest. Blue eyes like ice are surveying the room, half hidden by hair the color of a shined, copper coin. His arms are covered in colorful and detailed tattoos the likes of which I have rarely seen. They are marks I have only seen on strangers from the eastern islands of Brighal. Strange men with stranger customs, they do not come this way often and none have ever looked like this man.

Most importantly, the red-headed man looks like the gentle type. I approach the table where he is sitting alone, thinking I might have an easier evening ahead than the last one. I lean in close, and his head snaps up.

"Can I do you a service, sailor?"

He is shaking his head before I even finish my question and scans the room once more, suddenly more aware of his surroundings. "Not unless you know any sailors looking for work, miss."

Laughing flirtatiously, I take a seat beside him. "Miss? Such a gentleman. I am afraid I am not in the business of knowing men's trades. They are usually more interested in mine."

I put a hand on his thigh but before I can say more a gruff looking man with anchors tattooed on his neck shoves me from my seat like I am but an annoying object in his way. I can gain no purchase and fall on the sticky floor.

Enough sailors have slipped between my thighs for me to recognize the anchors marked on his neck as a common enough design. They likely hold some meaning, but it is lost on me.

On his hip, the newcomer carries a nine-tailed whip made of

supple, brown leather with a polished wooden handle. He proceeds to speak to the beautiful sailor as though I never existed there. The man with blue eyes shoots me an apologetic smile but says nothing in my defense. I do not really expect him to.

Dusting myself off, I whisper the foulest curse I know and a few others at the new man under my breath. Being pushed to the floor is hardly the worst that has happened to me since coming to Grand Port. It is probably not the worst that will happen to me tonight. Still, he did not even pay me to push me around.

I stomp off in search of someone who will give me coin for service but hesitate before the threshold. One of fifteen in the warm hall is one thing. Last I entered the streets I nearly died.

Bile fills my mouth, and my feet turn to lead. I might have convinced that pretty red head to my side. If the man with anchors on his neck is why I die in a gutter tonight, I will haunt him.

Trudging into the streets where I earn my keep, I find the air has grown even more frigid tonight than the last and the sun has not even set. My thin shoes crack the ice that has formed between the small stones in the street. I force myself to walk with my arms at my side despite desperately wishing to cross them for warmth. I unclench my fingers so that they gently sway with my arms, beckoning any interested party with my ease.

Most men only like uncomfortable women if it is them causing the discomfort.

Sailors have filled the shanties and alleyways of Grand Port after long weeks at sea with purses full of coins. I am trying to catch one on my line like a fisher of men when I overhear a conversation which, on any other night, would have gone unnoticed. I am not sure why fate has intervened, that I hear it now, intrigued enough to be distracted from my task.

An older man who is missing a few fingers and a few teeth speaks in a ragged voice to a younger man. "That ship blown full o' holes that came in to make repairs is settin' out in the morning. Looked like seedy folk. They won't find many people willing to take up with their lot here."

They are speaking of the same ship I saw last night. Everyone has been discussing the flagless ship for weeks, but tonight I listen closer. My fantasies of running away return in full force. With the right disguise, it would not be so impossible. I spend enough time with men to know how to walk like one. I am unremarkable. Perhaps no one would even look twice.

The man with anchors tattooed on his neck certainly did not.

The younger man with sandy hair and a nice pair of boots sounds excited and more than a little drunk as he answers his older companion, "There are plenty of rough sort in Grand Port, but no one wants to ride with pirates who are so clearly running from something. The men I heard were speaking of southern waters. They were running hard to have come all the way here and then to be nearly sunk..."

Pirates would be even less likely to notice me. They come and go at each port. I could disappear into wherever they stop next. I could change my name again.

The older, rougher man scoffs and speaks like someone who is tasked with teaching a lesson, "Who's sayin' they're pirates?"

The young man continues eagerly, unaware of his companion's annoyance, "They are not navy men, that's for certain, and merchants would have something to sell or buy. What else could they be but villains?"

The young man stands at the same height as me and an insane plan starts to form. I have been desperate many times in my life, but I have never felt a call for survival quite like I do now. A desperate ship in need of crew may look past my obvious lack of experience for an extra set of hands. Even hands as unused to hard labor as mine.

The men finally notice me standing nearby and the older one smiles wickedly at me. "You lookin' for a good time, girl?"

I try replacing a cringe with a smile and speak in a practiced, breathy voice, "Hmm, maybe if your young friend would like a go."

I try to lure the boy in and put one hand on my hip and the other on the young man's chest.

His older friend snarls, but the younger one grins widely at me and knocks the old man's shoulder. He is probably not quite twenty, handsome, and looks like he has a home to return to somewhere. Somewhere nearby if his fair coloring is any indication. I also think his boots might fit me.

The younger of the pair steps towards me and I reach for the collar of his shirt. He taunts his companion over his shoulder as I lead him away, "You've had your days in the sun, old man. Let the young dogs play."

I think his coat would fit me well enough, too. If I bloused his shirt a bit, no one would notice what little waist I have.

"Let's find somewhere a bit more private." I whimper sweetly as I pull him down the alleyway, "I feel shy."

My heart is pounding in my chest as I think of what I will do next. This is not rock bottom. These streets, these men, they are not the worst my life has ever offered me, but I do not have anything to lose. If I die tonight, I will still not be in my husband's house. I will not be beneath my father's roof. I will die with a name of my choosing. That is not rock bottom.

The man leans into my touch. "Whatever makes the lady happy."

Couples rut against walls on our way around the back of the brothel. The air is so cold that I can see my breath, but it does not stop others... or me. Most of them are so drunk they probably cannot feel it. My partner is already stumbling from drink as I lead him by the hand. From his swagger, I doubt he feels chilled.

I have been waiting for an opportunity to leave the brothel since I arrived. The fingers of the violent man from last night still a painful memory on my neck. The raised hand of the forgiving man who could have killed me in the street with no consequence sticks in my mind. His silver coins press into my skin beneath my corset.

The memories urge me to continue despite the tremble of my hands and quickened heart. Anywhere would be better than here.

As soon as we round the corner the young man has me pinned against the wall next to a stack of firewood. He kisses my neck, and I let him. Searching my surroundings for anything that will help set my plan in motion, my fingers wrap into his hair with one hand and grasp a small log from a pile of firewood beside me with the other.

If I do not get this right, he will sound the alarm. I try to imagine every time my husband took a swing at me. The bend of his arm and the fluid motion of it. I can do this.

The boy's hands begin snaking up my borrowed skirt and into the folds of my sex, I sigh in a practiced way, luring him with the only bait that I have. He closes his eyes and begins using his free hand to release himself from his trousers. His voice is husky, and his words slur from drink when he pays me what he might think is a compliment. "You're gonna feel so good."

I take a deep breath. He bites my neck, his fingers twining into my hair. I push him away from me and scarcely notice his fury before I swing the firewood as hard as I can with both arms. I hit him in the temple, sending him splayed to the ground before shock can register on his face. He looks peaceful save for the blood soaking into the dirt beneath his head.

For a few moments I stand above him, stunned and shaking. His breath comes in shallow starts, and his right temple, eye, and cheek are already turning a sickly dark color. Damn. Damn. Oh, damn me and all the fates and gods together, I might have killed him!

I am also supposed to be in a hurry.

I pull off his clothing from the bandana on top of his head to his socks and boots. All of them are simple, but well made. There is a jackknife in his pocket that I slip in between my breasts. I take his coin purse as well. Guilt churns in my guts over it.

Leaving the young man in the icy alley, naked with blood pooling around his head, I do not allow myself to look back to see if he still breathes. My mind begins to create pictures of a mother, a father, a younger sister, perhaps. I swallow the rising vomit and turn my thoughts away. None of that can matter and I am far from finished with my night.

Moving as quickly as I can without tripping over my own feet, I bolt down and away before anyone discovers my crime. Just like last night, I do not stop running until I come to the docks and the ships are in reach. The unmarked vessel is being loaded by borrowed barge to cast off with the next tide. I have no clear idea when that tide will come, but it cannot be long now, and I will not allow myself to miss this chance. Not when death chases me like a shadow.

The street lamps are lit by the time I weave my way through dark streets to the water. Most men are busy carousing in the main town, leaving this industrial place by the docks empty. I duck into the dark between two warehouses and pull out the stolen knife from between my breasts.

My hands are shaking. From the cold or from the knowledge of what I have started, I am uncertain. Nothing remains in Grand Port for me, and a few feet of my long hair is a small price to pay for freedom. In a different life, it was a sign of my devotion to the many gods in the heavens above. Now, I suppose I am beyond such things. If gods watch me, they long ago gave up on leading me to light.

Still, it is the only part of me that anyone would ever have considered beautiful. I have spent a lifetime vainly caring for my hair. I will have to find something else to like about myself.

With a steadying breath, I hold the stolen knife up to my braid. Another deep breath and I touch the cold metal to my hair and then pull it away. Tears spring to my eyes. It is too late to back out now. Someone will notice my victim sooner rather than later. It is hair. It means nothing.

I hate to part with it.

One more time, I pull my hair back in my fist. Eyes clenched shut, I saw through the top of my braid.

Slowly, I release my held breath in a shuddering sigh. My hair now rests in a pile by my feet. Carefully, I avoid looking at it or else I may lose what small grasp I hold over myself. I have no mirror to check but running my hands through it several times I am confident it is all roughly the same length by my ears.

Tears sting my eyes and run down my face. Panic rips at my chest. *What have I done?*

There is no time to contemplate it, but what I did to that boy feels very different from what I did to my husband. The boy did not do anything to me and I... I cannot think about it until I stop.

I wipe my eyes and step out of my dress. When I loosen the ties of my corset, I find the three silver pieces stuck to my skin so tightly that when I pull them off myself, the king's crown can be clearly seen dented on my ribs.

Shivering naked in the winter night, I start the task of replacing my dress with the young man's warm clothing. Using the small knife once more, I cut apart the cotton shift from under my discarded dress and bind my chest with it. I tie the bandana over my freshly hacked hair and pick up the slightly large boots. They are of a fine make and the tops of each one is embossed with a set of initials. *D.A.*

My tall, boyish figure has finally come in handy. The

stranger's clothes fit me well. I tuck the blade into the pocket of my stolen trousers and finish the look by dropping the three silver pieces from the kind man last night into my boot. Maybe they will be lucky. I could use some luck.

When I step back into the street, my reflection is illuminated by the flickering street lamps in the window of the docking office. I do not recognize the young man staring back at me. Perhaps he is a bit round at the jawline, but enough to pass to those who do not care to look too closely. His blonde hair is longer by his ears and short, almost to his scalp, in the back under a bandana that lies low on his brow.

The bruises on my face and neck aid in his disguise; he is just the desperate type who may take up with pirates. He looks nothing like Jane Polk, the woman running away from a brothel. He looks nothing like Jane Richards, the woman running away from her husband. He looks nothing like Jane Mason, the girl her father lost in a game of cards to a widower three times her age.

I do not know this stranger.

He could be anyone.

CHAPTER 3

A FAMILIAR ANXIETY WASHES OVER ME AS I LEAVE JANE BEHIND IN THE alleyway with her locks of blonde hair and a shredded dress. I have left behind a lot of lives lately. It has felt much the same each time. Like jumping off a swing and being faced with not knowing how I will land. I might break my ankle, but I have already jumped.

I half-jog to the docks, not giving myself time to think about the absurdity of what I am doing. I catch the first man I see by the arm as he rolls a barrel towards the barge they are using to load the anchored ship. Despite the chill air, he is covered in a fine sheen of sweat.

KENNEDY SUTTON

He jumps when I grab him and shouts at me like I have appeared from the air rather than run up beside him in heavy boots. "Gods and fates, boy!"

Inwardly, I smile at the title. At least in the dark I am fooling someone. The man has long, brown hair pulled into a bun on the back of his head and a full beard. I recognize the whip on his hip before I recognize his face. He is the man who pushed me aside at the brothel. It cannot have been more than an hour since.

He never looked twice at me then, perhaps he will not recognize me now.

Trying and failing to keep my voice steady and natural, all my words tumble out of me in a rush. "I heard in the streets that you need crew. Is it true?"

He gives me a once over from the tips of my boots to the top of my head. I stand a bit straighter under his scrutiny but keep my face in shadow. He shakes his head at what he sees and says, "Dumb to be running away from home, dontcha' think? What happened? Pick the wrong pocket? Young love, unrequited?"

When I do not answer, he runs an arm over his brow and groans out, "What's your name?"

With only a half second to think, I look at my new boots and spit out the first name that comes to mind. "I am Dixon Ables, sir."

The man looks at me skeptically, whether because he knows I am lying about my name or some far worse reason.

"I am smarter than I look. Stronger than I look, too."

Both statements feel like lies, but I finish with some honesty even as my desperation seeps into my tone. "I will work very hard if you will have me, sir." I will not be turned away.

The name Dixon Ables belonged to a long dead neighbor from my youth. I hope his ghost does not mind my stealing it. I look back down at the boots on my feet. *D.A.* I hope the man I took

18

these boots from wakes up. I hope he has been found and made warm again.

Grumbling, the man before me abandons his load for someone else to take up and finally responds. "Beggars and choosers and all that. Fine. We're in no position to turn down a pair of hands. Even soft ones. You can run errands until someone thinks of a use for you. Follow me."

I fall in after him, my entire body alight with something akin to fear but more exciting. It makes me crave jumping into an ice bath. In an attempt to clear some of that restlessness from myself, I ask, "What do I call you, sir?"

My voice comes out higher than I meant, but the man ahead does not appear to have noticed any change.

"You keep calling me 'sir' and you'll do fine, boy."

It is not lost on me that he has already discarded my fake name. I follow him onto a small rowing boat. He steps in first with sure footing even as the boat rocks beneath him. I tail after him, falling to my seat quickly before I trip into the dirty waters of the docks.

Alongside us are a few others leaving the work on the barge to the next shift of sailors in a pecking order I do not yet understand.

The boat rocks beneath me and no one even bothers to give me an oar, the look of me alone informing everyone that I would not know what to do with one. They all look like sailors. You can pick tar out of a crowd if you know what you are looking at, and tar always knows useless when they see it. It is a conversation heard in the streets of Grand Port every day a dozen or more times. These men are as weatherworn as sailors come. Sunburned and windblown with large, dirty, calloused hands. The ones that look at me mostly smirk and shake their heads much as the man who has brought me along did.

When we come to the ship, it is larger than I expected, having only seen it from shore. Looking up the hull with only a rope ladder to climb it, my stomach does a somersault.

One of the strangers beside me takes my hand in his to inspect my palms, laughs, and announces loud enough for all to hear, "Boy's never climbed a staircase, be ready to play catch."

The men about me roar with laughter and push me towards the ladder first. My body rebels against the idea of standing in the rocking boat so close to the water where I would certainly drown. My cringe is obvious and brings on more teasing, but also a few sympathetic looks.

My fear of the dark depths lapping at the side of the boat where I sit is the only thing that makes me brave enough to take the rope ladder in hand and climb. I force my eyes heavenward, up the hull, and pretend there is less at stake than my life.

I breathe a sigh of relief when I come to the ship's deck and have something sturdier beneath my feet, even if I still feel unsteady.

A few men look my way while working a hundred jobs I know nothing about, but never more than a passing glance. The man who brought me here finishes his climb and leads me towards the back of the ship, or is it the front? The raised bit.

A sailor shouts at us from across the deck, "Looks like you've got a mutt on your tail, Hugh."

I look back at the man who brought me aboard and memorize his face and name: Hugh, the man with anchors tattooed on his neck and a whip at his hip.

Hugh answers flatly, "A mutt would know more about ships."

I keep looking at my feet. My heart pounds out of my chest. That I have gotten this far is a miracle. If I can keep up the ruse until they lift anchor, it would be more trouble to return me than to keep me aboard. I make keeping my disguise until we are out of sight of land my first and only goal.

There are doors ahead set beneath the stairs of the raised

deck, but that is not where I am led. Hugh leads me up the steps and then through a hatch on the raised deck. I climb down a ladder after him into semi-darkness, only a single candle in a glass case lights the small space. Before I have let go of the rungs, Hugh tosses a roll of canvas from a pile at me. I fumble it to my feet and quickly pick it up. A hammock is what I have failed to catch.

A kid with shaggy, black hair is in a hammock only a few inches from me, watching with interest as he chews on something. Whatever it is, it makes the entire passageway smell sickly sweet.

On a door at the end of the narrow hall hangs a weathered piece of parchment where the names and marks of hundreds of men stain the page. Nine commandments to which everyone on the ship is held are printed neatly above the names of sailors, most of whom must be gone now, one way or another.

Hugh knocks on the door and is called inside by a voice that sounds familiar, but I cannot place it.

I try to calm myself with the reminder that men often sound alike. This ship has been docked for weeks. How many of their number have I met in that time? I recall a few faces from my nights working. Hopefully, the men who sought my services will not remember mine.

Left to wait in the cramped passageway with the boy who looks like he needs a bath, all I can smell is the candy he is chewing. I am grateful for that.

He catches my eye and smiles in greeting. "Ever been on a ship before?"

I shake my head.

"If ya' retch, ya' better not wake me with it." The boy grins mischievously and though he speaks teasingly, I can hear he is kindly meant.

My study of some of the marks and names on the page is so

intent that I jump when the door opens. Hugh has returned with a dipped quill in one hand and his pistol in the other. Behind him stands yet another familiar face. Hazel eyes look me up and down nonchalantly from behind a bent nose and short, brown hair. The cocked hat is on his head rather than in his hand and he is no longer drunk, but it is unquestioningly the man I tried to rob last night. The man who did not strike me and threw the three silver pieces which are now in my stolen boot.

My goal of keeping this up until we cast off now seems out of reach.

Hugh watches the new man pass and speaks familiarly like they have known one another a long time, "I'm right behind you, Ben."

Ben looks from me to Hugh, his amusement is only a huff of air between them. "You're always bringing aboard strays, Hugh. Best keep this one with Harry or he'll be eaten alive."

The man's eyes return to me, and I stupidly meet them. He smiles in what appears to be a mix of genuine kindness and disbelief. For a moment, I fear I am found out, but he only adds, "Maybe he will surprise us. You a quick learner?"

Nodding, I answer in a hurry, taking great care to keep my voice flatter than my usual. "Yes, sir."

He corrects me, "It's captain."

I wince at being so obviously out of place. "Sorry, Captain."

My stomach rises into my throat. This is his ship, and I tried to rob him. I look at my stolen boots and then turn my gaze around the small hall so he might not get a good look at me. I am lucky to be hidden in the dim lantern light. This was a terrible, stupid idea. One of my worst, and that is really saying something.

The captain clears his throat and I slide out of his way so he can pass me and climb onto deck. If he recognized me, he did not show it. I calm my racing heart. I could still make this work. Even if the captain remembers the girl from last night, he has no reason to think that she is now the young man, Dixon Ables. My coloring is the same as many in Grand Port.

Hugh instructs me to place my right hand over his gun. I do as I am told. Mistakenly assuming I cannot read it myself, he reads each commandment aloud to me. I listen quietly.

I. Every man shall obey the captain's command.

II. Every man shares an equal vote in affairs of the moment; equal shares of provisions, strong liquors when taken, unless scarcity makes changes necessary.

III. If any man runs away or keeps any secret from this company, he will be marooned with one bottle of powder, one bottle of water, a small arm, and shot.

VI. The captain shall have half of all prizes and one full share; Ship's surgeon will have two shares; the quartermaster, master gunner, and master carpenter will have one share and a half. All crew have equal shares. Ship's boys will have a half share.

V. If any man steals from the company or strikes one another whilst these articles are in force, they shall suffer forty lashes to their bare back at the crew's discretion.

VI. Any man to fire his arms, smoke a pipe without a cap, or carry a candle without a cover shall suffer the same punishment as the former article.

VII. All men should keep their arms clean and fit for engagement. Failure in this will be punished as the captain and company sees fit.

VIII. If any man loses a limb, they shall receive compensation in eighty pieces of silver per limb. If a joint is lost, forty.

IX: If at any time you meet with a prudent woman or take a boy, the man who meddles without consent shall suffer death as the quartermaster sees fit.

· · ·

At the same moment that Hugh reads the final article, the boy behind me adds, "An' you've got to kiss the coin!"

Before I can question what the kid meant, Hugh reaches around me to smack him on the ear. "Of course he'll kiss the coin, boy! Hardly needs saying."

I do not know what the coin is, but I would kiss the rude, leathery man before me to stay on this ship. Hugh turns his eyes back to me and the younger says no more, clearly admonished.

I swear on Hugh's pistol to live by the rules and then sign my new name with the quill. *Dixon Ables.*

The third article is seared into my mind. I have never signed my name to lies before, yet there it is.

If any man runs away or keeps any secret from this company, he will be marooned with one bottle of powder, one bottle of water, a small arm, and shot.

My plan of making it until cast off quickly changes to making it to the next port. I have no idea how to manage it, but I must. When we set off in the morning, my husband's ghost will be left behind me. The madam will never know or care what became of me. I will be replaced in no time with some other desperate girl. Whatever happens now, it is happening to someone new.

Hugh appears to agree with the captain's assessment and motions to the passage we stand in, so small that all three of us touch while in it. "You sleep in here with Harry, boy. Captain's right, forecastle's nowhere for you. It'd just cause trouble."

Hugh leaves and it is just Harry and I, so close I can feel his breath on my skin.

The boy with hair in his eyes holds out a dirty hand for me to shake. "I'm Harry Lewis. Nice to meet ya', Dixon."

I take his hand and he shakes it enthusiastically.

"Don't get no ideas or nothin'. You're bigger and older than me, but I've been at this longer. That was Hugh Digby. He's the quartermaster. Since you're not used to ships, I'll tell you that it means he's a sour, mean man who will beat you for your misdeeds, so keep it together. Captain's named Holt, but you just call him captain." He smiles brightly and I smile back. I get the feeling that young Harry Lewis means well to everyone.

I do my best imitation of a solute and answer him as I have seen navy sailors speak to lieutenants before, "Aye, sir."

Harry snorts at being called sir and jumps from his hammock to lead me out. "Follow me ta' kiss the coin, Dix. We can't set off unless everyone does, and you don't wanna be the reason we lose the wind."

Despite fear of discovery, I follow Harry up onto deck. He is a friendly kid and already has taken me under his wing, I think. Though he cannot be a day over thirteen, I am more than happy to accept his tutelage. If I have enough humility and do what everyone says, no one will spare me a glance.

The coin to be kissed is a silver plate, nailed to the helm. On it, some goddess, likely the goddess of luck, was once stamped plainly. She has been worn smooth by the soft touches and lips of many sailors. I kiss her after Harry. Whatever superstitions belong to this crew, they now belong to me as well.

Men tie ropes to purposes I cannot begin to guess. There seems to be an endless number of tasks to be done before we are aweigh, and Harry and I are invited to none of them. Another familiar face with beautiful tattoos and copper curls walks past me at a brisk pace and then climbs the lines.

Without thinking I ask Harry, "Who is that man?"

Harry chews his lip and then pops another boiled candy between his teeth. "That's Mickey Compton, the second mate." He hesitates before adding, "And master gunner, cooper, and navigator."

I wonder how long one must be on ships to learn so much. "He wears many hats."

Harry looks up at Mickey, squints, and answers as though I am the simplest person he has ever met, "He ain't wearing a hat, Dix."

I do not have time to explain the expression before Harry is back to speaking a mile a minute, "He and Digby share the other room below. That door and hatch used to lead to just the captain's quarters, but Captain Holt built the passageway, and the extra room 'neath the quarterdeck. Hugh sealed the door up when Mickey moved in beside him. I have had that space all to myself until now. Not that I don't mind the company."

I note the second mate's name and the term for the raised bit of the ship, quarterdeck. Silently, I curse my rotten luck to have met three men on this ship before sneaking onto it and having all of them share the same small space under the deck with me. Harry does not seem to mind that I have not answered and continues chattering while I drift into my thoughts.

The sails and ropes above me are fascinating. Harry is still talking about other things when I interrupt him, "How would someone learn to sail? Has anyone thought to teach you?"

Harry shrugs. "If you make friends with the right people, they'll teach you. You'll learn a lot just by being around. There is plenty to it all that happens right here with boards beneath your feet. Right now, they prefer using me to fit in small spaces rather than climbing up and getting in the way."

He smiles as though he is very proud of his birdlike bones before giving me more advice. "Don't go poking around anyone yet. Digby is really big on everyone sticking to their own job."

I wonder what my job is.

I do not have any business wanting to learn more about this ship. I will not stay long. If I am lucky enough to make it to the next port, I will be out of here and not likely to ever step foot on a ship again. Still, like a man possessed, I watch the men above me on the masts. I want to be among them. I want to know everything.

CHAPTER 4

WHEN I ARRIVED ON *SNEAKY LASS*, I DID NOT ANTICIPATE GAINING adversaries. The quartermaster, Hugh Digby, is ill tempered, even with those he considers friends. Most of the crew seems to think it is a success when he does not acknowledge them. He dislikes the swabs. He kicks at Harry. He *hates* me.

From my first day aboard, his hand has always rested on the nine-tailed lash on his hip in my presence. So far, I have not committed any act terrible enough to have him untie the instrument from his side, but I have learned that it would not take much.

My first morning, Hugh threatened me on the grounds of not

waking quickly enough to the pipe. Months of sleeping primarily during the day made the transition to rising with the sun difficult. I stupidly attempted to explain that. If the second mate, Mickey Compton, had not interrupted so I could dart off, I am certain that my ruse would not have made it past raising anchors.

The second morning aboard, I attempted to redeem myself in the eyes of the quartermaster by waking up with the pipe and going to his door to ask if he needed anything from me. It turns out he had spent much of the night on deck helming the ship. That time, only his drowsiness and my quick feet saved me. I was grateful that by the time the quartermaster saw me again he seemed to have decided waking him early was not an offense worth skinning me for.

I think Hugh Digby believes that I am the dumbest person on this ship. He is right, to a point.

The men around me are speaking an entirely different language than the one I learned. Not only do many of the sailors use so many colorful curses that I do not always know their meaning; every rope and stick of wood on this floating city have a name and purpose. Stem, stern, belaying hooks, harpins, fore and aft sails, and about a thousand different lines. The different decks all have names, and the names change depending on who is speaking. It is the top deck when the men are holystoning, but the same boards are the weatherdeck when Hugh is barking at me to get up to it faster.

When below the ceiling is not called the ceiling and when I called it such everyone howled, but no one would tell me what it *was* called. I had to ask Harry in the evening to learn that it is called the deckhead. The walls are walls or bulkheads, but if you are outside the ship, it is the hull.

The windows can be windows if someone other than me says window, but they can also be portlights or ports. Those ports are not to be confused with the many other things called ports on a ship. The floors are not the floors, but the vertical bits that hold up the floor and what should be called the floor is something different, but I have not managed to sort it out just yet as it is such a mundane thing I am embarrassed to ask, and no one speaks of it.

Right is not right but starboard, and left is not left but port. And even when left and right are perfectly clear, any sailor about will look at you like you are ignorant or mad for using it because it could be tricky if I mean *my* left not *your* left, but port always means port... unless you mean windows.

That is not even beginning to discuss breezes and tides and everything else. No one has thought to teach me anything, but I get shouted at each time I am found ignorant. I have quickly learned it is best to pretend I am mute and catalogue information in silence as I come to it.

Today will be different.

It is my sixth day at sea and I am determined to put everything I have worked hard to memorize to use. When the pipe blows on deck to wake up the crew, I shoot upright. I do not want to get yelled at by Hugh for being idle, which is a grand task. The grouchy quartermaster thinks everyone but himself is idle at all times. Harry is still rubbing his eyes as I pull on my boots, which now have some canvas shoved into the toes, so they fit properly.

Only Mickey Compton has ever thanked me for any service I have done. I would be willing to put money on him being twenty-two, the same age as me. He would pass as a gentleman easily if not for the tattoos that trail from his jawline all the way down his arms to his fingertips. He may just be nice or have a soft spot for ignorant ship's boys. Perhaps he is not yet accustomed to just ordering me about. Mickey is also the only one aside from Harry that uses my chosen name, Dixon.

He is one of the only men aboard that can get a smile out of Hugh Digby. It is clear to me, and everyone else, that they are lovers. They make no secret of it. I had heard that such pairings were relatively commonplace at sea, at least outside the Navy, but I did not expect such openness.

My time spent as a prostitute means I have met men with every possible variation of preference, but they usually keep it to dark alleyways and paid company. I knew of houses that catered to their type in Grand Port. I pointed the way to more than one curious man seeking one out since they knew I would be in no position to judge their pleasures against them. I wonder if Mickey and Hugh came to this ship in order to be together or if they met upon it. I would not dare ask anyone such a thing to find out.

The second mate, among his many other titles, was helming last night, navigating towards the main shipping routes. Unfortunately, Hugh will likely be in a foul mood for having to sleep without his partner. Regardless, the second mate will have messages for others before he retires. I want to be the person who passes on those messages best.

Harry is not well known for his memory, but my aptitude for it is already beginning to stand out. I do not plan on staying, but while I am here, my life depends on being useful. If I am competent then maybe they will maroon me somewhere friendly when I am found out.

I tuck my shorn hair under my bandana, take the ladder up to the main deck, and report to the second mate.

Mickey, obviously ready to collapse after being at the helm most of the night, smiles weakly when I approach. He had been writing in a journal, but I can see it is not the typical jotted notes kept at the helm, but more private musings. He fans the ink as I climb up.

"Mr. Compton, sir, do you have need of me?"

The second mate shakes his head at my formal tone. "You don't need to call me sir. No one else does. Tell the Captain we're moving southeast at seven knots. Last night the lookout spotted the lanterns of a sloop flying under blue birds, but they didn't see us."

I suppose a ship flying under the blue flags of the Goranese Navy would be news worth sharing among wanted pirates like those I have taken up with.

Nodding in understanding, I repeat the instructions back to him. The tired second mate looks appreciative and then his words are nearly consumed by a dramatic yawn. "Thanks, Dix. Knew I could count on you. Tonight, spend some time by me after the pipe sounds."

I know I look like a grinning fool, but the offer is exciting. I remember what Harry said about learning to sail. Maybe Mickey would teach me...

My thoughts die before they run away with me. I have no business learning to sail. Ignoring his request to not be called sir, I answer before running below deck once more. "Yes, sir."

Harry is still trying to rub the sleep from his eyes in his hammock. I listen at the captain's door to ensure he is moving around and awake inside. After accidentally waking Hugh earlier in the week, I am not eager to repeat the mistake.

I fear that if anyone would recognize me from Grand Port, it would be the captain. The quartermaster barely looked at me as Jane. Mickey Compton had avoided my gaze. Captain Holt looked in my eyes and knew I stole from him. Harry has handled most of the captain's chores so far. I have allowed it despite meaning I have to see Hugh more often.

Captain Bennett Holt is only a few years older than me, at most. It seems like an older man should oversee an entire ship, but it is becoming abundantly clear to me that the rules I was raised with do not apply well to my new life as a pirate aboard *Sneaky Lass*. Piracy is a young man's game.

Apparently, when they take ships or make port, he dresses flamboyantly and makes a big show of looking like a dangerous pirate who is not to be messed with. On any other day of sailing, no one would know him from any other sailor. He works just as hard as his men. He knows how to work every part of the ship from rigging to carpentry, so far as I can tell. Primarily, though, he decides where the best bet of the next payday will come from. The men vote on directions and plans for prizes, but almost all trust his calls above any others.

I find myself watching the captain a great deal mostly to ensure he is not watching me and have caught him staring in my direction more than once. I do not know if it is because I make stupid mistakes in his presence or because he suspects something is off about me. Both, maybe.

On deck, I have noticed he wears a silver locket around his neck on a thick chain that he toys with when he is idle. I wonder why he cherishes it, or if it is cherished at all. Perhaps it is just habit.

Harry's chuckle from his hammock shakes me from my musings.

"Gotta go in there at some point, Dix, and if you're not quick, Digby will trounce you for it."

I roll my eyes at my young friend, not pointing out that he is still lounging, and knock on the captain's door. Ushered in by a low grunt, I find the captain in a state of undress. In only his trousers and boots, I imagine he must be chilled. Each day we travel south it gets warmer, but it is still cool in the morning air. He looks up and I look down, not wanting him to get a good look at me.

The captain sighs impatiently. "Spit it out, Dixon."

I am so surprised he knows the name I have taken, that I look up at him, mouth agape, before remembering my purpose. "Captain Holt, Mickey wanted me to tell you that we are moving southeast at seven knots. Last night the lookout spotted a ship flying blue flags, but they did not see us nor care if they did."

At the mention of the Imperial Navy his hands rise to the locket about his neck. He rubs the face of it with the rough pad of his thumb. A nervous habit.

"Good. Tell Hugh to continue the course and watch the new swabs. I will not tolerate their drunkenness on my ship during the day." He continues dressing as though I am not present.

I nod towards the floor. "Yes, sir."

"It's Captain." He flashes a congenial grin, showing off his straight teeth that are a little too big for his mouth.

I could kick myself. "Yes, Captain. Sorry. Shit, I thought I would do better today."

The sound of his laugh reminds me of my brother's growing up. Hearty. "You're doing fine. It doesn't even matter. Go."

He winks at me, which I decide is close enough to words of gratitude. In fact, on a ship full of men who make me the butt of every joke, a wink is downright friendly. He seems like a genuinely nice person. I wish I had not tried to steal from him. His three silver coins slide against the bottom of my left foot, a reminder of his kindness and my wretchedness.

I leave to find the quartermaster and am both relieved and disappointed to be out of sight of Captain Holt. If not for my careful lies, being in the captain's presence would feel easy.

Harry nods in my direction when I pass, which brings up my mood a touch, too. It is nice to be a part of something. Even as one of the lowest ranks on the ship, I get more respect aboard *Sneaky Lass* as Dixon the ship's boy than Jane did anywhere.

CHAPTER 5

Days on *Sneaky Lass* are long, but not always busy. So long as the winds are fair, most of being on a ship's crew is as simple as that: being present. Apparently, some captains will make up work to busy idle hands. One of the perks of piracy is avoiding such measures.

I am relieved to have been invited to stay by Mickey Compton tonight. I am not eager to return below deck. I fear if I go below Hugh will make good on his threat to bloody my hide for catching me convincing one of the sailors to teach me more about the standing rigging.

The rigger in question, a man named James, with the darkest

skin I have ever seen, seemed to enjoy teaching me and said I caught on quickly. The quartermaster told me to know my place. I am in no hurry to see if Hugh's threat holds any truth.

We have spent our time sailing on strange courses to avoid as many ships as possible. It is even more clear to me now than in Grand Port that *Sneaky Lass* is desperately avoiding something. Be it navy or monster, no one has told me yet. Tomorrow we will sail the main trade routes. All I know is that the next ship we see, we will board and steal from. The men state it like there is no possibility of failure.

Mickey ties the helm in place with a length of rope and sits beside me on the steps. The sun has set, and I wish I had another layer of clothing to put on. I think most of the crew does. The wind coming off the sea makes everything colder. Each day we sail south, it will grow warmer. I am eager for it.

The second mate points out the sailor who had been teaching me earlier in the day and says, "I heard you met James."

I wince, knowing the quartermaster must have been speaking of me. "Yes."

"He's the best sailor on this ship. He's been at it longer than almost anyone. The only reason he's not captain is because he does not want to be. Well, that and he cannot read or write a word."

I find my voice, deciding to ask my question even though I do not know if I should. "Is that why Hugh was so mad about me slowing him down?"

Mickey smiles, as he easily does. "Don't flatter yourself, Dixon. You wouldn't be able to slow James down if you rode on his back. You want to learn something about sailing? We have a greater need of capable hands than boys."

My heart thrums to life. I have started trying to memorize all the parts of the ship. I have my work cut out for me, but when I give a message about the foremast repair, I would like to know what is being referred to.

Every single one of these men has something I desperately want. They have a trade. Unless prostitution counts, I am not likely to ever find one as Jane.

Despite every reason to decline, I nod. The rules on the charter were vague, likely for a reason. Keeping a lie from the company, big or small, results in the same fate. I may as well try to learn something.

I answer him honestly, "I want to know everything about this ship, sir."

Mickey throws his head back and laughs in a way that helps me trust him. "Ha! With that attitude you'll take my place in no time. I don't even know everything."

I do not feel as though he is teasing me but speaking in earnest. Part of me, a foolish part of me that does not understand the precarious line I am walking, hopes he is right.

He points over to the rigger, James. "You follow him around in every spare minute you get, and lord knows you have plenty. He's a good teacher. You show some promise and I'll put a word in for you."

"What will keep the quartermaster from killing me for it?"

The second mate shrugs, unconcerned. "That's none of my business."

"Why has Harry not been taught anything about sailing?"

The second mate runs his hands through his tangled hair and sucks on his teeth with a wet sounding pop. "I'll let Harry learn more about his trade once he can properly see over the rail. Kid can't keep a thought in his head. He knows plenty for his tasks."

I did not know anyone else worried about Harry aboard. I am glad to be wrong.

Before I can ask any more questions, he nods towards James. "Go ask him about something. You have to start somewhere."

I walk away from the second mate. As I approach my newly assigned teacher, I wish I had more clothes. Not for warmth, but to hide in.

The rigger starts when I tap his shoulder and then smiles at me, showing off front teeth chipped from years of biting thick sail-mending needles between them. I point to the tears forming where the canvas pulls between a sail and the mast it is tied to. The question has been burning in me since I noticed it. "How do you mend a sail? Is it like mending a shirt?"

James is tall and lean with long arms and legs, his skin so black that he blends into the night. The ebony stubble on his jaw matches his dark eyes. He has not worn shoes that I have seen, keeping his feet free for climbing the lines.

He gives me a shake of his head like a horse might try to shake a fly. "A bit like mending a shirt. You know, climbing aloft is the deadliest job on this ship most days. It's easy to fall."

The cadence to his voice reminds me of one of the women I worked alongside under the madam in Grand Port. It has only been a few days since I left that life, but it feels like it happened to a different person.

I answer honestly for once, "It's also the most important job on the ship, right? We do not move if you all do not make us move."

"Don't let the captain hear you say that." His white teeth glow against his dark skin in the starlight. If I had to guess, I would say he is flattered. His smile is contagious, and I find myself smiling back.

"So, the tears in the sail?"

"It won' be troublin' us for long. Shame we lost our best a few weeks back when a fight went bad." He looks grieved for just a moment, his eyes welling up in the lamplight and then the tears vanish. "I will patch it tomorrow with somethin' extra from around. It's like mending a shirt, but it's ten times as thick and the wind's got it because I'm not gonna have anyone take it down, and we won't stop before it must be done."

He waves a hand nonchalantly toward the torn sail.

Before I can think about it, my offer is flying from my lips. "I am fair at sewing."

James' smile is still in place. "You got a death wish, boy? Itching to climb the ropes? Not to mention you're a slow learner. I know, given you keep pesterin' me even after a warning from Hugh."

"I was just given permission from Mr. Compton to follow you around and learn all that I can." I try not to sound proud.

James hisses air through his teeth and shouts loud enough for the second mate to hear him, "That Mickey is always signing me up for shit."

His teasing does not feel insulting, but it is enough to remind me that I should not be making any trouble for myself. I forge on anyway. "I am on a streak of poor decisions lately. What is one more?"

The rigger is about to respond when the voice of the captain sounds behind us. "Ables, get over here!"

I tense at Captain Holt's thundering voice and James snickers at me for jumping like a rabbit before getting back to doing whatever it is he is doing.

Not taking the time to say goodbye to James, I rush to the helm where the captain is standing beside the second mate.

I watch my feet while Captain Holt barks, "You are distracting my crew again."

"No, sir... Captain." I mumble at the deck.

The captain continues, humor snaking into his stern warnings, "Look up and speak clearly. Don't act dumb when you're not dumb."

Looking up from my boots, I see no malice in his eyes, but I am on edge anyway. His shoulders shake in his fight to contain his laughter at my expense. Still, if he wants me flogged, I am through.

"I was asking about how to repair a sail."

The second mate acts as though we have never spoken before. Despite his hand over his mouth, the lines edging his delighted eyes hint at the grin he is hiding.

I have lost count of the number of risks I have taken this evening. "I want to learn, and James has offered to teach me."

Mickey turns back to me, dropping his hand and appearing impressed. Captain Holt shouts across to James from the quarter-deck, "Stealing boys now, James?"

Anxiety lands in my stomach like a stone as James looks up from what he's doing and nods. "Yeah, I'm teachin' him. Got a problem with that, kid?"

I wince at James' nickname for our captain. How long must one sail to be able to get away with calling our captain *kid*?

Either way, I am relieved when the captain answers me good-naturedly. "Seems not even Digby's sharp tongue can turn you away."

The second mate jabs the captain in the side. "I told him he could, Captain. I just wanted to see if he had the guts to stand by it."

Like schoolboys, Captain Holt punches Mickey in the gut and the second mate doubles over from the hit, breathless but still smiling.

The captain turns back to me and behaves more like a captain now than he had been a moment ago. "You can't do your job and learn another on no rest. Get some sleep."

He keeps eye contact with me. I force myself to meet his stare rather than turn away. Returning his gaze feels like a test that I must pass. Eventually his attention returns to the helm, leaving me to wonder if I imagined the contest.

"Thank you, Captain."

I dash below deck before I can tempt fates further. I am becoming too comfortable here and taking stupid risks. I need to keep my head down and make it to our next stop.

Harry is already asleep. I slip off my stolen boots, which already feel more mine than any shoes I have ever worn, and lie awake with troubled thoughts. The freedom of sailing appeals to me but, more so, having a marketable skill.

If I were a man and knew how to sail, I could raise my station. Despite all my hope in running away, I suspect my fate when I leave *Sneaky Lass* and Dixon Ables behind will differ little from every life Jane has been thrust into before. The only real change between my life in Grand Port and a future anywhere else will be warmer weather.

CHAPTER 6

THE NEXT MORNING, IT IS NOT A PIPE THAT WAKES THE SHIP BUT THE ringing of the large brass bell in the crow's nest. I had not been told that it means I should be on the deck, but I have caught on enough to know that it does not mean *keep laying in your hammock*. A fact punctuated by how the captain and the officers are out of their cabins and up the ladder to the deck in their underclothes. Harry and I scramble after them.

Not even knowing what the bell means, my blood pounds with it.

Without having to be asked, Pax, the carpenter, reports to

Captain Holt, "A merchant ship, a slow-moving galleon heading north, Captain. Right in our path."

The captain grins like a wicked child sucking on a stolen sweet, and the men grin with him.

"Looks like luck is back on the side of the *Lass*. Prepare the guns and boats; raise the black. Remember men: we are not in the business of fighting; we are in the business of taking. Look fierce!" The captain's bellow ignites a flurry of activity across all the decks.

Hollers and hurrahs rise from the crew, all hopeful for heavy purses. Captain Holt heads back down to his room, motioning for me to follow. With my guts tying themselves in intricate knots like those of the rig above, I follow without question.

The captain's quarters are larger than any other on the ship, but still cramped. He begins tearing away his cotton breeches and shirt. Waiting for instructions, I avert my eyes. I have seen plenty of naked men in my lifetime, but I do not know how they behave around one another. I would rather be noted as uncomfortable than forthright.

Above me I can hear the men preparing to do whatever it is pirates do when they set to pirating. Beyond what is listed on wanted posters on the walls of Grand Port, I can only guess at the details.

Captain Holt points to a chest, half hidden by his bedding, which has been left in a heap at the foot of his bed. "You're smart. You will know what I require."

I pray he is right as I quickly open the wooden chest to discover there are only a few different things it could be. He had said to look fierce, so I grab the articles that speak true to those words. A black coat with shined silver buttons and a high collar comes out first. Next a pair of black breeches, silk stockings and undershirt both in blood red, followed by an embroidered vest.

Finally, I lift out the black boots, folded over at the top and sporting silver buckles, all shined to near perfection.

Soon I realize my reason for being brought along is to help with dressing him. If the situation were not so worrisome it would be comical. It is clear the finery is seldom worn and not at all what Captain Holt is accustomed to. I note the hole in the jacket, vest, and shirt that line up with the fresh, puckered scar on his back near his shoulder. I suppose no one thought to mend them. Fortunately, the damage only serves to make him look tougher.

With each article he pulls on, I start the laces on one side as he tackles the other. I steady my nervous fingers with a reminder that I have helped many people dress in the past. Customers and peers, alike.

Finishing the laces around his stockings and the buckles on his breeches, he yanks on the shirt, which has more ornamental, gilded buttons down each arm than necessary. As they are only for fashion, they do not require fastening.

In my anxious state, words tumble from my lips, "All this focus on buttons, yet no one has mended the bullet holes."

As soon as the words leave my mouth, I realize I should have stayed silent. One would think after a lifetime of being told to be quiet that I would be better at it. The captain hisses out a laugh, it escapes through his tight lips, the corners of his mouth tugging upward at my frustration.

He moves away from my fingers as I finish the last button and grabs a thick leather belt from the wall. It holds four pistols in holsters and a naval cutlass, which all get strapped to his hip. It is the same belt I tried to steal his purse from in Grand Port. I hold up the coat so he can slide the tailored piece into place on his broad shoulders.

"Smart, indeed. I thought you might be accustomed to finer things. Harry cannot tie a proper lace to save his life."

I bite my tongue to keep my response behind my teeth. He does not need to know that I practiced dressing and undressing men quickly a dozen times a night for nearly a year. Nothing so fine as this, but the same concept applies. In my short time as part of the crew, I have learned that silence is not necessarily a bad response. Silence keeps me from saying something stupid. It is a shame I am not better at remembering that.

Captain Holt removes the silver locket that he wears on a thick, plain chain around his neck and places it carefully in the desk. It is a feminine piece of jewelry, entirely out of place on this ship. It looks like something a widow might keep a lock of hair in, or a lover—a portrait. From the same drawer, he pulls out several large golden and jeweled rings that he slides into place on his fingers.

In his finery, our captain appears to have grown ten inches taller and ten years older. He looks proud at my stunned expression as he dons his tall, leather boots.

"Piracy is often far more about putting on a good show, Dixon. Remember that. Now, go find Harry on deck. He knows how to stay out from underfoot."

Out from underfoot is precisely where I would like to be if I can manage it.

I follow the captain out through the cramped passageway and up the ladder to find Harry beaming as he pulls canvas off the cannons. A sailor brings up a barrel of gunpowder from the magazine. The air is full of the contagious excitement of men waiting to be hired and, finally, a ship came by offering pay.

The crew I have grown familiar with have changed. None so much as the captain, of course, but pistols have been buckled into place and sabers are in hand. Silver and gold rings have been placed on tired fingers. With each accessory, the men stand straighter and grow in confidence.

All eyes rest on the prize. The merchant vessel, with its slow, square sails and full load, has no hope of escaping *Sneaky Lass*. I know almost nothing of ships and even I know that much.

I check that my stolen jackknife is still in my pocket, as having it feels safer than not. Who knows, it might be lucky. The three silver coins still rest against my foot in my boot. I might be collecting lucky items. If I am careful, I will never know which is working, if any of them.

Just as the captain takes his place on the quarterdeck, the black flag sporting a white, skeletal hand holding a red apple is hoisted into place; everything appears more sinister beneath its shadow.

I feel out of place at first, but as orders are barked and I help Harry carry out what ones we can, I feel the rush infect me as well.

The captain and quartermaster make it very clear: our goal is for the merchant ship's crew to be so frightened that they give up without a fight. We will put on a big show, they will decide the cargo they carry is not worth their lives, and then we will split up. Some of us will keep the opposing crew in line and others will load everything of value onto *Sneaky Lass*. Harry seems pleased that part of the show will involve cannons, even if it is just to make a lot of noise.

Sneaky Lass is outfitted with eighteen large guns and a variety of smaller mounted ones. It is the first opportunity I have had to inspect the cannons. Each one is stamped with the seal of the Imperial Navy. Seabirds in flight over the royal crest of Goran. It dawns on me that this ship was once a navy ship, at the very least these were once navy cannons.

Beside me, Harry goes on and on about the how and why of each of the guns with obvious passion.

"The small one's are mostly for show. It's not enough to damage the other ship much, but it may start fires and will make a big noise. The Navy keeps them for stopping boarders, not that many would try to board us. That ship may have a big cannon or two, but prolly just small stuff to try and keep us from boarding 'em. See how slow it moves? That's because it's full. Prolly cotton or leaf, which is easy to resell. Wouldn't it be something if it's filled with gold!"

I have not seen, or heard, Harry so excited over anything in the days I have known him. Usually sounding much older than he is, the idea of piracy in action transforms Harry into an eager child.

I cannot help but meet his infectious excitement. "Your future may be as a master gunner, Harry."

The actual master gunner, Mickey Compton, takes time to roll his eyes at my comment from where he is organizing everyone nearby, but Harry glows.

We are nearly upon them when the Quartermaster shouts an order that I cannot hear over the clamor of the crowded gun deck. It is lost to me until several sailors around us repeat it. "Ready the guns."

More men call around me, but they are not orders, as much as reminders.

"Aim high!"

"Aim off!"

"Leave them crippled but floating!"

I watch Harry closely and follow his lead as we, and a few other young sailors, ready the cannons with powder and shot before more experienced gunners take over. The men go silent; the usual banter and song that fill the day is gone. Only the sounds of creaking boards and splashing waves fill the quiet. Gooseflesh rises on my arms and down my spine in defiance of the warm sun.

We all wait for the captain's order.

Harry covers his ears, patting them several times frantically to remind me to do the same. I press my hands over my ears as well, thankful for his reminder. In the few seconds of silence, I can hear my own heart thrumming like battle drums in my ears.

The cannons fire. My entire body leaps at the sound. The wood beneath my feet vibrates. Never, in my years on earth, have I experienced anything like it.

CHAPTER 7

My ears are ringing when I drop my hands. The deck is awash once more with activity as we start to reload. Cannons fire up and down the deck. Pistols and muskets fire into the air. Everyone around me is shouting and cursing, including Harry, who catches my eye and encourages me to do the same. Thankfully, I have years of experience with angry, villainous men and I call upon every single memory to produce the dangerous sneer I aim at the merchants.

Our ship sails closer and I begin to wonder if they will fight back. More shouts. Pandemonium erupts as the merchant ship returns fire. There is no aiming off. They have no qualms with sinking us. The ship quakes and the carpenter, Pax, grabs a few others and jumps below to check for damage.

The captain orders the boats lowered into the water and men jump inside. Harry pulls me to the rail. Before I have time to consider staying on *Sneaky Lass*, I am in a jolly boat rowing fast amid cannon fire towards a merchant ship.

Every warm body is needed with such a small crew.

Being so close to the water makes me more nervous than cannons or muskets. Only an inch of wood now separates me from the fathomless sea. I cannot swim. If anything were to frighten me away from a life at sea, it would be these small crafts. It is all I can manage to keep from trembling.

As we near the galleon, the cannons of *Sneaky Lass* are still firing so close it feels like the whole ocean lifts and falls with each volley. Ahead, our prey hauls down their colors in surrender. A ladder is tossed over the side for us and I am grateful since I am not certain I could climb up on a single rope. I certainly could not scale the hull of a ship with axes as the man beside me begins doing just for the sake of being fearsome.

Harry pulls a dagger from his filthy vest and, with it between his teeth, climbs the ladder after the rest of them. I make no secret of waiting. Despite my fear of the water below, I would rather catch the tail end of whatever lies above me. The shouts and jeers of my shipmates are intertwined with the howling screams of dying men and grateful cheers. It is terrifying. My skin pebbles all over and I do not know which of these men frighten me more. Fearsome pirates, screaming victims, or the men who cheer at such violence.

It is with great effort that I make my way up the ladder. I am last from the boat and my jackknife is all I carry in the means of weaponry on the deck of this new ship. If I am to stay, I would need to find a better-suited blade.

I squash any thoughts of staying.

Blood is pooling on deck, but not from merchant sailors. The tumult quickly falls into place like pieces of a puzzle. The sailors on the opposing deck merely stood aside, allowing our men to tear the officers on their ship apart to roaring applause and grateful shouts. Captain Holt is among those who have wrestled the merchant captain to the ground.

Captain Holt bellows at the merchant captain, spittle flying from his lips and landing upon the face of the terrified man. "Should I ask your crew what should be done with you?" Lowering his voice to a growl, he adds, "I often find a wicked captain's victims are an imaginative lot."

Sure enough, the merchant crew turns against their captain in an instant, shouting their many ideas for what end their captain deserves. Flaying the skin from his body is offered by more than one man, almost like this crew has some history with such a punishment.

The fair-handed captain I have come to expect on the deck of *Sneaky Lass* is not aboard this merchant ship. This is a different captain entirely.

The merchant captain struggles and screams to be spared, but my captain cuts a filet off the wicked, red-faced merchantman's arm like a butcher might cut chunks off a side of pork. The act is met with raucous cheers and calls for more blood. Their celebrations are so loud, the merchant captain's terrorized cries are lost to the roar.

I am the only person present who looks away. If I watch a moment more, I might jump ship for fright. Then I would drown, and all of this would be for naught.

Stepping over the gore, I swallow the searing bile in my throat, and fall in behind the dark-skinned rigger I spoke to last night.

When James notices me following his footsteps, he throws a smile over his shoulder at me, but it looks off. Men grow infected by violence. One bar brawl often turns into a night full of them. James has the eyes of a man seeking blood.

Something about my clear terror must break the spell, because James shakes his head and his brown eyes suddenly appear more his own. "Stay by me, Dixon. I won't let you get lost in the shuffle."

The merchant captain is still screaming. Captain Holt has given him to his sailors to do as they please to the man. My guts clench in tight knots.

"I do not understand why they have turned on their own this way. Surely our crew would defend one another. Why is this crew so different?" I begin questioning the experienced rigger if only to have a reason to look at him instead of the gruesome spectacle.

James points to one of the dead men on the deck, "You think Hugh Digby is a tyrant, but has he ever actually struck you? Have you seen him whip anyone since you came aboard? Seen anyone punished in any scarring way at all?"

I shake my head. I have not, but so far as I know, no one has done anything too terrible. Hugh is surly and ill-tempered, but from what I have witnessed, Hugh Digby is not overly cruel.

"And the rules on the charter you signed, are they unfair?"

Despite breaking one every moment I am aboard *Sneaky Lass*, they are clear and not too much to ask. I shake my head again.

James is doing a fine job pressing my terror into the back of my mind by giving me something new to think about. I allow his calm to soak into me.

"You're not like the rest, Ables. They don't usually pop aboard knowing nothing at all. Pirates start as merchant sailors like these or navy deserters and mutineers like Holt."

The new speck of information about our captain being a mutineer does not shock me but draws my interest all the same. I never once met a navy sailor who had anything good to say about his lot. They all complained bitterly all the time.

James leads me towards the ratlines before answering my question in full. "Based on how this crew all turned tail, their officers murdered sailors for looking at 'em wrong. That captain has rules that are unjust. It's the same on nearly every ship we take. Our captain is not a god and does not pretend to be but, I'd bet, this ship's captain thought he might be. If you had a chance to kill gods, wouldn't you? Rare is a captain not deserving of becoming governor of his own island."

"Governor?"

"Marooning, boy. That's enough of that. You and me are gonna take the ropes. Of all things to be short on, huh? I'll take the high climbs. You untie the low ropes, since you know the knots."

He winks at me. That he has noticed the meager skills I have managed to acquire floods me with pride. I am thrilled to be given something new to focus on, and not just because it gets me away from the danger on deck. I try to ignore the still-unfolding violence below and free the ropes from the lowest masts. Even I can tell this rig is in rough shape. The standing rigging is fraying in places it should not. Some places are so taught they might soon snap and others flutter loosely in the wind.

Below me, faster than I thought possible, members of our crew are already loading cargo from the merchant ship onto ours. The three boats we came on row to and from *Sneaky Lass* full of prizes. Now that the merchant crew is free from their leashes, it would seem most intend to join us. The seamen's chests are lowered down into the boats, too.

Faster still, James starts dropping his lines down to the deck long before I have even untied my first knot. Everything about piracy up until this moment seemed to be waiting and drudgery. Today, I see it is punctuated by swift and sudden adventure.

A strangled shout echoes off the deck from above. I spot James tangled in the ropes hanging by just his left arm with no recourse. The line he dangles from is frayed like it snapped beneath his weight. With a quick glance, I realize I am the closest person to him.

A few of our sailors follow the howls skyward, moving towards the lines to help. Before I can think of letting someone with more experience handle it, I grab the coil of rope I have collected and climb toward my new friend, as I have, at this moment, decided he is my friend.

The main mast of the galleon ship looms higher still with James desperately hanging on above me. Focused only on where my hands and feet go next on the rig and nothing else, I climb.

"Gonna get yourself killed!"

Someone growls from below, but I do not stop or turn to see who spoke. James looks like he is about to lose strength and I will not let him die. Perhaps it is a childish notion, but I like to think someone would try to save me if I were in a similar position.

I reach the lineless, sail-less yard. Having never been so high up in my entire life and shimmy across towards the middle. It takes every bit of courage in my guts to move out towards where James has fallen. The sail, which has been loosed from the yard by the same force that sent James falling, whips dangerously in the wind to James' right, a few feet below me. I would call out to him, but I do not think he would be able to hear me above the winds. How can anyone hear anything in these gales?

Taking great care not to look down, I make my way inch by painstaking inch along the yardarm toward the rope where James is tangled. One of his arms hangs limply by his side, otherwise he would be able to climb up himself.

After an eternity, I make it to the rope that James is clutching for dear life. For longer than an instant I allow myself to look down. It is a struggle to keep my focus on James and not the faraway deck where I would land a broken heap if I fell. I am dismayed to see that it will not be as simple as pulling him up, a task I already doubted I could complete. The rope he is dangling from is tangled through several other lines in the rigging. In fact, if James were to let go, I am not certain he would even fall. He might just get trapped like a fly in a spiderweb.

All the years I spent with my father yelling at me for being unladylike and climbing trees with my brothers afforded me no great fear of heights, which is either about to pay off or kill me.

Taking the rope off my shoulder, I tie one end to the yardarm before wrapping the other around my waist and each leg like a harness. Giving it a firm tug, the only thing to do now is trust the rope, which would be much easier if rope was not what sent James falling.

I am not afraid of heights. I repeat it over and over again in my mind like I might manage to convince myself that what I am about to do is not mad.

The same moment that I put all my faith in my own rope, others of our number have reached me. I can hear Mickey Compton shouting for me to stop. He is too late.

My heart leaps into my throat and black spots threaten my vision when my feet slide off the yardarm. Once the initial shock subsides and I am still alive, now hanging high above the deck, I slowly lower myself down to where James is dangling.

To some, I may appear brave. To most, I am certain I look foolish. As I focus on keeping last night's dinner in my guts, I believe both may be right. Or life has finally driven me well and truly insane.

As I get close enough to hear James' voice, I recognize the sound and rhythm of desperate prayer. His eyes are shut. I do not think he believed anyone would come in time. I feel a small bubbling of pride at having done so. I will allow myself to feel truly prideful if neither of us die.

I shout over the wind and prayers to get his attention. My voice quivers in such a way that if anyone listening thought me fearless, they would be dissuaded of the notion. "I have no idea what to do."

James' brown eyes fly open and make contact with mine. He did not expect anyone, but me least of all. I try to smile, but probably look like I am about to throw up. His shock transforms into determination.

"Can your little arms even lift your own self back up the rope?" Wonder twines through his voice.

I do not tell him that I was wondering the same thing. Every muscle in my body is on fire and so is the skin on my hands, which I can feel blistering as we speak. The threat of the long fall onto deck is enough to keep me holding on with shaking limbs.

"How do I get you back up with me?"

Despite the deadly predicament we have both landed in, James' smile through the pain he is suffering reassures me. He eyes the coil of rope I am using to lower myself down and seems to do some mental math about the distance back to the safety of the main mast.

"You got a knife, right?"

I nod. I do not know why I did not think of the small blade in my pocket.

Releasing my hold on my own rope, I allow my harness to take all my weight for the first time so I can reach out and grab the slack dangling below James. My friend watches with encouraging eyes as I tie one of the only knots I know, a bowline, and slip it around his foot.

I suspect James might laugh at my effort if not for his frightening reality. If my rope fails or his grip slips before I can get this done, he will die. At least this way, he will be left hanging by his foot.

Mickey Compton and another man I do not know the name of are above us on the lineless yardarm. None of them dare make any moves to join me. I have tied their hands in this regard. If they tried anything they would be just as likely to make me fall as they would be to help. Once James is cut free, they can get him up. That is what they offer, and it is plenty. I may need their help hauling me up, too.

My fingers are shaking violently as I dig the small jackknife from my pocket. It takes most of my remaining willpower to not drop the damn thing. The knowledge that doing so would mean I have done all of this for nothing steadies my hand.

Careful to not tangle my own rope into the quagmire, and make the problem worse, I begin cutting everything that is not James' lifeline in as many places as I can reach as fast as my quivering limbs will allow. The more I slice through, the more dangerous the loose sail to our right becomes, whipping free further and further.

Just as I begin to believe my sharp, but small, blade was never going to make it through all the hemp, James swings free from the mess and the sail that had been snapping about us falls further away. In an instant the men on the yard above us begin hauling James up.

With my job finally done, my courage fractures into a thousand pieces and gets blown away in the stiff wind that stings my ears. My knife falls from my shaking fingers as, with both stinging hands, I clutch the rope that is keeping me aloft so tightly my bones ache.

I lack the strength to climb back up the rope. After James is safely on the yard and inching towards the mast, I am hauled up as well.

When I reach the yardarm, sweat drips into my eyes and I realize somewhere along the way, I lost my bandana. A raw, adrenaline-fueled scream claws at the inside of my throat, but I manage to keep most of the sound inside of me. Only small, pitiful whimpers sneak past my clenched teeth.

Mickey roars with laughter as though this has been a fun

game rather than a traumatic event. The second mate claps me on the shoulder hard, which helps bring my soul back into my body. I do not know if he meant it to serve that purpose or not, but I am grateful for it.

"When I told you to follow James," Mickey pauses to catch his breath, "I didn't mean into disaster, Dix."

I have nothing to say to that and the second mate does not seem to expect me to. I follow him, inching along the lineless yard once again, and onto the ratlines to climb back down. I am breathing so hard I feel my chest may explode like an over hot pot. My consuming desire to be back on solid wood once more is my only motivation to continue moving at all.

Once I land on the strange deck, I fold into myself and put my head between my knees lest I vomit. If I stay here long enough, I may melt into the woodwork of this merchant ship and leave no trace.

A comforting thought.

A polished, black boot kicks my thigh. Following the leg up, I find the captain is shaking his head at me. "You may have tar in you, Dixon Ables."

I do not know what he means, but I choose to believe it is something good. If I could catch my breath, I may have thanked him. Instead, I bob my head and force myself back onto my feet. Exhausted as I am, I am relieved when everyone just continues the business of looting everything of worth from the merchant ship, too busy to notice when I vomit into the sea.

Once my stomach is empty, I decide that my first pirate raid is over. I survived and that is as much as I could hope for. Just as I am about to take my freshly coiled rope and catch the first boat back to our ship, I am hit in the back of the head with something soft.

I turn to pick up my own sweaty bandana. The quartermaster,

Hugh Digby, shouts at me, "You're not done yet, Ables. James went up to fetch those lines. Seems it's up to you."

He must be kidding. There are a dozen sailors who know what they are doing standing in arms reach of him and he chooses me?

Hugh puts my fallen jackknife into my palm and points up towards the remaining job before turning away from me, yelling over his shoulder. "Did I stutter, boy? Git. Be quick about it. We're done here."

My father locked me in the cellar as a girl. I was petrified and nothing could convince me there were no monsters in the dark down there. I do not know how long I stood in the center of that earthen room, a statue frozen by panic, heart pounding in my chest, before I began screaming. When my brother Michael found me, he comforted me and brought me back into the light.

The next day when I would not go into the cellar to fetch anything, he told me, *"You cannot let things get the best of you."*

Then, Michael locked me in the cellar again and again and again until I was no longer frightened.

I wonder if that is what Hugh Digby means to do by sending me up again when so many others could. Maybe he knows that if I am left on the deck to shiver much longer, I will never climb higher than a staircase ever again.

Hugh leaves me staring at the half-fallen sail twisting wildly in the breeze above me. There is nothing for it, then. Hoisting a rope higher on my shoulder, I head back to the ratlines.

A week at sea and I know I am meant to learn the ropes.

The pressure of being watched lands squarely on my back as I begin climbing up. When I finally turn to see if they are truly there, I lock gazes with the captain's hazel stare. He is studying me, in all his finery. As Jane, I became very accustomed to the eyes of men on me. Men always stare in the same way. Though to have that look levied at me as Dixon catches me off guard.

I am relieved to be far enough away that he will not be able to tell.

The men celebrate their spoils late into the evening. We gained more sailors today from the merchant crew. Despite an early morning encroaching on the festivities, I stay on deck to listen to my shipmates sing and new arrivals tell stories about their previous captain, now food for the creatures in the sea, and his monstrous treatment of the crew. Eventually, conversation turns to their oaths of honesty and where they have seen mermaids. .

With each ship we take, we will gain crew. Harry assures me that with each port, we will lose some as well. Captain Holt prefers to sail with close to sixty pirates aboard. With the unspoken misfortune this ship has come into of late, there was only a skeleton crew upon my arrival of less than thirty. With the new crew members, we are up to forty-one. I cannot imagine where twenty more men would fit. Sharing a space where I touch shoulders with Harry at night does not seem so bad when compared to how cramped quarters must be with so many men stuffed under the forecastle and belowdecks.

As is often the case with drunk men, the longer they drink, the more somber the songs they sing. I find my mind wandering back to my husband. I feel his ghost creep into my thoughts, and shiver.

I carry no quarrel with captain or officer, past or present. I carry my own reasoning for not minding the bloody ends I witnessed today. I like knowing that we killed those who made others suffer. The gods, if they exist at all, know well that if someone had come and eliminated the oppressors in my past and asked me to join ranks, I would have without question.

The captain's voice draws me out of my memories and musings. I had not realized he had joined me on the railing until this moment.

"You have left my ship, Ables. Where are you when you stare off at the water?"

Hand to my pounding heart, I stutter, "Sorry, Captain. I did not mean to be idle."

Keeping my face down, I pray that he was not staring at me earlier because he has learned something of me that he should not know. What would become of me if he recognized me as the thieving whore from Grand Port? Would the crew all get a turn before they dumped me in the sea?

"It's night and there is nothing that needs doing. You have not answered my question."

He reeks of liquor, like most of the men do tonight. Perhaps it is the smell, not the sad songs, that have led me somewhere grim.

Nerves flitter in my stomach. I do not want to lie any more than I am by simply being here, but there are few answers I can offer that would not reveal too much of myself.

Before I speak, I clear my throat and brave glancing at Captain Holt, who is far from the lamplight. It is hard to make out anything about his expression. "You ever find yourself stuck in your own past, Captain? The song brought me somewhere I do not like to visit. I should thank you for the distraction."

He nods and stays by my side for a few moments before murmuring, "A pleasure to help, then."

When I say no more, he wanders off towards the singing men.

I find the night feels colder once he leaves, and I make for my hammock soon after.

CHAPTER 8

IT HAS BEEN MORE THAN A WEEK, AND JAMES' SHOULDER IS STIFF AND painful from where it dislodged from the socket in his fall. He has not gone easy on me, as his eager pupil. My head is fit to burst with the new terms, knots, and directions he shoves at me.

It is my job to take up the slack his injury has created, and it must all be done properly. There are far more able bodies than mine nearby, but everyone is entertained by watching me give it a try, or a dozen, first.

James has begun pointing out ships when they are nearby and quizzing me about the specifics that make each ship different and alike. There are schooners, brigs, barks, sloops, galleons, on and on and a few different varieties of each. *Sneaky Lass* is a brigantine. Most of the men shorten it to brig and brig can also be a word for any ship. I do not think I will shorten it. Brigantine is a word worthy of her.

There are trade winds with their patterns, slatches, gales, fair winds, foul winds, and a dozen or more other variations of breezes. I always thought the wind was blowing or it was not.

The ocean also has a nature of its own, I must learn. The sea's currents, calms, swells, and breakers.

That does not even begin touching on the specifics of the rigging itself, which is somehow simultaneously straightforward and labyrinthine depending on what needs doing.

Each time I begin to feel as though I have gotten good at something, James throws in an additional step for me to mess up. I wish there were a journal and a quill to keep it all listed neatly in. When I mentioned the possibility of writing it all down, James dismissed me with a heavy sigh. He rolled his eyes so far in his head they were all white at the mere mention of it, like writing his lessons down would somehow diminish them.

One thing every man on *Sneaky Lass* contributes to my advanced instruction, knowingly or not, are all the ins and outs of swearing, drinking, stealing, killing, back talking, and whoring. Working as a prostitute in a port town, I thought I had picked them up, but sailors have whores beat by a wide margin in sinning. They gamble and drink and curse more aboard this ship than I have ever seen any sailors do in Grand Port. Apparently, some ships have rules against such things, *Sneaky Lass* is not one of them. These men are masters of ships and seas. When it comes to sinning, they are gods among men.

It would seem sitting idle is not as necessary as I had thought. If someone is in need of an occupation, it is no large feat for Hugh, Mickey, or the captain to set a man to a task. Keeping everyone busy before any fights can break out, especially among the new crew we pick up with each ship taken, keeps the quartermaster's hand near his whip.

There is a constant barrage of tarring, oiling, painting, scraping, or scrubbing to do at any given moment. The standing rigging is always slack somewhere. If one cable is finally set to right, another goes slack somewhere else to make up for it. The old hands go about their duties while shaking their heads at the recently acquired crew jockeying for position and favor. We have taken three ships in a week, which is apparently nigh-unheard of as fortune goes.

There is always a pile of junk, old ropes and cables, to be picked through at any given moment. With the ships we take it would be a simple enough task to take the oakum picked by others, but if we did that what task would Hugh Digby set before those who step too far out of line one too many times? Without picking apart old ropes to make the oakum used to caulk the ship seams or spinning rope yarns, what task would he give me when he thinks I look too content? Tedious as it is, I far prefer tedium to standing still. I quite like how, while working, my mind goes blank. Since joining the crew of *Sneaky Lass,* I have scarcely had a spare moment to go into the darker parts of my memory. I have landed in my hammock too exhausted to even dream.

I have not moved my hammock to the main sailor's quarters beneath the forecastle, relieved that no one recommends it now that I no longer share jobs with Harry. The privacy allows me to better keep my secrets, and I would miss the company of the friendly ship's boy, having grown accustomed to falling asleep with his shoulder touching mine.

We are heading for a place called Azure Cove. When I had said the name sounded idyllic, my shipmates laughed at me. Apparently, it is a place to unload stolen goods and wet one's cock, but it is not good for much else.

The only thing barring me from staying on this ship when we

arrive at Azure Cove is that, as much as I would have liked to leave everything that is Jane behind in Grand Port, she is still here. Hidden beneath stolen clothing, poorly shorn hair, and the young man I named Dixon Ables; Jane is still with me. No amount of pretending will make Dixon real and sticking around until someone figures it out for himself is a terrible idea.

If any man runs away or keeps any secret from this company...

The third rule on the charter I signed bounces around my skull. Marooned with next to nothing would be my lot, if I am lucky. If this crew decides to stick to the rules for a wretch and a liar such as me. They could do far worse than a lonely beach.

It is a poignant reminder that I cannot stay aboard *Sneaky Lass,* no matter how fervently I might wish to.

As we continue south, the weather grows warmer. I leave my coat with my boots in my hammock most days and climb barefoot on deck in just trousers and the linen shirt and vest I stole from the unfortunate boy in Grand Port. Beneath it all, a binding on my chest holds my practiced lies together.

Despite James' insistence that I will learn by doing, each evening before heading to bed, I review everything he told me during the day. At the very least, I count the sails, rigging, pulleys, and masts and list their names in my head.

Sitting on the ratlines and looking out at the black waters is one of my favorite ways to pass the time. The deck is quiet this time of night, and I never tire of the way *Sneaky Lass* pushes the water out of her way.

The hair on the nape of my neck stands on end, and I know precisely who watches me. Steadying my breath, I turn to find Captain Holt fixated on me yet again.

When our eyes meet, I fight the urge to turn away. I always feel he is testing me with his stare. A woman may be expected to demurely glance down, but Dixon meets his gaze. He is staring so intensely that it takes a few heartbeats before he realizes I am staring back. He nods and looks away.

What does that nod mean? What does he know? Has he just answered some question for himself about me, or was he merely acknowledging me?

I return to watching the waves. It is not my place to approach the captain, but I find myself wishing I could ask what on earth he is looking at. Even as Jane, no one would ever have described me as exceptional in any way. I am not even the most attractive man on this ship, as that title falls squarely with Mickey Compton. The captain is certainly not ogling because I am particularly capable since I spend most of my days being hazed by the crew for my ineptitude at tasks I have never tried before.

I am so lost in my musings that I am late in hearing footfalls behind me. Captain Holt climbs the lines and stands so he is eye level with me in my makeshift seat on the ratlines. Almost every night he finds me somewhere and we have the queerest, short conversations. Each one leaves me wanting to speak to the captain again. I feel, somehow, we understand one another. I am nervous in his presence, but he appears even less certain than I feel. The lamp is at his back, but it is bright enough for me to see him wringing his hands. If my limited experience is any guide, he strikes me as shy.

He finds his confidence eventually.

"I thought I would come to see what it is you look for so intently in the night." He looks out at the onyx waters. "You watch the sea each night like it has answers for you."

His observation makes me uncomfortable. I am not seeking answers from the water. Watching it helps silence my thoughts. The ocean is more tedium, and tedium keeps me from straying down roads I should avoid.

"I just wonder how deep it goes and how far it stretches on. I wonder if there are monsters and mermaids like some say. Maybe that makes me simple but wondering about it keeps things quiet."

From the way he scrunches his face in thought, I can see that it is not the answer he was expecting.

I keep sharing, "If you must know my thoughts right this moment, I wonder if we would eventually sail off the end if we went far enough."

The very corner of his upturned lip is visible in the dim, flickering glow from behind us while he watches the water. "Ah, the question of every romantic sailor, then?"

I roll my eyes and then, worried over my disrespect, look at him. But even if he had been looking at me rather than the darkness, I doubt he could have seen it in the gloom.

"I think I understand your mind, Dixon Ables. As far as I know, there is no end, but pirates tell tales." He smiles into the night thinking about stories I do not know. "I fear even if we sailed so far that we wound up precisely where we began, we would not find answers to our questions. Though, how can I be certain? I've never done it."

Gathering my own courage, spurred by the idea of spending a lifetime sailing as far in one direction as possible, I ask, "Why not? You have *Sneaky Lass*. She could go anywhere you like."

Anywhere. Captain Holt has all the freedom in the world, and he has never done it? If I had his choices in life, I would never touch land again.

My imaginings of the edge of the world and what it might be like to find it are interrupted by the captain.

"Exploring is only a fancy. I'm beholden to the crew, and they cry for vengeance and coin. There are plenty of both nearby." Absent-mindedly, he starts rolling the silver chain of his locket around his fingers. "Not like you. You seem like the sort of man who would jump off the edge of the world if you found one."

I cannot hold back my laugh at his apt, yet grim, description of me. Perhaps all his studying me is doing him more good than my watching the sea has done for me. My laugh still etched into my words, I say more than I meant, as I often do with the captain. "If that is what it takes to outrun Grand Port and all I left in it, then I would. Vengeance and riches be entirely damned."

For the first time since coming to my side, he turns to me now, looking away from the water to study my face. "That is a true pirate's tale."

His eyes reflect the stars back at me. He is waiting for me to tell him more. No matter how much I enjoy his strange company, I cannot.

"Morning comes early, Captain." I start my climb down.

His head bobs, acknowledging my descent. He stays in place, watching the wake in my stead.

My feet are dragging so hard I fear they might gather splinters as I move to the hatch that will take me to my hammock when Mickey calls me over to join him by the helm. "Hey, Dixon. Come over here, I have a story for you."

Despite the fact that Mickey would understand if I chose not to, intrigue wins over my exhaustion. I plop down beside the second mate.

"What story?"

"You ever hear the story of Tiana, the woman warrior of Hiacin?"

The second mate levels two icy blue eyes at me and I get the feeling another lesson is being presented, just not one about winds or sails or tides.

I shake my head.

"Good, I love sharing stories to new ears." Smiling, he claps his hands together, eager to spin one of his stories as he often does for the crew. "The country of Hiacin was not always part of the empire though many tried to conquer it before Goran succeeded. A long time ago, it was under attack and every able-bodied man was called to serve and protect the borders.

"Tiana had no men in her family. It was only her mother and her two sisters, but she desperately wanted to fight. She knew she was a strong warrior and clever enough to do it, but women were not allowed to serve in the armies of Hiacin. It was believed that their place was at home tending to children and shops and farms. Tiana did not like being told her place."

I can see where this story is going. Mickey's gaze is somewhere out over the deck, not at me, but I cannot tear my eyes away from his face. He knows. He knows everything about me that matters, and this tale must be his way of sharing it.

He continues like I am not struggling to contain the mounting panic beneath my skin. "She disguised herself as a soldier and arrived at the army camp. As I said, she was very skilled. She quickly moved up the ranks, making many friends, and enemies, along the way. It was not until the final battle was won that she revealed herself."

Fear for myself is quickly replaced by fear for a warrior woman I have never met, who may not even be real. Almost frantic, I blurt, "Why would she do that?"

The second mate snorts at my shock. His sparkling eyes are filled with delight when they find my face in the lamplight. "Why else? She had fallen in love with one of the generals and wanted him to know he could love her back."

The tension loosens the knots in my body I had not realized had been tied. It is just a story. A stupid love story at that. I shake my head at the tale I have decided has nothing to do with me.

"She may have been skilled, but she was stupid. Did they saw her in half? Rape her? Put her head on a spike?" My voice is flat at the images my mind cooks up for the poor storied woman.

The second mate looks at me with disappointment, and perhaps a little insult. He answers me as if I had been very wrong

68

about the tides rather than human nature. "You are thinking like a man from Goran but know little of the men of Hiacin."

"Men are the same everywhere, Mr. Compton. This ship or that, Goran or Hiacin. Even a world away. They are all the same." I speak with absolute certainty.

Mickey shrugs one shoulder and closes his eyes, unbothered by my observation. The corner of his lip is turned up just slightly.

"That'd be an easy thing to think if you only ever met men in a brothel in Grand Port."

The blood drains from my body and I feel terribly cold. I peer out over the deck, my eyes landing on the captain, who is still on the ratlines where I left him.

The second mate finishes his tale easily, as though he has not just torn me asunder. "In any case, when Tiana came clean, they changed their rules. She had proven that she could fight as well as any man. There is a statue of her in nearly every town in Hiacin, or there was. Perhaps Goran has thought to tear them all down by now."

I clear my throat to speak but I cannot find my voice. I try again and manage only a whisper. "That's a strange tale, Mr. Compton."

He is smiling, as he so often is, when he looks at me again, but his eyes are serious. "What you make of the story is none of my business, Dix. I just wanted to tell it. It's a fine night for stories."

"Yes, sir." My voice squeaks out, quaking.

"Morning comes early. You should head below." He dismisses me now the same way I dismissed the captain.

That no one has said anything about my hammock remaining in the passage between quarters with Harry makes sense now. If the second mate knows and is not interested in getting me marooned, he would make excuses for me to remain. In the morning I might have more emotions to sort through, but in this moment, I am trembling with pure terror.

CHAPTER 9

ARRY CRIES IN THE DARK BESIDE ME UNTIL HE FALLS ASLEEP EVERY NIGHT. His tears are as predictable as his snores.

I do not know if comforting Harry is the right thing to do. Aboard this ship, emotions are far from anyone's priority.

The entirety of my wretched day has been spent trying to remain as far out of the second mate's path as possible. The man has not spilled my secret yet, but he could. I carry a vain hope that if I stay far away from him, he might forget about me entirely. The trouble is this ship is a small world and I share an even smaller passageway with the man below deck.

If he gives me away, I will have to leave. And though it has always been true that I have to leave, the choice being ripped from me would sting.

Simply put, I could use some comfort tonight. Since no one can comfort me, I might settle for trying my hand at comforting Harry.

"If you ever want to talk about whatever it is, I will listen." I say softly into the darkness to my young friend.

Harry sniffles, and I imagine him wiping his tears on his grimy shirt. The action alone would defiantly say, *I was not crying.*

He remains silent for so long that I have managed to soothe my own aching mind and heart some by the time he answers.

"I was on the street a long while before Hugh caught me stowin' away. He said I could make it up to him by working on the ship. We both knew he was doin' me a favor."

The parts of his story that he has chosen to share are few, but I know enough of grief to be able to piece together the rest. Thinking about Harry has helped slow my racing blood.

My words are tentative, but sincere. "I am sorry about your family, Harry."

He counters, "I have a new one now."

Harry does not say it to dismiss his own loss or my care. It is a fact. Even though he cannot see me in the dark, I nod. To those of us with no one, the friendships here could be easily mistaken for something far more loving than it is.

I lie awake for hours thinking about family. Would these men leave me alone on a beach somewhere? Mickey Compton clearly knows and does not seem eager for me to be dead. Does he speak for the others?

No. Men are the same everywhere. I will not be taking the risk.

Sleeplessness plagues me until even Harry's snoring has become less a familiar comfort and more an irritating reminder of my inability to properly rest. I would much rather be out on deck in the cool air than spending any more time tossing and turning in my hammock.

Mickey is still at the helm, writing in a journal by lamplight. He nods in my direction when I climb up but does not say anything. From what I have gathered in our few conversations he struggles to find any sleep at all. I do not know what could be keeping the second mate awake. Nothing seems to faze or challenge him as far as I can ascertain.

The ship is run primarily by those who cannot sleep by night. Some nights there are more crew on deck than others. Tonight, it's just me, Mickey, and one other man who watches the sea.

With smooth seas and easy wind, there isn't anything for the crew to be doing anyway. I could find work, but my attention is pulled again. I would rather watch the water, where the sky is reflected so perfectly in the gently rippling sea it feels like we are sailing in the heavens themselves.

The hatch on the quarterdeck squeaks on its hinges, startlingly loud in the silent darkness. In the lantern light where Mickey writes, I can make out Hugh Digby climbing out.

Mickey's face lights up upon seeing the quartermaster. I can only see Hugh's back, but something tells me the joy is mutual.

I stay perfectly still on the masts. Their relationship makes almost no sense to me. Mickey Compton is easily the nicest man on this ship, perhaps the nicest I have ever met. Hugh is like a walking blade. No one should get too close, lest they get cut.

As though to prove me wrong, the quartermaster steps behind Mickey and wraps his arms around the other man's shoulders. Mickey visibly relaxes into Hugh's tanned arms like it is the most natural thing in the world. All my assumptions about the cruel quartermaster are challenged in a single embrace. Whispered words I cannot hear, easy smiles, and soft kisses on calloused knuckles and sunburned necks pass between them. Perfectly innocent, in stark contrast to their professions and setting.

I feel guilty, at being a voyeur to their intimacy, but I do not want to move and break the spell. The night's stars pale in comparison to such an exotic sight. A happy couple together because they want to be is a rare thing, and not just at sea.

Next to the guilt rests a jealousy I struggle to quiet. No one has ever held me like that. I doubt anyone ever will.

CHAPTER 10

I HAVE SPENT SO MUCH TIME HIGH ABOVE DECK THAT I NOW FEEL MORE comfortable on the masts than anywhere else on the ship. James teases me for it, reminding me often that being made to stay aloft for long stretches is a punishment given to unruly sailors. Still, I prefer to remain up high. If anything, it makes me less noticeable and since Mickey's story, I have been working hard to make myself scarce in all the ways one can on a ship.

Harry has joined me today to avoid notice as well. In his case, it is because he tossed one of the captain's shirts over a lantern and nearly started a blaze that would have seen us all dead. Plus, he ruined one of the captain's shirts.

It was an accident, but the captain kicked him up the ladder onto the deck and had the crew vote on whether he should be caned on his bare bottom like a rotten child or not. There was only one vote difference in his favor, and it did not stop half the crew from bruising him up regardless.

Harry scurried up beside me like a frightened cat and has been beside me in silence ever since. Beyond the occasional sniffle or huff, he has been still. I have let him keep me silent company, finding comfort in the companionship words could not offer.

Eventually, Harry speaks so softly I can scarcely hear him over the wind. "It really was an accident."

I rest a friendly hand on his shoulder. "I know you would not try to sink the ship on purpose, Harry."

He throws a hand up in the air, keeping the other on the wood and canvas before him. "Half the crew thinks that I meant to see us all turned into flames and ashes! Hugh's gonna have me doing nothing but swabbing and stoning the deck for days to make up for it. Might even make me pay for the captain's new shirt."

His grumbling and indignation might condemn him to others, but it makes me smile. Harry has a firm sense of what is fair, and I find it admirable.

"They all know it was an accident. They are just brutes who never learned how to forgive anybody."

"My ma wouldn'ta beat me for an accident. She would say accidents are wisdom gained." Harry has never mentioned his mother before. She sounds like a far nicer person than my own mother was.

"Sounds like she was wise enough to know. You will not toss a shirt aside without thought again."

Harry shakes his head dramatically, the corners of his pink mouth lifting just enough to show a hint of dimple in his barely fuzzed cheek. "Not me, Dix!"

It has been a quiet few days with no ships coming or going.

Below, Captain Holt watches the sea, his agitation clear from his clenched fist to his rod-straight back.

Harry catches me looking. "What are you staring at?"

"The captain. What is he looking for?" I do not suppose telling the truth could hurt.

Harry hisses through his teeth before beginning his climb down, away from me. When I give him a questioning look, the boy levels eyes full of disappointment on me before shouting, freeing a hand to gesture wildly at the heavens. "Damned fates, Dix, I'm not tempting the lucky lady by telling stories."

For weeks I have been on this ship eavesdropping, and anytime anyone gets close to naming the predator to our prey they either trail off, point at the heavens, or wave an angry arm towards the coin at the helm and mutter prayers.

I know that I could ask Mickey Compton and he would likely tell me, but for now I am giving the second mate as wide a berth as possible when trapped by the ocean on all sides.

The captain paces. I recognize the tension in him as something I have often felt in myself, like there is too much emotion coiled inside me with no outlet. A pang of empathy flares within me, followed by a wave of pity. The feeling is as consuming as it is confusing.

Captain Holt slaps his hands on the railing, probably hard enough to make his palms sting, and then jerks them away. His gaze reaches the sun edging down the horizon before swinging back to the *Sneaky Lass* and her crew. As he often does, he scans the ropes for me. This time, when he finds I am watching him, he averts his eyes without the customary acknowledging nod.

It has been a too-hot day with very little to do. I let too much time pass above and, upon returning to the deck, I discover my ears are ringing from the wind and my knees are weak. Though perhaps the latter is more from the decision I made on my descent rather than from being aloft so long.

For the first time, I approach the captain rather than waiting for him to come to me. Even as I tell myself that the answers he can give me will belay my boredom, I know that the real reason for my approach is that I desire to offer him the same sort of quick and strange distraction that he often gifts me.

The surprise on his face is genuine when he realizes I am leaning on the rail beside him. "Would you like to tell me what has set you to pacing like a dog in a pen?" I try to strike a balance between sincerity and curiosity in my tone, but I do not know if I succeeded.

Captain Holt blinks at me a few times before chuckling to himself. That he did not expect such a phrase from my lips is apparent by the rise of his brow.

"A dog in a pen? Aye, that's apt."

That does not answer my question. I cannot tell if he is being evasive or is locked so deeply in his own thoughts that he did not hear it.

I inhale the fresh, salty air, solidifying my resolve to ask Captain Holt the same question I asked Harry.

"What are you looking for?"

"That's usually what I ask you."

"Yes, but I look for something more..." I trail off, lacking the word for what I search for. I motion out to the sea and the sky and then myself with an open hand.

It must be enough explanation because the captain grins knowingly, giving me the courage to forge on. "You are clearly looking for something specific." I point to the small spyglass he is holding in a clenched fist.

Curiosity is an affliction I have carried since childhood. I have always wanted to know everything, even when ignorance would serve me better. I want to know what chases us, and now that I have dropped the question in his lap, I do not know if I can put it away again.

When he does not send me away, I summon courage and continue, "Is it the thing that chases this ship, that no one will name aloud? Given your clear nerves, and as a new member of this crew, I would like to know more about what monsters we face."

Captain Bennett Holt puts the spyglass into his pocket and sighs at my persistence, which is better than having made him angry.

"You're not the superstitious type, Ables?"

I am not. I think if powers exist, they like to torture poor human souls regardless of how we behave.

"I only believe in gods and fates when it is time to curse them, Captain. As for luck, I have not run across much of it."

"Not a believer in the coin at the helm, then?"

I am more a believer in the three silver coins in my boot than the plate at the helm.

"I believe it is there to kiss and that I would be ended in an instant if I did not kiss her and the wind stopped." I meet his manner and respond as nonchalantly as I feel about it. I can only hope we are truly as friendly as he seems.

The roar of Captain Holt's laughter is unexpected in a nice way. I find myself laughing with him. When the merriment settles, he smiles with his entire face and it makes him look positively jolly.

"I believe you'll find the superstitions will grow on you like barnacles on our hull the longer you stay on the sea, Ables. For now, your clear head is refreshing."

I doubt superstition will grow on me, but I do not tell him as much. My curiosity, however, is far more relentless than barnacles. I will not go unanswered.

"So, will you finally tell me?"

His eyes shine and my heart leaps into my throat with the anticipation.

"There is a navy frigate that chases us. Her captain's named Gates and he searches for me."

Feeling empty at such a lackluster answer in comparison to all the avoidance I have been met with, I try to sort out why that would be frightening to a bunch of pirates and fail.

"The Navy is all then? That is not so frightening as everyone made it sound. Of course the Navy would be after this ship. We have stolen shiploads of goods just since my arrival."

"This ship does not chase us because we are pirates or because of orders on high, but out of personal spite. She nearly blew us to pieces last we met and took a lot of good men with her. I wouldn't put my crew through meeting *Three Queens* again anytime soon, and it might be inevitable."

I know the ship *Three Queens*. I saw it once. I received letters that included its name and sent letters into its holds. The air shifts around us as I become as pensive and agitated as Captain Bennett Holt had been.

At my silence, the captain turns away from the horizon to face me instead. "Have I made a believer of you? It would seem someone walks over your grave."

"Frightening to hear you speak of vendettas is all." I try to shake away ancient memories.

"You know something I don't, Ables?" The captain is unconvinced, his tone as serious as sin.

I get the chance to tell so few truths that part of me wishes to to tell Captain Holt the truth, and it feels like one I can spare. Every man on this ship has a history, and I do not suppose it would be held against me among thieves. At least, I hope not.

"A few lifetimes ago now, I knew that ship."

He looks me up and down, making me nervous. "A few lifetimes? You're what? Not a day over twenty, surely."

I inwardly applaud how well my ruse is working and do not

correct him. "I was only a child when I knew someone on the deck of *Three Queens*."

Captain Holt looks surprised and whispers towards the heavens, "Fates."

"I do not believe in fates." I remind him with a wink.

Captain Holt knocks his shoulder into mine. "You're an odd one, Dixon. Who did you know in the Navy? It usually runs in families and yet you come to my ship not knowing how to tie a half-hitch."

I search for a way to walk between the truth and lies.

"My brother was five years older. My mother paid for his apprenticeship on *Three Queens*. By the time I would have been old enough, she was dead, the money was gone, and my father had no thoughts left for me. I was not smart enough to run away to the Navy on my own."

I have purposefully not thought much of Michael until taking my place on *Sneaky Lass*. Remembering him always hurts for more reasons than I can properly count, and none I can get away with confiding in the captain as Dixon.

I tell Bennett Holt the same likely-true, but unproven, thing I have often told myself. "He died years ago, my brother."

Biting his lip, my uncomfortable captain attempt to comfort me. "I'm sorry to hear that."

Michael, left me to something far worse than fates, he left me to our father's handling alone. The part of me that misses him is far smaller than the part that would rather him be dead, if only so I never have to explain myself to him.

"You need not be sorry. We were close and then we were not. Now, he is dead."

My retort snaps out more biting than I meant. The captain raises a brow, putting his hand on top of mine in a way that would not be suggestive if I were telling the tale of Dixon Ables, but I am not. I am speaking as Jane and he does not know it.

"I'm also sorry you clearly suffered, though, I doubt you would have suffered less in the Navy."

How little he knows.

I let his hand sit atop mine longer than I should. It has been years since someone last tried to comfort me with a touch. So long that I do not remember the last time.

I flip my hand so I am holding his rough fingers before he can lift his hand from mine. It feels like the natural next thing to do. I hold it for just a moment before letting go, returning my hand to my pocket.

"Thank you, Captain." I do not know if I mean to thank him for the touch or for his sympathy.

My mother had a ring when I was small. It was actually four rings interlocked, and if each was moved in the right order they formed a braided band that sat on her smallest finger. She always managed to solve it eventually, but beforehand, she would stare at the four rings in the same way Captain Bennett Holt is staring at me right now.

Nervous under his gaze, I try to return to my original purpose of drawing the captain from his discontent. "It would seem this enemy of yours is not floating behind us tonight. Thank you for telling me. I have been lost to our plight since arriving."

The captain is not a traditionally handsome man, but he wears a handsome, lopsided grin when he responds. "I am happy to instruct you, Dixon. It is our collective duty to instruct new hands, though we've all mostly saddled you on James."

Despite knowing that I should not, I want to spend more time with him. It is, at least in part, because he seems interested in spending time with me.

"In that case, I have another question. I have been hesitant to join the rest playing spades because I do not know the rules and think some may cheat me. Would you mind? It would keep you from pacing so."

Perhaps it is my imagination, but Bennett Holt looks very interested in helping me. It is not the first time I have suspected his interest to be more than friendly, but it is the first time I have been certain of it.

His eyes alight and he grins with his whole face again. I think I would do anything to make him smile at me like that. Lines form on his cheeks to follow the upturned corners of his mouth and the tip of his tongue is pressed between his teeth.

"I did not think you were terribly interested in making friends, with how aloof you tend to be. I feel honored."

"I am not aloof. I just do not know the rules. You have surely heard how they all torment me for my ignorance in sailing. I do not intend to see if it holds true in card games, too."

"Shy, then?"

Men are not shy. Damn. Do I come off as shy?

Not waiting for my answer, he walks towards the hatch that leads beneath the quarterdeck, still grinning. "I'll get my deck and be back."

I watch his retreating back, dangerous notions floating around my heart. Our next stop is mere days away. I will disembark and playing cards with the curious captain will no longer matter.

I hope.

CHAPTER 11

WITHOUT WARNING, THE BRASS BELL CLANGS ABOVE MY HEAD, THE surprise pushing a bit of the biscuit I was eating down the wrong pipe. Above my cough, I hear shouts that first sound like gibberish, as the shouts of my shipmates often do, which slowly become clearer.

"Land, ho! Azure Cove in sight!"

The entire crew erupts into cheers. My heart thrums fast. I should be relieved. This is where we will sell our haul of misbegotten prizes, divvy up the money, and I will be on my way to starting another life as Jane. I have successfully managed what had felt impossible. I survived on a pirate ship and kept up my disguise. But as the opportunity for escape draws closer, the desire to leave *Sneaky Lass* moves further away. Even as logic howls a hundred reasons to go, my heart holds firmly to the rig.

I squint over the sea and find nothing, which I suppose is why I am not the lookout. Captain Holt is on the main deck giving orders; calling all hands to the deck to move canvas from the jibs to the topgallant, changing our course to the east side of the stretch of beach that houses Azure Cove.

Beside me, the men who have been to Azure Cove before are chattering excitedly about their favorite brothels and whores in the port, while the men who have not been here before absorb every detail, drinking in the recommendations. Soon, we will get paid and they will spend their money before it can grow warm in their hands. Everyone is anxious to be off the ship—save me.

The moment my feet step back onto dry land all the problems I ran away from will come flooding back. My chest tightens until my breathing is shallow and labored. My husband's ghost, bottle in one hand and his belt in the other, will stand on the dock waiting to whip me for running. The boy whose clothes I am wearing will be demanding the return of his boots. Madam Hattie will have her palm out for me to pay her back for the dress I ran away in. Of course they will not be, but the panic will not be so easily quelled by reason.

Within an hour, the land the lookout had spotted becomes a reality in the distance to the rest of us. The ship is bustling with new work in preparation to drop anchors. Sails are stowed, knots are untied and retied in new places, and the heavier prizes, bales of cotton and the like, are moved to different parts of the ship so we can maneuver more easily into the shallows. All the while, men take moments to pause their work and look wistfully out over the sea towards the trees and sand, imagining a warm woman, strong booze, and the wonders of fresh food.

We have sailed far enough south that the hard winter that we left behind in Grand Port is milder here, if it ever comes at all. As we get closer I can see the trees are not the pines of my former life, but oaks that spread their branches out wide, catching moss that dangles low by the ground. The elation, as usual, is infectious. I join in the conversations as though I do not plan on slipping away.

Pax the carpenter, on my right, speaks to no one in particular with an air of nostalgia at the thought of his favorite whore.

"Juliette's plump bottom is going to be mine! That woman worships me. She will be my first stop."

It is interesting, and enlightening, to be on the other side of conversations about prostitutes after spending so many months of my life as the topic. Pax speaks of this Juliette with awe and wonder. I had regulars in Grand Port. I wonder if they ever spoke of me such.

I answer him even if he does not seek my opinion. "I think my first stop is going to be a good place for a proper wash. Perhaps yours should be as well. Juliette would worship you better."

Pax howls with laughter, showing off his missing front teeth and the rotting rest. He cups my shoulder hard in his big hand. "Fancy boy like you would think of that. You're probably right."

I knock him back, having done Juliette a huge favor.

Even if I have lost the ability to smell it, I know we all reek worse than hogs. My washes have been even quicker and more secretive than the minimal hygiene practiced among the crew, stealing moments when Harry is sleeping to rinse where I can, taking time to retighten the bindings over my chest. My courses, not an easy thing to handle in the best of circumstances, were a special sort of disaster aboard the ship. I fear the filth may be a large part of what hides my sex from the rest of the sailors, but I am ready to find some secluded place to truly wash the grime away.

The captain puts a hand on my back, and I jump. When I turn, he simply motions me to come with him. Each time I have been alone with the captain I have waited for him to call my bluff. He never has. And since he taught me how to play spades, we have been speaking even more like friends.

I follow him to his quarters where I am meant to help him into his fine clothing. In his cabin, I tie knots and fasten buttons. The jovial mood on deck and the continued success of my disguise has me speaking without thinking, and before I can stop myself, I share my thoughts.

"It must be exhausting to be an actor on a stage." As soon as the words leave my mouth, I refocus on my task of buttoning the gilded buttons at his knees.

"Sorry, Captain. I did not mean to say that aloud. Just that it's all so unlike you, the silver and gold."

Smiling wryly, he responds how I have come to expect, his tone light. "It is fine, Dixon. You are doing me a favor by dressing me when you do not have to. Speak your mind. I find I often like what goes on in your head."

I am shocked by the compliment as he holds out his arm and I begin fastening the gilt buttons that run to his wrist. I do not know why he would like anything in my head.

My father, my husband, my madam and every man in Grand Port told me to be silent. I can count the people who have liked anything I have had to say on one hand.

When I grow quiet, he pushes me to speak, "Tell me, why do you think it would be exhausting?"

I release a long breath, feeling lightened by his request to hear my thoughts. I had not known how heavy a burden silence was until it was lifted. "Well, all I meant was that not being able to be oneself seems like it would be tiresome."

I am pushing some of my own exhaustion with disguises onto the captain. I watch my fingers and wait for him to tell me all the reasons I am wrong.

86

He hums quietly in agreement, which makes me look up once more.

"As usual, you have read my thoughts. It does not help that I find being at port tiresome already. Azure Cove, especially so. We've come here a lot the last six months out."

Since he does not mind my speaking, I push the conversation, "Why do you not like Azure Cove?"

He shakes his head and lets out an annoyed huff, "I imagine you'll see why once we get there. Some places are better suited for pirates than others and Azure Cove is rougher than most."

I help him slide on his coat. He looks in the mirror and catches my eyes reflected there. He speaks to my reflection in the small mirror on the wall, "Be careful in the town, Ables. Azure Cove has few decent people in it. Go armed, and you should stay close to this crew."

His concern catches me off guard and I find myself desperate for anything to do rather than look at him. The part of me that worries he knows my secret flares, as if he just noticed all the reasons Dixon should be weary; how useless Dixon is with weapons, how nervous he is around the men when they drink, how sick he gets in the face of violence.

I go to the peg on the wall and grab his hat for him. He holds it at his side and his shoulders sag. Then, like an actor in a grand play, he places the cocked hat on his head, straightens his back, and becomes someone else before my eyes.

"Remember what I said." He levels a pointed stare at me.

"I will." He walks towards the door, and I fall in step behind him.

Though the men always show Captain Holt respect, they hush quickly and stand at firmer attention than usual. He cuts an exceptional figure at the helm of the ship in his long coat and hat. I can only imagine how hot he must feel in the sun. His resolve to put on a show is a wonder, even the heat of the day does not touch him.

The captain calls over the clamor, "Men, Hugh and I plan to go to Port and make a deal with a—" He pauses for a moment, searching for the right words. When he finds one, he smirks. "—a legitimate merchant."

Some of the men snigger and one hollers.

The captain continues, "Once we have made the deal, we will unload, and you will all get your share and a few days to spend it."

More cheers from the men resound around me, including Harry who jumps and lets out an excited, "Hurrah!"

The captain steps back and Hugh Digby steps up and says one last word to the men, "Look out for good sailors at port, men. We are still running on bare bones. Find anyone that can abide, run them by me."

The ship runs on a fair system of pay. The captain's full share and half of prizes makes sense, it is more for the ship than for him as he purchases crew provisions, port fees, repairs, and whatever else is needed that we do not steal along the way.

I was pleased to find that, though not mentioned in the charter, James receives one share and a half. I have been told that James is the closest the ship has to a boatswain, so he clearly deserves the pay. Harry and I get a half because we do not know enough to be very useful yet. Maybe next we stop—

No. I will not be stopping again.

I signed my name to the rules upon arrival and they are followed to the letter.

Hugh pushes a small tower of silver coins across the table to me and, even though he dislikes me, I trust him enough not to count it, just like all the men who collected before me. It may not be a life-changing amount of money, but my husband never let me touch any at all and my madam took almost every coin I made. I have never had enough coin at once to warrant a purse on my hip unless it was stolen. I slip the silver into the drawstring leather purse I stole from the young man in Grand Port, and then tuck the purse into my boot beside the three silver coins the captain tossed Jane in Grand Port.

The men make straight for the local taverns and whores, taking the small landing boat back and forth. James insists on my coming to shore with him for a hot meal. I want to decline. The coin I have should be enough for a bath and a room alone with plenty to spare. The spare will be needed to sort out whatever my life will be now that I am leaving *Sneaky Lass.*

My heart pounds louder in my ears at the thought. My mind quickly fills with a dozen terrible scenarios and even more questions I cannot answer. Images of cruel pimps and rotten customers slipping between my thighs makes me feel sick. It is my inevitable end. Why did I bother leaving Grand Port at all, only to end up doing the same thing somewhere new? Can I keep Dixon? How long could I keep up this ruse? What would I do if I managed it?

Before we leave the ship, I grab the spare set of clothing I earned being a part of the boarding party for one of the ships we took. I tuck them into the band of my breeches to change into after a long-awaited and thorough wash.

Harry and Mickey come with us, among others. I have been mostly avoiding the second mate since his story, but in the small boat there is no escaping him.

For now, he is lecturing Harry like a mother might. "Remember you are not to leave my sight at port after nightfall. You are not to even return to the ship without me, understood? Break my rules and I'll ensure you never step foot on land again, got it? Azure Cove is no place for you."

Harry nods.

"Not gonna let the kid have any fun?" James speaks disapprovingly to the second mate.

Mickey Compton levels his blue eyes at me when he answers James, and speaks as though I am as young and foolish as Harry is. "Not all ports are as safe for some of our crew as they are for you and me, James."

The rigger laughs and keeps rowing towards shore, but I do not join in his fun. I am watching Mickey's warning look.

Those dozens of questions and unseeable futures return to pound against my brain with their full force.

I wish I had stayed on the ship.

CHAPTER 12

THE CITY OF AZURE COVE IS FILLED WITH CHEAP AND SINFUL entertainment for pirates. It is also filled with mud, poverty, and squalor. The air is foul with the stench of human waste, as it is tossed from the windows above without care. My boots sink and squelch in the muddy ruts that appear to be the only roads. I do not think I will find any way to feel clean in this place. The air itself makes me feel sticky all over. Most of the buildings make the shanties where I worked in Grand Port look like lovely garden homes. The buildings are all crooked, rotting into the sandy soil and peeling paint when they are painted at all.

As far as I can tell, there are only two types of people in this port: pirates and whores. There must be more infrastructure somewhere. It cannot just be a haven for villains and those who entertain villains. I find nothing to prove that theory in any of the places James leads me.

Many of the prostitutes forgo clothing altogether. Some lean out of windows and motion us over with slim fingers. One smokes a pipe, squatting close to the earth, legs spread, wearing only a pair of muddy boots. She has tally marks tattooed on her back. I have no idea what they could be counting, but it is nothing good.

One woman with seeping sores on her neck and brightly rouged lips informs me how she could teach a boy of my youth how to use parts I do not actually possess in ways I never even heard of despite my time in the trade. Blood rushes to my face at her words and James guffaws, endlessly amused.

When we enter a rough looking tavern called *Twin Mermaids,* I am just relieved that everyone inside is clothed to some degree. James abandons me for a woman called Scarlett so I approach the man working behind the bar.

"Can I pay for a bath, hot food, and room for an hour?" Then, looking about the room, I specify, "No company, please."

The hall is so loud with rough looking sailors, giggling women, and a group of men playing drums and singing that I can barely hear the barkeep's reply.

The man reveals his perfect, white teeth behind a thick mustache when he smiles. A startling sight in a place such as this. His teeth might be the only clean and proper thing in all Azure Cove.

He hands me a key and shouts over the noisy patrons, "Third door at the top of the stairs. I'll have water brought, but it won't be as hot as the food."

His strange accent is so thick I barely catch the instructions. I pay him with a silver piece and if there was to be any change, he kept it.

By the stairs, a woman is holding a fan made of white feathers. She hands one of the feathers from her fan to a man who leaves her with a curt nod, tucking it into his collar where it can be easily seen. She looks at me expectantly when I approach the stairs alone. I know her type and purpose. The men with white feathers will be seeking one another out tonight in this hall, a secretive means for men to give away their preference for one another.

One look at me, at my more feminine features and empty arm, and she saunters closer. I wave her off, feet moving up the stairs in a greater hurry than before.

I am pleasantly surprised by how much quieter the room is than the hall. I avoid the bed, not wanting to catch any of the pests that may live in such a mattress. Instead, I sit on the floor and lean my head against the wall.

When I shut my eyes the room sways in the same way the ship does at sea, like my blood is still moving with the waves even though I am now still. It is disconcerting and makes me feel ill. I did not get seasick, but it seems coming back to land holds its own kind of discomfort.

Hot food is brought in first. A large bowl of unidentifiable meats and greens I have never seen or tasted before is set on a table in the corner. It is so full of sweet, unexpected spices that I nearly cough when I bring it to my lips. After so long of the mostly flavorless rations on *Sneaky Lass* it is nearly too much for me.

I take another bite anyway, and by the third, I am more accustomed to the array of flavors meant to cover up whatever the stew is made of. The meat is stringy and I pretend it is fowl, but it is definitely not fowl.

It takes a lot longer than I thought it would for water to be brought. As promised, it is not warm when it arrives, but it is clean and not seawater. A large washtub is brought in first with a bar of lye soap placed beside it, and then a young girl dressed in rags with a dirty face comes in over and over again with a small pail to fill it. I feel guilty making her do so much work just to get myself clean. Each time she enters the guilt grows worse.

When the tub is halfway full I tell her that it is plenty. She doesn't understand me. I think she might be from a place where my language is not spoken, perhaps stolen away. Maybe she is deaf. I push a coin into her hand and shut and lock the door behind her so that she gets the point. Her job is done as far as I am concerned.

Even in cold water, washing away the sea feels like washing off a layer of skin. I might actually be doing just that with how the lye-heavy soap stings where it touches. I cannot bring myself to complain about it even in my own mind. It is what I asked for and it is not so uncomfortable that I would stop short.

With the grime goes Dixon and the armor I have been very successfully hiding behind these short weeks at sea. The sting of the lye soap is nothing compared to the sting I feel when I consider staying here. Would Azure Cove be so much better than marooned? I do not think so. Would I not just become one of the women we saw on our way in? One of the women in the hall below? Like the stolen girl who brought this water to me?

Like a bad apple, sometimes, you do not know it is rotten until you take a bite. I was like that once not long ago. All rotten inside.

Dixon is alive. Really alive. Even just washing him away, I feel rotted again.

There is no mirror in the room, but I do not need one to be surprised at what I see when I look down at myself. I hardly recognize the wiry, tan semi-sailor I have become in only a few weeks on a ship. Where my clothes protected me from the sun, I still carry the same fair skin I was born with. Where my clothing did not cover me, I am dark like the shell of a nut and freckled so densely one would never guess what lies beneath them. I decide that I likely cut a rather handsome figure. It is a foreign feeling. As

Jane, I never felt beautiful. As Dixon, I think I like the view of myself more.

I run my clothes through the tub next, scraping away as much of the grime as I can and running the bar of soap over them several times until little is left. My hands are itchy and raw by the time I am done, and I have created a few more tears in my shirt than before, the fabric not completely surviving my rough washing.

The humid air of Azure Cove means my old clothes will take hours to dry, so I simply wring them out as best I can and carry them out with me in the same way I carried my new set in.

When I leave the room and re-enter the raucous brothel hall I do not bother trying to find James in the masses. The captain sits at the bar drunk and wearing his typical ship-worn attire among friends. The man beside him, who I do not recognize from our crew, wears a white feather in the ribbon on his cap to give himself away to other men as potential company. I do not see a white feather on the captain.

A naked woman sits in his lap and the captain spanks her for her boldness then kisses her when she gasps at his gall.

I do not know how I feel about any of it, but it makes me feel some confusing way that I do not want to try untangling tonight.

Kicking myself for noticing the captain at all, I leave in the hope of finding my own way back to the ship quickly. Bennett Holt is the reason I should stay right where I am, with how he looks and wonders about me. The captain was right, though. There is little to like about Azure Cove and his reasons for disliking the place are obvious. Those dozens of scenarios and questions about what might become of me here have one clear answer. Nothing will become of me in Azure Cove for I will not be staying. I will find my way back to *Sneaky Lass*.

The dark alleyways and muddy streets are filled with villains tonight, and it does not ease my nerves that I am among their number. My disguise will only buy me so much safety. Every laugh from a distant group of drunkards or shout from a bar fight makes me jump.

As it turns out, my anxiety is warranted. Three men fall in behind me, smelling my fear like dogs do. They keep their distance, yet it does not take long for me to know for certain that they are following me. I start walking faster but there is nowhere to go. I am too close to the water, and the businesses of the town are behind me. The men begin closing the gap and I duck into an alley to try and lose them.

The next street is even darker than the last and the men are still behind. While they are in the alley I start running. The men laugh and make chase. I feel like a hunted rabbit.

In the dark, I can hardly make out any landmarks from earlier in the day when I arrived. I only know that if I run long enough in this direction, I will reach the water. It will not do me any good since I cannot swim.

I do not shout. I would probably just bring more danger down on myself. I must keep my head because, just like always when I am on land, I am alone.

My heart pounds in my ears in time with my boots stomping the pebbled path beneath me. I can hear the men calling for me, they are so close I can hear their ragged breathing just as clearly as my own.

They mean to rob me, certainly. To be robbed would not be so bad, but if they discovered more in the process, would they even bother to let me live after they had their way? The thoughts have me moving faster than I knew I could go.

Ahead, there is a warehouse door hanging open and askew. The men are gaining on me, and though the threat of collapse scorches my lungs and spreads down through my legs, I push my body inside the decrepit building. It is dark inside, lit only by the moonlight streaming through the doorway. The building is filled with broken barrels, lumber, and a lump that might be a man. If it is a man, I cannot tell if he is dead or asleep.

I slide along the wall slowly, wincing at every sound my boots make on the creaking floor and every shuffle of clothing against the wall behind me. My leg bumps against a mostly intact barrel and I duck behind it. The men who chase me burst into the building at the same moment that I retrieve my jackknife from my pocket and flip it open. They stop dead in their tracks when they see all the places I could be hiding.

The longer I hold my breath, the fear of fainting roars louder with each beat of my pounding heart.

After what feels like an eternity the men turn and leave through the same door they entered, grumbling about a good chase.

I release my breath but stay crouched and silent for so long that my ankles and calves begin to shake. Tears sting my eyes and, though no one would see them fall here, I manage to keep them at bay. I must keep my head about me. I am not safe yet.

The possibility of staying all night plays in my mind, only the possible corpse for company. It would be safer if I did, but I do not want to. I want to go home, and home floats in the bay.

Creeping towards the door, I check all directions as far as I can see in the dim light of the half moon and then walk towards the water again. The leftover fear still swirls just beneath my skin. It takes a lot of convincing to keep my pace steady and not to run ahead. I will be staying on *Sneaky Lass* for as long as she will have me. Whatever may happen to me on the ship cannot be as bad as my life would be in the desperate pit called Azure Cove.

It was a good call to duck and hide. I am not far from the beach. If I had kept running this would have been the end of the line. Now, I am unsure what my next step should be. Frustratingly, I can see the ship and her lanterns on the water; I just cannot get to her.

"You can come back with me."

I yelp in a very unmasculine way at the sound of the captain's voice before sighing with relief to see his silhouette against the moonlit sky and not that of a stranger who snuck up on me. He has left his finery behind on the ship and stands before me now looking as weatherworn as any other of our number. As drunk as the rest, too.

"There are other men on the ship who can return the boat to shore." He adds.

"Do you know if Harry made it back alright?" I try to cover up my own fear with concern for a shipmate.

He shrugs, but upon seeing my wide-eyed expression he answers me well enough. "Mickey won't have let anything happen to that little villain."

Clearing my throat and steadying my heart, I try to save face, "I have no other choice but to accept your offer, Captain. I cannot swim and I cannot stay here."

He leads me by the arm towards one of the smallest boats used to carry men here from our ship. If I took it alone then it would be stuck on the water, unable to help others come and go as they please. I am not confident in my ability to row all the way out to where the *Lass* is anchored anyway, certainly not in my state. Trembling all over and jumping at every cricket's song.

Bennet pushes the boat towards the water and speaks with a drink-slowed tongue, "You have company in your plight. Most sailors can't swim...I can swim." I think he means to sound impressive in saying it. I can hear his smile in his tone.

He trips over his feet twice in his task and chuckles at himself, cursing his own clumsiness. Even if he did not reek of booze, he would be clearly drunk. Intoxication would have been enough for me to avoid him in any other circumstance, but tonight, he is the safest person I have come across even if he smells like my father and raises gooseflesh on my arms where he touches.

Better the single drunk man I know than the hundreds on this island I do not. I step onto the boat and he takes up the oars despite my reaching for them first.

He begins rowing with a simple explanation. "I will get us there faster. I am merely doing you a service, Ables. You can make it up to me in some other way another time."

Owing favors to anyone is not my preference. I look up at the moon and perhaps he can see more of my anxiety than I thought in the dark, because he adds, "I'm jesting, Dixon. We happen to be going to the same place at the same time."

I drop my tense shoulders with relief and the captain notices. It would seem liquor loosens his tongue, his words slur slightly from drink. "Here, I thought you were eager to sail to the end of the world and jump off it. Are the streets of Azure Cove more frightening than all that?"

From his tone, it is as though he came to Azure Cove on purpose to frighten me back onto the ship. It is not the case; Azure Cove has been his target for weeks. Still, if it had been a plan, it would have been a good one.

I know he expects an answer, so I keep it short. "Did I seem frightened?"

"Like a rabbit in a trap." I avert my gaze away from the captain and say nothing back. He continues in my place, filling the silence. "Not that I blame you. Azure Cove can be a scary place. You did not bring your weapons like I told you."

"I do not own any weapons, Captain." I quietly answer him, feeling more like a scolded child the longer he goes on.

He just shakes his head again and we are both silent for a time. My whole body is still trembling from what happened on land and I tuck my hands between my thighs to hide their shaking.

Captain Holt watches me while he rows. I do not think he will remember much of this come morning, so I keep talking in an attempt to clear my head. Those men and what might have happened had they caught me still circles me like crows around carrion.

"Even if I had a weapon, Captain, it would not do me much good when a group of men want to rob me. I cannot take them all at once. I barely know how to hold a pistol, let alone fire one. I have never so much as touched a sword. You think I am useless on a rig; you should see me with a weapon. You would think me proper tar. I had to hide and wait for them to lose interest."

Captain Holt looks puzzled. He struggles to find the words he wants to say through his drunkenness. "Where was James? I thought you two came to shore together?"

I had not thought about James since leaving the brothel. I swallow my annoyance at the rigger for abandoning me so easily. It is not his job to protect me, and I left without him fair and square. "He is slipping between the legs of a woman called Scarlett, if he got his way. We parted as soon as we arrived having different interests in mind."

Captain Holt pulls in the oars and throws them at his feet, shouting, "He promised to watch you!"

Like a boy throwing a fit, Bennett Holt throws his hands in the air and groans, "Gods and fates."

Underneath my surprise at his outburst, I feel insulted. I decide to voice my frustration if only to hide my new discomfort from being on a boat, inches from drowning, with a drunk and angry man.

"I do not need anyone to watch me, Captain. I am used to being on my own. I—" The words *I am fine* rest on the tip of my tongue, but they feel too terrible a lie for even the likes of me to tell. I swallow them down.

It is one thing for me not to know how to defend myself, but another entirely for Captain Holt to think it.

The captain levels a look at me, more sober now in his anger.

"You weren't carrying any weapons and you don't know how to use one. You could have been killed." His emotional response has me stunned and by the look on Captain Holt's face, I would be willing to bet he has said more than he meant. Calmer now, he adds, "What I mean is you're an asset to my crew. Your usefulness to me does not stop these villains from preying. James was meant to stick by you."

I am torn between being pleased at being described as an asset and being angry at being described like a tool for the captain's use. My retort holds a hint of hysteria, the fear from my night still racing through my veins. "James left me to my own devices because he knew I could handle myself."

Captain Holt laughs at me, but there is no humor in it. It is not a cruel laugh, though, but a knowing one. "You just said you were mugged."

Struggling to keep the scowl off my face, regardless of whether he could see it in the dark, I ultimately fail. How dare he? I have been more alone the last year than he can imagine. More alone than almost any man can imagine. A small, damaged piece of me wants to bite him. Not with words but physically lash out with claws and teeth and show him how well I can handle myself. Weapons or no.

I do not like the captain much when he is drunk. Tonight, he is drunk on whiskey, I think it might be a favorite of his. The smell makes my mind twist everything he says into a more sinister knot.

Correcting him louder than necessary, my voice bounces off the smooth sea. "I got away, did I not? I do not know a damn thing about fighting, but I am faster than you or anybody. I have had to be. You will do well to remember my strengths since I am an asset, Captain."

I cannot count how many times I have shaken alone, terrified or hurt in the dark wishing someone would care about me or my circumstances even a little. Now, here someone is doing just that, and I am biting at him for it.

"I am sorry. I do not know why I am shouting at you."

Bennett takes up the oars once more, still eyeing me warily. After a moments' hesitation, his voice rings from the darkness to soothe my ragged soul. "Forgiven. It's been a trying night for you."

The moment it is in reach, I take the rope ladder in hand and climb up, still angry with myself for getting into a dangerous situation and at the captain for seeing it coming. I am also angry at myself for letting all of that be known and I do not like that I yelled at him for no good reason.

I am relieved that the drunken captain waits until I am all the way up to tie the small boat into place beside the ship and climb up behind me. By the time he stumbles onto deck, I am halfway up the ratlines.

CHAPTER 13

I WAKE WITH SHAKING HANDS AND SWEAT DAPPLING MY BROW FROM YET another of my common and recurring nightmares, one where someone is holding me under water.

I look over to ensure I did not wake Harry, who was already safely asleep on the ship when I arrived last night. My heart leaps in my chest to find my young friend grinning, only inches from my face, sitting up as though he has been eagerly waiting for me to rise.

Upon seeing my open eyes, Harry whispers urgently and reaches into his vest, "Dix—"

Before I can even catch my breath from my drowning nightmare, Harry pulls out a faded piece of parchment and tosses it at me. "Is this you?"

Harry seems so anxious that I begin unfolding it just to please him. My breathlessness only grows worse when I find myself staring at a portrait of a woman with the name *Jane Polk* printed beneath it. Her hair is pulled back in a long braid. The artist drew her lips a bit thinner than mine and the nose a bit wider, but she has a mole near her right eyebrow just as I do. The woman in that portrait killed a boy in Grand Port. The youngest son of a wealthy merchant, as it turns out. Her crimes are listed beneath my fingers in ink. It does not say it on the flier, but I know Jane Polk took his clothing, his boots, and his purse.

The boy's knife still rests in my pocket.

I look up at Harry, stunned, and murmur more to myself than my young friend, "I never meant to kill him."

I killed him. Oh, gods and fates and Luck forgive me! Guilty tears sting my eyes and I only manage to keep myself from falling apart because Harry's grin only widens wickedly at my confession. He begins talking fast and with a great deal of excitement and I force myself to hear him over the condemnation echoing in my mind.

"It is you! I saw men comparing bounties and they came across this. You can probably imagine what they had to say 'bout a murderess and their cocks. I took the flier once they left. You're lucky most of the men on this ship don't bother lookin' at the boards. That boy you killed musta been a somebody for your face to be all the way here in Azure Cove."

Harry seems thrilled by his discovery of my past, which is apparently more dastardly than even I knew. He keeps speaking but his words all blend into noise. Terror and bile grip my throat tight like the hands of an angry man. I killed that boy, but a part of me already knew that. My blood rushes with a question I must now ask in earnest.

What does this discovery mean for me?

I interrupt him frantically, keeping my voice low and my eyes on the doors on either side of the tight space we share. "Harry, no one else can know I am not Dixon Ables. I am sorry for the lie, but I must keep it up. I have nowhere to go but this ship."

In stark contrast to my fear, Harry brushes me off by rolling his eyes and grinning. "You honestly think I sleep an inch from ya' each night and haven't sorted out that you have a cunt? I'm not stupid, Dix."

"You will not tell anyone?"

"I haven' yet, have I? So far as I know, no one knows nothin' but me and it'll stay that way so long as I'm keeping secrets." He waves a breezy hand before growing more pensive, and then says more quietly, "I thought you were gone for sure when I saw the poster. I thought you'd disappear into the..."

He waves his hands in a chaotic sort of gesture that I find describes Azure Cove quite well.

At the admission of his worry over me, I can already feel Harry beginning to pull back into himself, closing back into a shell like a nervous hermit crab. I want to reach in and pull him out. I want to ease his mind.

"I am not going anywhere. Any danger I run into here cannot be as bad as Azure Cove. I am staying right here on *Sneaky Lass*." Leaning in conspiratorially, I tell him the rest. "Mickey knows, too."

He meets my eyes briefly, looking a bit braver, and then examines his feet. "Mickey is good. He has enough of his own sins to not go giving away yours. As for me, you're one of the only people who give a damn if I live or die, Dix. I can do the same back. I'll fight anyone who wants to mess with you, myself."

I have never felt more cared for in my life than in this moment with Harry. A murderess and a pirate. I do not deserve his care, but I will take it anyway.

Then, like the admission never occurred, Harry changes the subject. "Few crew are headin' to shore this morning and I'm gonna go with 'em. You coming?"

He pulls on his boots and starts towards the steps. I shake my head.

"No, I would rather pick oakum and tar ropes than step foot in Azure Cove again. Be careful, Harry."

He mumbles something about me being a chicken as he leaves, but I catch the smile in the dim glow of morning from the hatch above. Despite the obvious danger, I find some relief that Harry knows and does not care. A small weight has lifted from my chest.

CHAPTER 14

THE SECOND DAY ANCHORED PASSES SLOWLY. I STAY ON DECK AND CHECK the ropes and tar the lines that get the most wear. I shine every metal piece on this ship until it sparkles, and rope runs cleanly through it. I hardly know enough of ships to know what work there is to do but I manage to keep busy all day with the same tedium I busy myself with while we sail.

By evening, I have done everything twice over that I can find to be done, except pay seams in the hold and I have no idea how I will pass an entire day tomorrow without ending up covered in pitch and bilge water. I could stone the deck, but in the sun's heat

I would rather do anything else. Perhaps the captain or Mickey have a book I can borrow to pass the time with.

The captain spent the day coming in and out of his cabin, smoking a pipe on deck. He mostly watched the sea, but occasionally his eyes followed me. I found myself working a little harder when I felt his eyes on my back.

Some of the men come back to sleep off whatever they had been drinking before rowing back towards port, but the ship remains fairly empty throughout the long, hot afternoon.

I eventually settle in my usual seat on the ratlines to watch the calm water beneath us. Small, silver fish catch the fading sunlight as they dart around the hull in the green sea. The water around Azure Cove is murky, fitting for such a place, and so the fish quickly vanish only inches from the surface.

After a long day of working in silence, Captain Holt's matter-of-fact statement from over my shoulder is unreasonably loud. "You did not leave the ship all day."

I turn to face him and see we are alone on deck. The setting sun illuminates everything just enough for me to see his features.

To my surprise, he climbs up the ratlines to stand eye level with me as he has done once before. I meet his gaze before I respond in my own defense.

"Neither did you."

"I was sleeping, mostly. Thinking about our next heading, too." He looks away from me in the same shy way he has in the past.

There is still an unfair flicker of resentment in my heart towards the captain from last night, and also shame. I was rightfully frightened by strangers and then he showed up, behaved precisely like himself, and I shouted at him for it. He was only trying to keep me safe.

I decide to risk teasing him since he approached me first. "The girls in the brothels seem like they would hold more appeal than maps and charts. The rest of the crew is playing hard while they can."

He smirks at my response and fine lines form at the corner of his hazel eyes. I have never noticed the fine lines there before. "Those ladies are also more appealing than paying ropes and oiling eyes, yet here you stayed."

Telling the truth seems like the easiest route. "The girls here are not my type."

I am still watching the water when I realize my reply was strikingly like what he told a very different version of myself in Grand Port. He was not wrong about my desperation then. I was desperate enough to kill a boy and join a crew of pirates.

When I look up from the sea, Captain Holt's eyes burn in a familiar way. I have seen the look on hundreds of interested sailors in my past. Remembering the woman with her fan of white feathers mistaking me last night, I stammer in my haste to save face. "Working girls, I mean. Not girls in general."

He smiles nervously and nods, absent-mindedly rubbing the silver locket around his neck as he so often does. The oval locket looks as though it used to have an engraving on the front, but it has been worn smooth by the pad of his thumb. I wonder, not for the first time, what it holds that he cherishes.

"Of course. Not everyone can be so sinful as me." He looks out to the green waters of the bay and the fading light, leaving me to guess his meaning.

"What does that mean?" I am not a fan of guessing games.

"I just mean I have a wide array of preferences. There is something to like about most everybody if you're me." He looks over at me, scanning my face for a reaction or judgment. I cannot guess what he sees as I keep my own expression as unreadable as I can. Eventually, he gives up and shrugs. "Less so in Azure Cove, but that's more the place."

Growing up, there was only ever one way to be attracted to

anybody. A year in the brothels of Grand Port taught me better. Bennett Holt's nonchalant shrug while expressing his desire for people of every ilk is something I have not encountered until now. "You are very accepting of yourself."

"I've spent all my adult life in a position above the rebuke of most on this ship. Such a life has its advantages."

My awe at just the thought of such privilege is not lost on Bennett. He smirks at me. "I know. I'm a lucky one."

I try to change the subject away from sex and end up saying more than I intended, as so often seems to happen in Captain Holt's presence. "I have very little interest in liquor and being on dry land makes me feel nervous now. I do not share the crew's enthusiasm for whores nor drink."

"Said like a man running from something,"

In the twilight, his eyes appear to sparkle with mischief. I think he has purposefully brought this up to keep me talking about myself. It is working.

"Do men become pirates when they wish to stay where they are? Running is not the word I would use, but it is fitting enough. I will not be going back to Grand Port. If that is the course you mean to chart, I will be finding a new ship." Looking up to the emerging stars just twinkling to life to avoid Bennett Holt's curious stare, I mutter under my breath, "I am saying too much, Captain."

I do not know why I said all of that beyond a friendly ear and I have been toiling away the ghost of that young man I killed in Grand Port all day.

Thankfully, he says nothing on the matter of my opinion of Grand Port. "Tonight, I am just Bennett. My crew is dispersed, my duties set aside, and it is nice to have a conversation with someone other than Hugh."

I wish I could unburden my heart and speak more openly. The dream from last night has stayed with me throughout the day, as has the knowledge that the previous owner of my boots is dead by my hand.

Against my better judgment I continue speaking, I have not had many kind ears to listen to me in my life. I will take the opportunity when I find it. "I found Hugh when I was willing to slit my own throat rather than stay in Grand Port. Now, it feels like what I escaped stands on beaches and watches on docks. This ship feels like hallowed ground where ghosts cannot reach me."

"You're well-spoken. I, too, am most comfortable miles away from land. Miles away from Azure Cove, especially." He nods knowingly. "So, with your dislike for liquor, you will not share a drink with me? It has been a long day working alone for both of us."

I know I should say no, but one drink will not loosen my tongue and I think it may help soothe my restless mind enough for sleep. I also want to spend more time with Bennett. Captain Holt is someone I want to impress with my work and avoid otherwise. Bennett, I find myself wanting to make him smile in that infectious way that he does. It is a stupid, girlish notion that I should run from rather than towards. I think of Mickey's story of the soldier who fell in love with the general. It worked out okay for her, but I have never been lucky.

I find myself nodding anyway. "If you are Bennett tonight, then I will share a single drink with my shipmate."

He starts climbing down and around the ratlines. I slip through them and land beside him with a thud.

In the captain's quarters at the back of the ship, the moon is shining directly through the windows, illuminating the room alongside the two lanterns. I note that there is already an open bottle and a used glass on the table and recognize the sickly-sweet smell in the room immediately. Bennett Holt certainly has a favorite drink. My mind is immediately awash with painful memories of people and places I would rather forget.

I hate whiskey. It smells like my husband's house. My father's house.

Bennett pulls a second glass out and I start wondering if it is already too late to change my mind. If the captain has already been drinking this is a more precarious situation than I knew. If we are to drink whiskey, I am even less interested.

The captain pours a small amount of amber liquid into a faceted glass and places it in front of a chair at his table. I sit down and hold the glass, but do not drink from it. The captain pours himself another drink and takes it back all at once.

"You do not typically drink, then? I haven't seen you partake with the crew." The captain has always been accommodating within reason, and I believe he would be fine with me asking to drink something else. He likes to hear my thoughts and I do not think he would mind hearing my opinion on whiskey... but what if he asks me why?

I hold my drink on the table, my fingers tapping nervously at the faceted glass. "No. I have not had a drink in years."

The last drink was on my wedding night when my husband and I sipped from the same cup to signify our union. The memory of what came after the ceremony makes me shiver.

The men in Grand Port would often buy me drinks, but I never actually drank them. A drunk whore is as good as dead.

I am pulled from my past once more by the captain, or Bennett as we are friends this evening. "You don't like the taste? Or is it that you don't like drunk people?"

The way he reads my mind makes me want to take the drink just to cloud my thoughts so he cannot see them so clearly. When I hesitate to answer he smiles in his disarming way, I recognize it as the way he smiles at Mickey when giving the second mate an especially hard time.

Bennett adds, "I noticed it last night, too."

"There is nothing more dangerous than a drunk man." I do

not like that he remembers last night, or that I sound defensive even to myself. What man openly admits to being afraid of anything, let alone anything as mundane as drunk men? The men on this ship are drunk more than they are not. I give myself away with every breath I take.

I wet my finger in the drink and run it along the rim making the crystal sing so that I do not need to look at the man across from me. The delicate, faceted glass is out of place on the ship, much like the locket he wears.

Bennett's voice is soft like one might speak to a frightened feral cat. "I won't hurt you, Dixon. No matter how I indulge."

His simple admission feels too vulnerable for our relationship as captain and crew. It feels especially wrong since he believes he is saying it to a man who does not actually exist. I know he is telling the truth. He did not hurt Jane when she tried to steal from him. Cruel as the captain can be when the circumstances call for ruthlessness, I think Bennett carries a gentle soul.

I find myself staring at my dirty fingers on the glass and thinking of a way to make a hasty exit. "I believe you, Captain. Without me, who would stay aboard and boil pitch?"

Bennett lifts his brows, seemingly surprised by my aloofness. Perhaps Bennett is unaccustomed to anyone he chases, be they man or woman, turning him down. He corrects me, "Bennett tonight. Have your drink."

He pours himself another glass and I quickly drink my own down to empty. With the burn in my throat, the smell and taste is suddenly all around and inside of me, making me gag. I think I might throw up. I think I might *want* to throw up. Maybe it would make the whiskey smell go away. Tears sting my eyes by the time I manage to stop coughing, but a veil of panic rests on me that had not been there before.

I hate whiskey.

Bennett's brows are raised once more when I look up, this

time concerned. His hand is on his knee like he was about to stand and come to my side and aid me. Breathlessly he asks, "Fates, are you alright, Dixon?"

I shake away the ghosts that hound me and swipe my tongue over my teeth like I might wipe away the taste. It is no use. I nod and wave a hand like he should keep talking because I am still choked.

"You're really not much of a drinker."

"No." I cough the word more than say it, but manage a small smile meant to reassure him.

It must work because he smiles back. "I know you have noticed my watching you. I apologize. I've been trying to figure you out."

His admission and apology surprises me. So does his clear nervousness in my presence. When I finally look up, the candle-light makes his hazel eyes look red. Clearing my throat, I manage to squeak out a reply. "I hope what you see impresses you, Cap... Bennett."

He admires me and boasts, "More than impress me. I have never seen someone take to a life at sea so quickly. You're deter-mined to learn and that's a good thing on a ship when you know nothing."

Even in my state, I smile at the compliment. Perhaps a different woman, one who lives in my past, would have blushed. I look down at the rug beneath us only to have the captain reach across the table and lift my chin with his fingers, which are even rougher than mine from a long life around wood and hemp.

His eyes soften. The flickering shadows of the lamplight cast across the planes of his face add to none of this feeling very real. It is a dangerous game considering how the smell of whiskey keeps trying to drag me into nightmares. Bennett leans closer to me and it is alarmingly clear that he wants to kiss me, probably more than kiss me if I know anything about men.

He is looking at me like I am something that should be cared for. Last night when I was not cared for, he had been angry and now...

It is the drink, certainly. Not that Bennett could not possibly care for me, I know we are at least friends, but this look is not meant for me. The gentle turn to his lips, asking to be kissed, that is not for me either. Not for Dixon or Jane.

I have never been kissed by anyone who I wanted to kiss back before. I would rather keep it that way under the circumstances.

"Thank you for the whiskey. I think I should return to my hammock. Morning comes early and all." I say my usual parting line, hoping to turn him off me completely.

The captain's face is flushed from drink and when I stand from his table to leave, he catches my wrist gently.

"Not many people have turned me away, man or woman, crew or not. I have seen the way you look back, Dixon. Do not say I am alone in my infatuation."

He stands to look me in the eyes. His voice, no longer tentative, bounces off the walls of the small room. I want to pull away, but panic grips my heart and holds me in place much more firmly than Bennett does. Some rational part of me knows this is nothing to him. He is just flirting. He is thinking I am just a shy crewman on his ship. The smell of whiskey and the way he looks at me with lust feels familiar in a bad way, though. It is a way I was hoping to always avoid with this new name.

Before I can stop him, he moves towards me and kisses my lips.

Kisses Dixon's lips.

Pulling away, I am reminded of his grip on my wrist. He still holds my arm like he had been ready for me to wrap his arm around my middle, wanting me to step closer into his embrace and tangle my fingers in his short brown curls. I have played that role with so many men who paid me for the pleasure. He had thought Dixon would give it to him for free. Maybe if this room and everything in it would stay still, I could pretend to be Dixon and do so. I cannot, though. I am Jane and I am terrified.

In my boot, three silver coins rest against my foot. The reminder of this man's kindness is not enough to convince the terrified beast inside me.

"Get off of me!" I twist out of his still-gentle grasp.

This is the man who paid Jane Polk for trying to steal from him. Yet still, my breath comes in quick gasps. The small room keeps shifting from the captain's quarters to my husband's house.

The taste of whiskey is rancid on my tongue, as surely as I can smell it on his breath and feel it in the air.

I try to steady myself as I back away closer to the door, but each word comes with a gasping, panicked breath behind it. "Tomorrow, when your head clears, Captain, you will see that my leaving now is best."

The use of his proper title seems to remind the captain of his usual self. He takes a step back from me and the gap between us in the small room feels as deep as the sea. He looks as disturbed as I feel.

"I'm sorry, I overstepped. I thought..." He shakes his head. "Are you alright? You do not seem yourself. I'm sorry, I overindulged and made assumptions. You need not do anything you don't want to do."

Whether he means he has indulged too much in drink or in me, I cannot tell. My mind wants to run away where his liquored breath cannot find me.

He looks hurt that I do not return his affection, but his feelings are far from my mind. In my racing thoughts Bennett is my whiskey-soaked husband keeping me like a canary in a cage. Bennett is one of the bleary-eyed men who paid for what lies between my legs in Grand Port. Bennett is my liquor-mad father about to beat me for not following orders he never gave.

This will inevitably end with Bennett's hands on my throat, his knuckles connecting with my face, and me begging him to stop. I do not think it has ever ended another way for me.

There is a knot between his brows as they furrow together trying to sort out how he has misread me so disastrously. I loathe that he has not misread me at all. I hate that he knows why I watch him and speak so freely with him. I abhor that he knows I trust him, and like him, more than I should. If only he behaved as mean as every other man in Goran. This guise would be so much simpler if he were terrible.

He continues trying to placate what is certainly terror painted on my face. "I'm a wicked sinner, Dixon. Forgive me. I've made a fool of myself."

To my surprise, I find myself torn between wanting to comfort him and wanting to twist the knife in his chest so that he will allow me to leave. Cruelty might get me out of here faster. I allow all the anger I have felt at countless men in my life to seep into my words. "I am not for your pleasure, Captain."

"I did not say you were." His shame radiates off him in waves. His remorseful tone is enough to startle me from my dark past. He is admitting something to me, and I am breaking trust with him by being unkind. Perhaps it is for the best. "I just thought—I thought that—"

I take a deep breath and square my shoulders, ready to tear him down, even if it means I must stay in a pit like Azure Cove.

"You know nothing about me. If you did, you would not be interested. I promise, the problem lies with me alone."

My attempt to let him down while also comforting him fails as I notice him flinch. Struggling to regain my composure, a tear slides down my cheek and I wipe it away before it burns a trail to my chin.

He glances out the window and then back at me. His eyes are pleading. "You don't know me either, Dixon. How can you know that? I want to know you. I want to know why you are so unlike everyone else. Why you walk as you do, and stare as you do. I'm sinner enough to admit I share affection in too many directions and too easily. You need not share my sinful affection for us to be friendly."

I know why I am unlike the rest. My secret coils about my chest tighter than the cloth I use to bind my breasts. I keep my voice as steady as possible, trying desperately to sound certain, but I know I do not sound like a sailor, or a man named Dixon.

"The name I signed under the charter on this cabin's door is all you need know about me or any man on this ship. I would like to go now."

I do not dare look into Bennett's eyes because I fear I will see recognition there; recognition of the woman I am desperately running away from, but whom I can never fully escape. Her breasts must be bound, her monthly bleeding must be hidden, and her voice must be masked. She is concealed in a hundred humiliating ways each day on this cramped ship, and concealed is how I prefer her.

My careful charades feel like they are falling away as a curtain pulls back from a stage. I leave before he can answer me. I move past my hammock. Past Harry, who watches me with concern, and back up onto deck.

The cool night air refreshes me and quiets my panicked heart. I climb up to the very top of the furled topsails and wish I could scream into the night. I stand in the breeze, clinging to the wood and ropes until my heartbeat steadies and the scream inside me dies away. I do not even cry.

I wait until the moon has climbed to its peak in the sky and then sinks once more.

I wait until the captain has climbed out onto the deck below me, looked up to find me, and then left in a boat with a few others for land.

I wait until I feel nothing at all and then wait an extra hour or so just in case some feeling comes back.

Then I climb down to find my hammock.

CHAPTER 15

THE CAPTAIN WAS GONE IN THE MORNING AND DID NOT RETURN TO THE ship until nightfall. Sailors have been trickling back all day, looking worse for wear but content in their poor decisions. Some new faces come along with the same men I have grown accustomed to. All the new sailors swear to follow the code with their right hand over Hugh Digby's pistol and sign their names on the captain's door. I watch as they find their places and kiss the coin from the ratlines.

When Harry climbs on deck, he has a pipe and a pouch of tobacco to go along with it. He sits down and puffs away. Though I like the smell of it, I decline his offer to share.

"Fine, you can just watch me enjoy my spoils." Harry blows smoke in my face. "I still can't believe you didn't leave the ship after the first night."

I motion to my relatively clean clothing, trying not to think of all the reasons I have to avoid Azure Cove and instead focus on reasons I have to remain on *Sneaky Lass*. "I got my bath, what more could I want?"

He shakes his head at me and takes another puff from the pipe, staring out at the sunset on the water before poking me with the end of his pipe. "Is your plan to hoard your lot 'til ya' can one day wander away as a rich gentleman? 'Cause you should know it's more likely that the silver will just weigh you down when the ship is sinkin' to the bottom of the sea."

I do not actually know what I will do with the money. I suppose I will need every copper for when I find a place to make a new life, but the thought of ever actually leaving seems further away each day.

Glancing around me to ensure no one is listening, I speak solemnly, "All I know of the future is that the only person in charge of mine is me."

Whether he can relate to me or not, he puts a reassuring hand on my back. I get the feeling that while he is a rough-edged young pirate now, his family had probably been raising him to be someone quite different. He is too kind for any other explanation.

"You're not gonna cry like a woman now are ya'? 'Cause I can't abide it." He warns me with a playful tug at the corner of his chapped lips.

He dumps the ashes from his pipe into the sea, pulls a sweet from his pocket and heads back below deck, pausing before turning to me once more. "Remember to kiss the coin, Dix. I won't forgive ya' if you're the reason we sink to the depths."

I nod and watch as the cabin boy kisses the coin near the helm before disappearing below. If I was going to stay in Azure Cove, now would be my only chance. Scanning across the green sea to the blight on the land that is Azure Cove, I kiss my fingers and run them across the smooth face of the coin before busying myself beside James.

As soon as the captain's boots land on the deck, he begins barking orders to prepare to cast off with the next tide. After my embarrassing lapse last night, I keep expecting the captain to reveal his knowledge of my identity to me. He never does. Perhaps he does not care, or perhaps my emotional outburst was not as obvious as I thought it would be. Maybe he did not see the posters bearing my portrait in town. If anything, he behaves as though I do not exist. I remind myself it is for the best, but it hurts all the same. I find myself missing his eyes on my back.

It is not until land falls off the horizon that I begin to feel like myself again... or rather like Dixon again. Days slip by in a haze of heat, salt air, and work. I squeeze myself into the mold of a sailor. The ship feels like a living organism. Every part and person are an essential piece of keeping her alive. My place is on her sails and I am growing better at playing my part.

Days drift away and along with them the attention Captain Holt once spent on me. The absence of his gaze makes me feel cold. In Grand Port, there is oftentimes a false spring where everything would begin to bloom only to be frozen in a late cold front. The trees and all their buds would look so desolate encased in ice. I have that same barren feeling inside me now.

I know I should be relieved that he has taken my advice and steered clear of me, but I am not. Does he know? Is he punishing me? Why am I like this over him?

For weeks before Azure Cove the captain and I had shared quick conversations. Without those small punctuations to each day, everything blends together in tedium.

To add to my worry, Mickey seems to have noticed how strained I am with the captain. For all I know, Captain Holt has told the second mate what occurred between us in his cabin. "Dix!" Anxiety balls in my throat, momentarily cutting off my air when the second mate waves me to his side.

Not bothering to avoid him, I sit down beside him near the helm and rest my chin on my knees. He looks me up and down and laughs at me pityingly.

"Oh, don't look so eager to hear what I have to say." His easy teasing makes me smile despite my dark mood.

I even risk jesting on my own behalf, "Is it another story to make me question all my poorest choices?"

Mickey lies down beside me, propping his head up on his arms. "No. Your poor choices are your own. You just looked lonely."

I am sure I did. I was waiting for the captain, as I have grown to always wait for him in the evening, even now that he does not come.

"There is a difference between being alone and being lonely." I confess to Mickey what I often tell myself,

He smiles knowingly. "Aye, but you look lonely. You used to talk to Ben at night."

"You mean Captain Holt? Titles are important, Mr. Compton. The captain may be the first to tell you so."

The second mate is unfazed and repeats himself with a small correction. "You used to talk to Captain Holt at night."

"Yeah. I did."

I allow my shoulders to slump. For a brief moment, Mickey and anyone else who wants to look can see how miserable I feel.

Urging me like a girl looking for gossip, Mickey pries, "So, what happened?"

I keep my eyes fixed on the vanishing edge of the world to keep from scanning the deck for the captain. "He became too drunk and said stupid things. I became too frightened and said stupid things. Now, we do not talk."

"He knows, then?"

I look at Mickey from the side of my eyes and play dumb. "Knows what?"

Shaking his head, he answers his own question. "Guess not."

The captain cannot know. It is better that I scared Bennett Holt off early so that I do not get any ideas about changing that fact. We are all better off pretending Jane does not exist. I imagine I will be dead before I ever want to find Jane again in all the mess I have become. I am not even certain which Jane I would seek out. There have been so many versions. When I envision any future for myself, whether strolling the streets of a city or sitting in the ratlines, I can only picture myself being Dixon.

After a long and uncomfortable silence, I reassure myself aloud of the same thing I said to the captain in Azure Cove. "No one needs to know anything about me but the name I signed on the captain's door."

My friend sits up and gives me a pointed stare. Mickey looks like he is about to argue with me and then he shifts into an easier version of himself and shrugs. "If you say so, Dixon."

My tongue will not be still and gives away my insecurity. Perhaps it is Jane rearing her many ugly heads at being buried so unceremoniously.

"Why do you care that the captain is not speaking to me?"

His eyes slowly glide across the deck and land on the quarter-master, Hugh Digby, who is watching us both with interest.

"Hugh says I have a bad habit of getting into the business of others. Working on a ship is pretty dull. I must fill my days with something, or I will go mad. Is it so terrible that I like to fill them observing people?"

"No, but that does not answer my question."

He runs his hands through his tangled mane and smiles handsomely across the deck at Hugh Digby who is waving him over.

Mickey motions for him to wait a minute. "Watching the captain speak with you is interesting. Ben has a lot of types, and you don't really fit into any of them. You make him pause in a way most people don't. I've been bored without it. I think the captain's bored without it, too."

I am unable to decide if I like his answer or not. "So, I am ruining your entertainment, then?"

"Precisely."

I do not know what to think of Mickey Compton most days, beyond his presence is comforting and each time we share a conversation my assumptions about life on this ship are challenged.

Hugh looks impatient, but I selfishly keep Mickey for myself a little longer, allowing him to hold off the frost. "What will you do now, then? To pass the time?"

Mickey purses his lips and shrugs. "I could give you a tattoo."

Eyeing the many colorful adornments on his hands, arms, and neck, I cannot keep the wonder from my voice. "You can give people such marks?"

He holds up his arms, pushing back his sleeves to his elbows, and admires his own skin. His skin is more cleverly adorned than the fabric used to make the wealthiest woman's dresses. Orange fish swim beneath blue, swirling water, the water turns to sky where grey seabirds soar. "Oh no, not like this. But I did Hugh's anchors, and most of the marks on this ship that you see. I don't know so many eastern secrets as these blooms and birds. Do you want one?"

I do not think so, but seeing his skin makes it a little tempting. Unsure of my answer, I ask another question. "Who did yours?"

Mickey is an open book and answers easily, "A lover a lifetime ago. They're beautiful, aren't they?"

Sailor's marks often hold meaning. How long they have sailed, what position they hold on a ship, on and on. There are probably dusty books on the subject. "Do yours mean anything?"

He shakes his head. "They don't have to. They're beautiful. Those days when I cannot look myself in the eyes, I can look at these and think there is something worth loving about me."

The way he says it is laced with sadness in the same way cider can be bitter after it is sweet. "You are the most beautiful man on this ship, Mickey. Inside and out."

All traces of morosity vanish and Mickey waves me off wearing a smile I recognize. I have painted the same one on my own face more times than I can count. It is a smile that says, "*Do not look too closely and all will be well.*" I wonder what brings Mickey to grief?

He stands and starts walking towards Hugh, answering over his shoulder, "If you're not careful, you'll make me blush and give Hugh more reason to dislike you. Since you don't want any birds or anchors, I'm being called."

"Goodnight, Mickey."

He jogs to his lover's side.

CHAPTER 16

WE ARE BACK IN THE TRADE ROUTES AND THE MEN SPEAK OF PRIZES AS though we will come upon a ship filled to the masts with gold and jewels. So far, it has mostly been sugar, but it is amazing what a few days at port did for morale.

Despite Captain Holt no longer spending his attentions on me, I watch him often. He is nervously searching the horizon all the time, which makes me wonder if he heard news that disturbed him in Azure Cove. For days he has been pushing for more speed and I have learned more about sailing from his insistence than in all my prior weeks on *Sneaky Lass* combined.

James knows how to best catch a breeze just by feeling it.

Occasionally he will test me to tell him what we should do to get the top speed. I am only right a small fraction of the time, but I am improving. When asked for details on how he makes the calls, he gave a cryptic answer about feeling the air and the ship and that I would learn it with time.

There is probably a book full of information somewhere that would serve me better than my gut reaction, but James is the teacher I have and I possess no books of my own. Maybe I am giving myself too much credit to think I know enough of sailing in the first place for a book to be of use.

Bennett looks over at me and then away quickly when he finds himself under my gaze. He has been agitated like this before and I was able to draw him out from it, but I doubt I could again. I have damaged him since. If I can make it better, I would like to. I miss the conversations once shared and I have been lonelier without them. I miss him.

I repeat my new mantra in my head to keep myself in place. *It is better this way.*

If gods exist, they must be laughing at me when I give up and approach the captain. I clear my throat to catch his attention. "Captain?"

I let his title sit in the air between us and choke on the silence. "Ables."

His tone is cold, and I understand why it would be. My body aches at his cold shoulder. There is no denying it, my heart aches, too.

It is better this way.

Yeah right.

I do not know what I hope to gain out of speaking, but I try. "You will put the lookout out of his job."

After days of avoiding me, his eyes meet mine as he struggles to find an answer. His face shifts through several expressions before settling into a mask of annoyance. "It is none of your business when I rest, sailor."

Despite having expected no answer at all, I find that his dismissive tone hurts far worse than his silence would have.

"You are right, it is not."

I should leave. Instead, I stay nearby much like he used to when I would try to dismiss him on the ratlines. The tension between us is taught like the cables in the rigging. He is working hard to watch anything other than me.

Deciding to be bold because at least anger is something, I try one more time, "It just seems like perhaps someone should care enough to remind you to do so."

"Must you always be a puzzle, Dixon? Can you not just leave me be?" His voice an exasperated whisper so others will not hear.

It is better this way.

This coldness is good. I am undeserving of his kindness and affection. The man he showed both to does not even exist.

I try to force my feet away from this spot, away from Bennett Holt, but they remain held in place by my own selfish wishes.

"Is that an order, Captain?" I wait for his confirmation, not knowing what I hope he will say.

Captain Holt looks me dead in the eyes, before returning to what he was doing before I interrupted.

"Leave me be." His flat tone is an unmistakable order.

The way my heart sinks in my chest tells me that I was hoping he would ask me to stay. Now I know for certain that he was right in not being alone in his infatuation. I am a lovesick fool and it is going to get me kicked off this ship if I am not careful. Dixon, if I mean to continue as Dixon, must be loveless always.

I catch Mickey watching me from the railing nearby and feel my face heat at having him witness me having been so thoroughly rebuked.

Slinking below deck, I try to rest my eyes but sleep does not come easy. My guilt over my secret, and the captain's new aloof attitude toward me keeps me awake. I do not believe Bennett meant me harm, even if he did come on strong. I hurt him anyway.

In my hammock, I unfold the poster Harry brought to me in Azure Cove and study the face of the woman I used to be. The list of crimes below her name is far from complete. It should include 'cruel, lovelorn liar' somewhere in her description.

Folding it again, I hide it carefully in my set of spare clothes before willing the darkness to quiet my mind, if only for a short while.

CHAPTER 17

WEEKS PASS WITHOUT A WORD FROM THE CAPTAIN, AND I HAVE NOT approached him again. I still feel foolish enough for my last attempt. Instead, I have occupied my days learning as much as I can. If I am going to be so foolish with my heart, I should at least try to make up for it by being a good sailor.

Determined to better myself, I have not shirked away from any task no matter how daunting. Paying seams, ankle deep in bilge water, trimming and waxing sails, on and on. The ship is a cracked cup, always in need, and I intend to keep it filled.

Pax, the carpenter on our ship, is always drunk and sings filthy songs while he works, but he has not minded teaching me a thing or two about replacing rotten boards and stopping leaks from one deck to the next. On one quiet afternoon, Pax taught me how to throw boarding axes at a makeshift target made from an old crate. Most of the crew got a kick out of watching me give it my best effort and fail miserably. I was not nearly so frightening as the carpenter, who was so off target, being stumbling drunk, that the crew was in terrible danger.

I have trailed Mickey, too, mostly during the taking of prizes, but also so I might learn something of gunning. Of the two boarding parties, I would rather be in the second mate's boat than the captain's. I could stay behind, but that would cost me pay and personal prizes like clothing and the quartermaster often stays behind to helm on *Sneaky Lass* during the work of piracy. I would rather be tied to the captain's belt, even with his avoidance, than be left to Hugh Digby.

We have taken ships and returned to Azure Cove and the rocky beaches surrounding it a few times now and will keep doing so until it is time to move on. It would seem the crew has entrusted that decision of when we will leave this area to the captain.

I have not left the ship any of the times we have dropped anchor. My purse has grown heavy with all the coin I am not spending. It has occurred to me that I could use the money to get off and find new employment. I tell myself all sorts of lies for why I have stayed, but the true reason is obvious to me. I want to stay here. I have made friends here. I am liked well enough here. The captain is here...

We have left Azure Cove just this morning when the bronze bell tolls, something in the response of those around me tells me that the bell does not signal another merchant ship on the horizon.

My fears are confirmed when the man on high climbs down and shouts, "She's flying the blue birds, Captain."

There is a pause that could not have truly lasted more than a few heartbeats while the man adjusted his spyglass, but it feels like an eternity. *"Three Queens!"*

The captain's eyes alight. He stands straighter and runs to the helm. "Outpace them, men. We do not have the numbers for a fight, but the wind is with us."

Captain Holt turns to look at his crew and when his eyes land on me, I spot an almost imperceptible flicker of anxiety.

Our gazes remain locked on one another as he gives his next word. "This is a fight best avoided."

His eyes leave mine, but not without one last concerned glance over his shoulder. I do not have time to make any guesses about his expression.

Some men might have scoffed at the idea of avoiding a fight but enough sailors on this ship have seen battle with *Three Queens* to not question the order. Also, as Captain Holt so often says, the men who choose piracy are in the business of taking, not fighting. A chorus of affirmative, "Ayes," echo across the ship.

James finds me and sends me up the lines. "Listen for orders. It's gonna be a long day if the captain is planning what I think he's planning."

I climb up, heading for the topsails, still furled. James follows behind alongside many others with the same idea in mind. I can see Harry far below me on deck running from one sailor to the next, doing whatever needs done. The captain is next to the helm leaning over a desk with a map on it. Usually, the job of navigation falls to Mickey and Hugh, but today the captain knows best.

James looks ahead into the sea and then calls again, "He's gonna lead us through the cays. Everything's gonna be moving quickly to keep us from running aground. Keep your eye on me, boy."

I nod, not fully understanding what James is talking about. I work up the gumption to ask, knowing that I will sound ignorant to any sailor around me, "What are the cays?"

James shakes his head, always a little surprised by what I do not know. "Tiny islands. Reefs. If you don't know where they start and end, then you run aground. The coral may even eat up the hull an' sink the ship."

The horror on my face makes James boisterously laugh despite the tension in the air, "Our captain knows the way, Dix. He's done this before. *Three Queens* will run aground, and we will get away to find our fortune. You just watch and see. There's a reason Ben is captain."

James' words reassure me some, but they do not hold their usual magic.

"Would a ship that runs aground sink?"

James answers me only by rolling his eyes.

Together with James and my shipmates, we finish the topgallant sails before I begin climbing down to the fore and aft sails. I can now see the cays coming into view, hardly more than specks of land just above the sea line, surrounded by green, choppy water...

As far as the eye can see the islands poke just above the waves in a line that spans miles appearing as an impenetrable wall of barely concealed land in the middle of a deep ocean. Captain Holt's plan becomes clear to us all. If we get through it by some miracle, the rival ship would surely be left on the other side.

The captain, after searching the chart and the horizon, begins shouting orders about sails that are echoed and repeated by the men until everyone has heard.

Then the captain belts out another command in direct opposition to the last as we near the cays, setting into treacherously shallow water. Now we are to slow down to a crawl, putting away all the canvas we just freed.

More sailors climb aloft. Together the crew can move canvas sails faster than I knew was possible. I am surprised to find Harry has climbed to my side in a moment of quiet between tasks.

He is grinning widely and looks at the oncoming islands with an excited spark in his young eyes.

"I think if the captain could get away with it, he would throw the guns and anchors over so that we could lift out of the sea." Harry makes a hand motion like a ship making a great leap and a sound effect of *Sneaky Lass* making a big splash when it lands again. Despite the stress in the air as the enemy ship approaches, I giggle at the image Harry paints.

James is watching the oncoming islands, ignoring us entirely. I respond to Harry, grateful for his distraction.

"That would certainly be a way to get over the cays." I turn my eyes upward towards the cloudless, blue sky, making Harry laugh again despite the circumstances.

Harry pokes me in the side with his elbow. "You would all have to hold onto the ropes damn tight up here."

This time even James cracks a chipped grin at Harry's antics. The quartermaster shoots us all a dangerous look and we jump back to work. Harry climbs back down to the deck carefully skirting the quartermaster, sticking his tongue out at the sour man behind Hugh Digby's back. Just before I turn away, I catch Mickey Compton nearby smiling at Harry's games as well. Something about the second mate being collected enough to grin eases my nerves.

James and I return to canvas.

It could be that the captain has purposely slowed us so he can better steer, but *Three Queens* appears to be running on magic rather than wind. It moves faster than any ship I have seen. Certainly, it moves faster than a navy frigate loaded with heavy guns should. For a moment, I wish to be on their rig to find out how.

James' voice snaps me back to the present, "Stop dreaming, Dix. The cays approach and orders will be coming. Climb down, now. We'll be needed to hold fast."

The sea laps against the hull of our ship, which is sitting high in the water, but not nearly high enough from the looks of it. The line of sandy beaches is now so close that I can see the small shrubs that grow in the shallow earth there. Captain Holt's eyes are back on me for just a second before he takes the helm and starts steering our ship far to the right.

The captain's shout makes every man jump into action. He calls for everything to be moved starboard.

James, me, and several other sailors pull the main gaff to catch the wind and help push the ship the right way. It is just a matter of holding fast against the wind. We all trust our captain, but it looks as if our ship is going to sail directly into the sandy island in front of us rather than beside it. Around us, cannons and anchors and everything else is being moved by every able body on every level of the ship.

We miss the first cay by what could not have been more than inches. Then Captain Holt takes another sharp turn towards the port side. We all follow the same procedure as before, rushing to the opposite side of the ship, holding fast on the sails. My hands burn from the strain it takes to hold the rough ropes in place, even with so many sailors holding alongside me.

The captain yells again like his orders might sway the sea itself, "Keep us off the ground."

The command is echoed by the crew, growing more succinct with each repetition, "Hold Fast, men!" "Ho!"

It does not feel like we will have much choice in the matter of running aground or not. The ocean and the beaches, more than ever before, feel alive and angry at our determination to conquer them; if they want to catch us on shore, they will.

Every sailor not holding onto a rope is pushing everything moveable on deck to the port side now. The ship nearly capsizes, it leans so far over. Most everyone lands on the deck as the ship slows and slides along the sea's bottom, a terrible noise rising from below

Pax, the carpenter, begins dropping down the hatches, grabbing able men to follow him before most of us have realized we have hit our heads. In my boot, which I never thought to take off in the rush, three coins rest. I begin pressing my thoughts through the soles of my foot into those coins. Those coins that are certainly lucky, absolutely lucky, luckier than any other charm on this ship.

Let Luck, if she exists, be with us today because I do not want to be sunk or stranded.

We come out on the other side of the cays slowed but still floating. A collective sigh fills the deck from every man upon it. Even if we got stuck now *Three Queens* has turned away and lies far behind, not willing to risk such a dangerous path. They will have to go around for miles.

None of us cheer until Pax climbs back up and raises his arms into the air in triumph. By the skin of her teeth *Sneaky Lass* has made it in one piece.

The luckiest damn coins in the whole world rest in my boot and my first superstition grows.

I put the spyglass back and return to James' side.

Sails are moved back into their normal positions along with the cargo. James sends me to help re-tie the jib sails. The work of the day is far from finished. We have avoided the immediate danger, but it is only just past noon, and the ship is disordered on every level. Tonight, there will be time to celebrate.

The captain is more capable than I knew. When he looks up to meet my stare he smirks arrogantly. He has earned the opportunity to feel prideful. I feel the wall of silence between the captain and me come crashing down. Even though I have been hoping for that very thing, I find anxiety creeping into my heart and stealing the breath from my lungs as I wonder what will be said.

CHAPTER 18

As night falls and the cays settle far into the distance, I find myself hesitating to leave the tallest parts of the ship. Captain Holt is drinking alongside the men as most of the work is long done, but we are both waiting for the other to make a move. He paces, not moving too far from where I nearly always descend. I once described such agitation as him appearing like a dog in a pen. Tonight, it is far more predatory than that.

Biting his nails, he appears nervous. The anticipation of reunion is like a taut cable between us.

After nearly two weeks of trying to end this silence, I now

wish to extend it. If gods and fates exist, they are likely frustrated by my inability to know my own mind.

Now, long after the sun has sunk below the edge of the world, I have no more excuses to stay aloft. My entire body feels like every ounce of moisture has been blown away by the wicked wind. Only a few sailors are left on deck and when I get close to stepping back on the warm wood, Captain Holt approaches me on the ratlines just as I knew he would.

"You seem a natural on the rig. I've never seen anyone spend time up high just for kicks."

I resist the urge to look away, meeting his gaze as intensely as he gives it.

"Thank you, Captain. I have good teachers. As for climbing high, the wind helps clear my head."

A small smile tugs up the corner of the captain's lips. "James Seaman has been with *Sneaky Lass* almost as long as I have, longer even than Hugh. He was voted the captain last year. The only reason he is not in charge of this craft is because he didn't want to be. He can't read, but he could have put Hugh and I in charge of such things. He turned it down. Said the rigs were where he felt most useful, not stuck on deck like I am."

Captain Holt takes a deep breath, like he has run a long distance. He looks away from me and back out to sea. I wish I could bring myself to ask him why he has suddenly turned his cold shoulder away from me, but trepidation holds my tongue hostage. "Your being on deck is what got us through all that today." I compliment him in the hopes that he will hear my forgiveness and my apology.

"I know those cays like the back of my hand... well, that's not true, but I've performed that trick precisely once before. I have been keeping near to them for days now just in case *Three Queens* thought to make chase again. I heard talk of Gates in Azure Cove last we stopped." Sounding clearer headed, he looks proud, like a small boy who received a pat on the head.

With the return of his friendship, I find my heart opening to him unwittingly. I feel the difference between the aloof Captain Holt and the man, Bennett. I admire both for different reasons, but Bennett is the one I missed when I pushed him away.

"It is a mystery to me how you can have any bearing of where we are at all. I know enough of our direction from the sun, but it is all just featureless ocean to me. I would not know how to find those cays again if my life depended on it. Once out of sight, land may as well not exist. I think I prefer it that way." It is easy to err on the side of flattery, though I am merely speaking the truth.

"From what little I know, a preference for being lost sounds just like you."

Well, that is apt enough.

When I do not answer, he nervously chews his lip, the action barely perceptible this far from the lamp lit by the helm, as if he has something shameful to say. Then he decides against it and returns our conversation to the Goranese Navy. "I do not know what we will do when we have to face them again."

The vulnerability in Bennett's voice is unexpected. I want to comfort him. Guilt for my cruel words towards him our first time in Azure Cove has been eating away at me and I wish to make amends. I tell myself the lie that it is because he is my captain. It would be best for him not to dislike me, right? I know the truth as well as he likely does. I want to comfort him because I am smitten, lovelorn, and stupid.

"When we must meet them, we will meet them with more knowledge than the first time. That is not nothing." My words reassure more than just the captain. Next time Bennett tries to meet me, I will also have more knowledge to guide my way. The thought helps the tension ease from my limbs.

Bennett shifts our conversation once again. "Dixon, is it only recently that you have decided being lost is better than being found?"

Depends on what he means by recently. A little more than a year?

I know the precise moment I chose being lost was far better than being *Jane,* but I am not prepared to tell Bennett Holt or anyone else.

"You sound like a poet." I deflect.

He raises his hands in feigned surrender and tries to make amends. "No offense meant. You just seem too well off to have spent a lifetime on the run."

His anxious reaction gives me some relief. At least I am not the only one who is nervous around our newly rekindled talks. "Twenty-three years is hardly a lifetime."

It has been twenty-three years. At some point my birthday has come and gone without a single thought from me or anyone else.

He beams in triumph, his teeth catching the yellow lantern light. "Now I know something about you besides your signed name on my door. I had guessed eighteen until we spoke some. Then I moved my marker up to twenty, and only because you spoke of life like it'd hit you a few times. Twenty-three years old? You do not look it."

My façade grows thinner each day. I should not have given away my age. I hardly pass as a man at all, let alone a fully grown one. Still, Bennett's countenance makes me want to tell him even more. I knew I missed him, but with the return of his teasing and probing questions, I realize the hole his silence left me was deep enough to get lost in. I do not think anyone has ever cared to learn about me before. Even Harry and Mickey do not ask many questions, though maybe they just know better than to expect honesty.

I try to come up with an explanation for what my madam

described as my *gangly bones*, and a lack of any stubble, ever. "Men in my family have always been slight."

Lies upon lies; how many will I tell before the Gods strike me down where I stand?

His eyes alight with more interest. "Ah, and what did the men of your family do? Not a bunch of seafaring men, I would guess?"

I should walk away from him, but his presence keeps me glued in place. Despite my better judgment, I decide speaking to him longer would be worth any punishment. "Innkeepers, shopkeepers, and farmers. One navy man. Reasonable professions until me and my adventurous streak."

At least it is not a lie. I sometimes fear I will forget how to tell the truth while wrapped in so many deceptions. The heavy burden I carry at all times lifts ever so slightly, even for only a few honest words.

The captain ponders this while looking out into the vast, onyx dark. He runs his hand through his hair and then rests it on the back of his sunburned neck before answering. "What made you think of an adventure at sea? Is it what you expected?"

I find myself eager to meet him with honesty once more. "I did not expect to love it as I do. As for why I joined your crew, it was for the same reason so many men jump onto your ship, Captain. I had nothing left on land. I would not even say I thought of it. The opportunity presented itself."

Fearful that he will see my losses and my sins as clearly as if they were drawn on my flesh, I look back up to the constellations above. My husband, dying in his own sick by my hand. That boy in Grand Port, naked and dead in the cold. The dead babe buried under the oaks with no headstone and no casket. They all have me lost rather than found.

He shakes his head like he thinks me unbelievable. "Are you always so vague or is it just with me? Thieves and beggars make up our lot, and you don't fit among them."

Last week he had asked if I insisted on always being a puzzle. I do not know how to answer him.

Bennett pauses for a few heartbeats and then looks away from me with regret painting his features. He finally mentions what we have both been avoiding. "I know I shamed myself in Azure Cove. Please, don't hold it against me."

The remorse in his voice is not lost on me, nor is the level of humility it must take for a captain to apologize to someone like me on his own ship.

I try to make my own apologies without saying as much. "I have nothing to hold against you, Captain. In the eyes of this crew and in the eyes of the heavens, if there are any eyes there, all would see you are the superior man between us."

Bennett crosses his arms and smirks up at me. "Now which of us sounds like a poet?"

Laughing more heartily than I have in days, I correct him, "No, I sound like a preacher. Though unlike men of gods and fates I speak the truth."

Bennett Holt is full of questions tonight and I wonder if he has been saving them up during our silent standoff. "I don't know much of preachers. Are there holy men in your family of slight, hard workers?"

I think of my husband and the perfect mask he wore in front of his congregation. At night, he would slip off his disguise and lose himself in drink. While he was lost, he always found himself beating me.

"No holy men, but there were preachers." Sighing, knowing full well what he will think of my answer, I answer his first query with a small smile. "I am this vague with everyone."

This time Captain Holt chuckles and I suppose my answers may seem funny to someone who does not know my history.

When his laughter fades, his tone becomes more serious, almost pleading. "Truly, do you forgive me? I drank too much to forget my worries and landed you in the deep of them instead. I meant what I said, but I should've kept it to myself."

There is regret in his eyes, but also a small simmer of the desire I have seen time and time again in his gaze. I cannot remember any man ever apologizing to me before in all my life. Perhaps someone has bumped my arm and said it in passing, but a true apology when I have been wronged? Never.

I no longer wish to lie to Bennett or let him live with unnecessary guilt. I allow a slip of Jane to shine through my disguise, knowing it is folly. "Is it an act of overstepping to kiss someone when they want to be kissed? I was cruel in my handling of you. I bit at you the way a frightened animal might. I fear drunk men and I hate whiskey, not just the taste, and it all fell on you."

A weight lifts off my chest when I finally admit as much. He seems to feel lighter as well, his straight, white teeth appearing too large for his mouth as they do when he is joyous.

Having learned nothing, he asks more of me. "Then you will come to my cabin again, have one drink?"

His eyes gleam, but not in a way that makes me fearful. He has something to prove, whether to me or to himself, I am uncertain. I can relate to the feeling.

My lonely heart accepts before my mind can stop it. "So long as it is not whiskey."

Captain Holt cups me on the shoulder and stands up straight, pushing off the railing of the ship. I hesitate before falling in behind him. Now he knows a bit more about me. Perhaps, in return, I can learn something of Bennett Holt.

Passing where my hammock hangs empty beside Harry, I can feel my friend's eyes trying to cut through the darkness as the sound of my footfalls follow Bennett's to his cabin. The press is still there when the door closes between Harry and us. Captain Holt heads directly to the cabinet where I know he keeps the glass bottles of liquor, probably a much finer quality than what the rest of the crew drink, not that I would know the difference.

"Not whiskey, then. What of rum?"

I sit down at the table and nod. He pours two glasses.

I start asking my questions right away to convince my mind I came here with a purpose other than the kind company of my dangerous crush. "You have learned something of me, will you be telling me anything of yourself, Bennett?"

He takes his glass and the crystal looks even more out of place in his large, dirty hands. "Ah, back on a first name basis? I will answer one question if you will answer one for me. What would you like to know?"

The game he proposes is dangerous but I remind myself I can always lie. I have become adept at it.

"How did you come to be a pirate in the first place?" My question is my acceptance of his terms. "James called you a mutineer."

Bennett huffs and looks towards the door like he has a mind to find James and reprimand him.

"Of course James would be out spreading rumors about me! A mutineer makes me sound like the brains of the operation when I was far from it. The answer is simple enough. I was first lieutenant on a navy brig called *King's Glory*. The captain was a beast and had made enemies of most of us." He pauses to sip his drink and then stares past me rather than at me. "There was mutiny. If I didn't join it that'd be the end of me, and our side won. We tore him apart, the ship was renamed *Sneaky Lass,* and for a long time we sailed specifically targeting navy ships."

I interrupt him, excitement flaring through me as pieces of a puzzle begin clicking into place. "That explains why *Three Queens* is out for blood."

He sips his drink with an affirmative nod. "We took everything and killed everyone who did not wish to join ranks. When Captain Eaton died two years back, the title of captain fell to me by vote. James is liked more, and Hugh is more deserving, but here I sit anyway."

Pride laces his voice, but the way he takes another swig from his glass and eyes the bottle like he wants more tells me otherwise. He finishes his drink but does not pour himself another. Flipping the glass upside down on the table, he pushes it back and forth with his fingers, making a sticky trail on the worn wood.

Bennett is fidgety. I had not taken notice of his struggle to remain still before now. His knee bounces and his hands always must find some way to keep themselves busy. When he realizes he is making a mess of the table, he picks up his locket again and toys with the chain about his neck.

Bennett shakes his head at the bottle, a physical gesture for a silent decision. "*Three Queens* is a special case. Captain Gates has been out to skin me since I killed his son last summer."

Suddenly, Bennett Holt seems like a different person. I always knew pirates murdered and stole. I have been relatively unbothered by my small part in such acts, save the gore left behind. Somehow, I never equated their victims as someone's son, father, or brother.

When I killed my husband, I did not care that anyone may miss him, but when I think of the young man in Grand Port who I accidentally killed for his clothing, my stomach churns guiltily.

"Do you feel sorry for killing his son?"

He looks at his empty glass and rolls it on its rim with the pad of his index finger, wearing an uncomfortable expression. He reminds me of the rules to our game. "The terms were one question apiece."

I wince realizing, only after the fact, that it may be a painful question to ask him. Apparently, I am full of those. "You are beginning to see why I prefer to stay quiet."

He looks up at me and does not speak until I lock eyes with him. He speaks softly, like he is trying to prove to me he is not upset. "The beautiful and upright son of farmers, innkeepers, and preachers on a ship of murderous pirates. You are an enigma. You never need to stay quiet in my quarters."

I do not know how to respond to his assessment and, instead, I move on with our game. Yet another first tonight, I do not think I have ever been called beautiful. I guess I still have not. It is how he described Dixon, not Jane.

Upright is a term that describes me even less.

I shake his compliments off my mind, pick up my drink but hesitate to bring it to my lips. "I suppose you should ask your question."

Bennett, guessing the reason for my pause, points to my full glass. "If you inhale, take a swallow, and then exhale, you may not gag."

Following his advice, I find much more success than in Azure Cove, even managing not to cough. He gives me the raised look a teacher gives a pupil before surprising me with his question.

"Why do you care if I feel guilty for killing Gates' son?"

Damn. That is quite a question.

The feeling I have is obvious to me, but my vocabulary leaves me at a loss. I think of the tiny, blue babe who I loved even though he never took a breath. How soft his skin was, how perfect the little bow of his grey lips. When I think of my child, I am unable to feel like Dixon, or Jane, or even a person. I just feel broken. I have not thought of him in weeks, outside of my terrible dreams, now I have been faced with him twice in one night.

I choke slightly on my words, trying to find a tone of nonchalance and failing. "Do you mind if I answer strangely?"

He looks at my eyes and then turns away as though he is frightened by what he found there. I wonder what he sees.

Reaching into his pocket, he pulls out his pipe and a small pack of leaf in a leather pouch. As he stuffs the pipe and tamps down the dried leaves, I get the feeling he is doing this ritual on purpose to avoid looking at me.

"I want you to answer however you like. If it helps you, know that your answers almost always seem strange to me. It is what keeps me coming back to ask more, even if it is not good for me."

In that, we are alike.

It takes me a few moments to gather my thoughts. Bennett takes a splinter of wood from a small satchel that hangs from the same hook as the lamp, sets it aflame, and uses it to light his pipe. He is so engrossed in the ritual of it, he starts when I finally speak like he forgot I was here.

"I wonder if you love a son more the longer that he is on earth, or if the love remains constant from the moment they exist and then forever."

Tears burn on my eyes, but I manage to push them back before they fall. Bennett is not looking at me anyway; he is looking at his empty glass and blowing smoke. Given the intensity in his face, I imagine he will finish that bottle of rum after I leave. I keep speaking before I lose track of my thoughts.

"I have never met a father who would miss a lost infant, but I have never met a mother who fully recovered from it. Maybe a man loves his children more as they grow, but a mother's love is constant from the start." I exhale as I finish my drink. My entire body shivers from the burn in my throat and the terrible taste. I do not know why anyone drinks this for pleasure. "I know that does not answer your question. I do not know why I care if you feel guilty or not. I just feel it is important."

Bennett is wearing a thoughtful expression as he stares out the windows at the back of the ship. Distantly, I wonder if the panes of glass that are so clearly windows in this room are called ports like the rest on the ship. I will not be asking.

I stand to leave, already forming a mental pact with myself to not do this again. "I am sorry. Both times you have invited me to your cabin you have started by wearing a smile but I always leave you wearing a frown."

He turns back to me, his lip turns up a fraction. "And yet this time I feel the weight is lighter as you go. I will invite you again, if you will allow it. In truth, the danger today made me realize that I want to know you better."

I push in my chair under the table, happy that he is not as downtrodden as he looked, my pact to avoid him vanishing before I ever finished forming it.

He stands, as well, and takes a step towards me. I feel the pull between our bodies as though a taut rope connects us. I step towards him, and he closes the space between us so that my bound chest is touching his.

I am tall for a woman, and he is not a particularly tall man. If he were barefoot like I am, we would stand eye to eye. I find myself tilting my eyes to meet his, and hope my expression is neutral and not some version of anxious. Whether for him to close the gap between us or for him to step back, even I am not certain.

Holding his pipe between his lips, he sounds cocky when he asks, "So, it is not an overstep to kiss someone who wants you to kiss them back?"

The captain uses my words from earlier in the night against me, much to the delight of my hopeful heart. I nod, swallowing the lump in my throat.

"So long as no one smells of whiskey."

In the next town, I will jump ship. I want to kiss Bennett before I go.

He pulls the pipe from his lips and exhales, ready to tease me again, and I press my lips to his. It is quick and chaste, but I taste sweet tobacco on his lips. His arms wrap around me without thought, his hand still holding the smoldering pipe by the small of my back. My body responds in all the ways which remind me that I am not Dixon, I am Jane, and Bennett cannot know.

It would be so easy to continue. If my secret held no consequences, ones the man I am kissing would be forced to administer, I might be dumb enough to let his hands wander.

He parts his lips for me, and the kiss deepens. My own arms instinctively move towards his shoulder and...

It is too tempting.

I pull away. His expression is a mix of stunned and wanting, a mirror of mine, though I know there is an added flush to me that he lacks. Another reason to curse my pale complexion.

My throat is tight when I step back, as I try not to stumble. "Thank you for the drink, Bennett. Morning comes early."

Bennett nods, regarding me in the same way my mother pondered her puzzle ring.

I leave. Harry, despite his worry when I entered the captain's quarters, is snoring softly.

Crawling into my own hammock, snippets of the conversation play through my mind in order to pull my observations about the captain together. I have met so few kind men in my life. Men who would apologize to me, who keep to only one drink in my presence, or bother listening to my thoughts that often run through circles and riddles.

He called me beautiful, and when he said it, I believed him.

Frustrated with my foolish heart, I remind myself that he did not call *me* anything. He called Dixon beautiful. The beautiful *son* of farmers.

I am a foolish girl risking everything over one man who has shown me kindness a handful of times. Even so, I find myself hoping Bennett will invite me back soon.

Falling asleep to thoughts of the captain, this time they do not keep me awake but sweeten my dreams.

CHAPTER 19

THE MOMENT THE PIPE BLOWS IN THE EARLY MORNING HOURS, HARRY hisses into the air between us, eyes on the captain's door. "He wants to put his prick in your ass, and he'll be surprised by what he finds under your breeches, Dix, unless you told him more than you're lettin' on."

Harry begins kissing the air with puckered lips and nearly falls out of his hammock soundlessly laughing afterwards.

"You want him to put you on all fours!" He whispers the words through a teasing smile, but I can tell he is truly concerned. Worse than jibes, I know he is right and is being far wiser than I, despite being only slightly more than half my age.

Still, my pride makes me argue. "There is no danger of that. He would never take what I do not offer. Watch your tongue."

Right now, I wish Harry did not know so much.

Ignoring my chiding, he rolls his eyes. "He's a pirate captain. It's his job to take what's not offered."

"Perhaps he would not care." I say it more to myself than to Harry, but I sneak a look from the corners of my eyes for his reaction.

"The gods have little mercy for liars, Dix. For pirates, even less. I didn't expect you to have such a woman's heart. You'll have my vote for leniency if asked, but gods and fates could you not go trying to get caught."

As with every other thing he has said this morning, he speaks with more honesty than I would like. I defend myself once more, playfully now that I have given up on poking holes in his flawless logic. "I do not believe in gods, and what do you know of the hearts of women, Harry?"

I put my jackknife in my pocket and tie on my bandana as if to say, *I am done talking about this with you.*

Harry pulls on his boots and mumbles, "More than you, apparently."

Even though I am late to deck, I lean back in my hammock and cover my eyes with my arm. I guess I am not done talking about it because I mutter into the room, "I am the greatest fool on this ship."

I hear Harry pop a sticky, boiled candy between his lips. It clacks quietly against his teeth when he says, "Yeah. That's what I was saying."

Emphasizing our lateness, the captain calls for Harry from behind the closed door. Harry puts a sweet in my palm on his way by.

The sky is cloudy, and the water is grey and choppy. Pirates are a superstitious lot and the sudden change in weather has the crew jumpy and whispering amongst themselves about omens and creatures from the deepest parts of the sea.

James clicks his tongue and shakes his head at the nonsense, proving that not all sailors are so easily spooked. At the very least, James puts on a braver show than most.

He grumbles beside me, "At least the wind blows. If the wind had stilled these men would be crying to the heavens for forgiveness. The fearful lot."

His words reassure me that there is nothing to truly fear. It would be easy to be sucked into the hysteria otherwise.

The bell tolls and cuts off whatever James was going to say next and my stomach sinks. Perhaps I allowed myself to relax too soon.

The men pick up the call. "Merchant ship!"

The grey, featureless sea made it so we snuck up on the ship by accident

Captain Holt calls my name and waves me back down below decks. I look to James apologetically, but the rigger has already moved on to his next task.

In the captain's cramped quarters, just as with the first time we boarded a ship, I go to the chest and pull out the fine clothing.

With each piece he pulls on I start the fasteners, quickly and deftly tying a sailor into an outfit better fit for a king. Before I slide the jacket into place, Holt slips the silver locket from around his

153

neck and places it safely in a drawer at his desk. I make a note to ask about it in our next round of drinks.

He straightens the jacket and dons his hat. The captain looks every part the dastardly pirate and I experience the familiar feeling of shrinking in his presence. I smirk to break the spell. He did tell me last night I never have to be silent in his quarters.

"Perhaps I should pierce my ears and get a few tattoos. Otherwise, I cannot meet your criteria of looking fierce."

Captain Holt smiles, relieving my worries over potentially speaking out of turn. "All the tattoos in the world could not hide your pretty face, Dixon Ables."

There is not a drop of uncertainty or shyness in his voice. The clothing making him behave as confidently as he looks. It is all part of the act, but I struggle to hide my disbelief at his compliment.

He laughs at my expense and turns to leave. "Back on deck or James will have my hide for keeping you."

I follow him out the door, proud to have been asked again to assist in putting together the character that Bennett Holt plays on the stage.

As soon as his feet touch the deck, Captain Holt is calling orders. "Run up the black. Take your places, men. Remember we are in the business of taking, not fighting, so look fierce."

I start to jog towards the rigging when I am stopped, a pistol is shoved into the waist of my trousers, making me jump. The captain gives me a lording look and answers my confusion with his hand still holding the waistband of my trousers.

"You cannot expect to protect yourself with that letter opener you carry, Dixon. Let this be your first step towards ferocity."

Struggling not to gape at him for listening to me and taking an action that might help me in looking fierce, I turn my mind to defending my knife. It may be small, but after what I went through to obtain it and how long I have carried it, I feel the need to defend its necessity. Straightening, I step towards the ratlines. "It is a sturdy little blade, Captain."

In front of the crew, he is not in a position to tease me as I believe he would privately. He lets me jog off without further comment.

The ship ahead is flying the blue birds of Goran but is mostly unarmed, heavy and slow with prizes for the taking. It is the first ship we have come to since escaping the cays and leaving the waters around Azure Cove. Captain Holt orders for the guns to be manned and ready, but not fired, much to Harry's disappointment.

Even as we approach, the crew of the other ship stands with their arms raised on deck and hauls down their colors. Our men continue to snarl and howl, but their outbursts are progressively less infectious and less boisterous as each man begins to realize this is no plain merchant vessel. They appear to be mostly passengers, even some women among them in plain dresses with children clinging to their skirts, fathers standing in front to shield them. This is not who we are sailing to steal from.

The crew is large enough now that I could choose to stay behind if I wanted. Some do, those who would rather play it safe even if it means fewer prizes for them. The thing inside me that pushes me to join the raid is difficult to pin down, but it has something to do with the way the ships we take look upon us all with such fear. I like being feared. I have never been fearsome before and I am not terribly fearsome now, but to act like I am is a welcome change from subservience.

We sail up close to the ship and then jump into boats. It is always different to be in the boats in the open ocean than when taking the boats to land. There is no telling what is beneath us here. No telling how deep the water is. It makes me feel sick. With the dangerous game I play with the captain, I might not get a chance to stay long enough to grow accustomed to it.

I am grateful and eager to climb aboard the merchant ship where the passengers are lined up against the railing.

Captain Holt shouts across the deck politely, "Might your captain come speak with me, man to man."

A portly, older man in rather plain clothes aside from his well-shined boots steps forward. He is bald on top with silver hair by his ears. He walks proudly across the ship and announces loud enough for all our men to hear, "You will not hear a complaint against me from these men, pirate. I ask for mercy for us all. We will cooperate."

Captain Holt calls to his crew, "Make way for their captain, men. Wait for orders."

Sensing that no drama will break loose at this moment, the passengers are ushered below so only the crewmen remain on the merchant ship's deck. Hugh Digby stands between our men and theirs with a pistol in each hand, pacing the deck like a hunting wolf to keep a clear boundary, daring anyone to cross it.

The quartermaster's show of strength seems unnecessary. Our crew is at a loss of what to do with themselves under the strange circumstances. Thankfully, it does not take long for the two captains to re-emerge.

The portly captain shouts to his crew, "Keep everyone beneath the forecastle and unload the cargo onto *Sneaky Lass*. No personal effects are to be taken. Hop to, no amount of tobacco or gin is worth our lives."

The crew of the merchant ship grudgingly abide by their captain's orders. Some of the sailors are more pleased than others to be giving up without a fight.

I am relieved that there will be no bloodshed of families as I watch the cargo brought onto deck and then taken by our men on the boats.

Alongside a few shipmates, I stand at the backs of the

merchant sailors, weapons held at the ready. I hope no one notices how my hands shake.

When all that we care to take is unloaded, Captain Holt, wearing a wolf's smile, nods to the other captain. That is when a shot rings out.

A man stands on the merchant deck holding a smoking pistol and one of our sailors lies dead by Mickey Compton's feet.

Suddenly, the subdued pirates around me regain their vigor, drawing their guns and cutlasses once more. I am filled with fury over the betrayal, but as shouts rise and threats are made on the women and children in the hold, I find myself stepping further from the howling crowd and towards the railing and the waiting boat.

I turn to Captain Holt to control the fervor of the men, but he stands as though he will allow it. The captain's face is a mask of calm, hands clasped neatly behind his back.

It is Hugh Digby who shouts above the clamor. "Men, it is not the women's or children's fault that this sailor acted brashly and offended us. Captain Holt, what do you suggest the punishment should be for spitting in the face of our mercy?"

No one else noticed it for what it is, but I do. Hugh is practiced in buying Bennett time to consider what should come next. His question allows Bennett to form an answer without even a moment's uncertainty.

The captain bellows over his riotous crew, "Line up their sailors, shoot the first man. Take a finger off every second. Take an ear from every third. Let each of them share in the loss of our comrade. Let them limp to land with their tails between their legs like the cowards they've proven to be!"

The captain punctuates his command with a pistol shot into the air. The men of *Sneaky Lass* whoop approvingly and line up the crew of the offending ship to carry out the gruesome task. Not a single sailor is to be spared.

I try to climb the ratlines to avoid having to see what is about to occur in too much nightmarish detail, but Mickey grabs my arm and puts me behind a kneeling sailor.

Captain Holt approaches the line of men with a pistol in hand. The portly captain of the ship is first. My captain growls at the man, his lip curled into a disgusted sneer, "Your men broke our agreement and so I feel no remorse in starting with you."

He shoots the other captain in the chest at point blank range. I can hear the man gurgling on his own blood even from my distance. Every pirate on deck cheers except for me. I am too busy counting down the line. Shot. Finger. Ear. Shot. Finger. Ear. Shot. Finger...

The pirates take turns, some even keeping the ears or fingers as grisly souvenirs. Hugh stands nearby to ensure that no one gets overzealous with his weapon.

I am fearsome. These men should fear me. I silently give myself stern reminders.

When my turn comes in line, someone shoves a sharp blade into my quaking hand. With everyone staring, waiting for my move so they can cheer again, I have no choice.

I am fearsome.

I try to imagine the terrified man kneeling in front of me to be an animal I plan on having for dinner, but I would not cut a hog's ear off before slaughtering it for dinner.

These men should fear me.

I slice through the man's ear with more ease than I would expect a human body to part with a piece of itself. His screams are drowned out by the cheers of the men around me. I drop both the knife and the ear on the deck, hands shaking too hard to keep my grip. As soon as the eyes of the crew move away from me, I climb the ratlines of the merchant ship to view the remainder of the spectacle from above. If I could swim, I would jump into the sea and make for the *Lass* that way rather than remain.

Gods and fates, forgive me.

When all is done, we climb down into the boats. Prizes are tucked safely in the hold and a much smaller crew is left on the other ship in our wake. They will barely have the hands to make the ship sail.

Sailing is one thing I am finding I have a knack for, but piracy is a whole other matter. Now that the adrenaline has faded from my body, I feel queasy each time I think of what I did. I began with such certainty today. I cannot find that feeling again. I like being feared and acting fearsome, but now...

Do I deserve to act mighty when I am so frightened inside? Perhaps *Sneaky Lass* is not the place for me afterall.

Once back on deck, James takes pity on me when he finds me quivering by the rail like a leaf on a windy day.

"Climb the rigging, Dix. Let it go before you're sick all over deck. It's not fair to the men swabbing." I climb up as instructed and let the sea air blow away the sins behind us.

I find Mickey Compton hanging upside down with his knees around the lines beneath the yard and he sways in the wind like the sails do. We are not high up, but if he fell it would certainly kill him. When I approach, he sits up, his face red from the strange position.

"Just trying to clear my head." Mickey sounds apologetic. Like he wishes he could summon a smile for me as he typically does but cannot.

I stand on the line where he was hanging and hold onto the wood in front of me bouncing my fingers on the taught canvas like a drum in the way James gets mad at me for. "Is it working?"

The second mate hangs again and shouts over the wind. "It makes it so I can't think."

Following his lead, I hang upside down like a bat from the line. My body and mind are now so accustomed to the height and danger of the rig that I do not even think twice before falling backwards. Nerves ball in my stomach at first. If the rope snaps, we would die. I giggle childishly at how reckless I feel.

"You are right. This helps."

His eyes remain closed. "Hugh hates it when I do this. All he can think about is what would happen if I fell."

Despite the obvious risk, it seems absurd that Mickey Compton would allow himself to slip. "You will not fall."

He answers with the same amount of confidence as my statement. "Neither will you."

I look over at him, but his eyes are still shut. "What makes you say that?"

His face remains completely serene, and his voice is clear like a ringing bell. "You wouldn't fall. I think you'd let go."

CHAPTER 20

Night falls and I watch the men wander to their beds. Unlike most nights when we take prizes, tonight there is little celebrating. Harry seems even more disturbed by the day's events than I am and has been silent all afternoon. Crossing the ship's deck, I sit beside him against the rail.

My young friend is silent for a long time before stooping his shoulders and finally whinging. "I don't feel right about it, Dix."

Neither do I. Once whoever I became on the deck of that ship today had faded away, my emotions have cycled through feeling guilty, then sick. Now, I do not feel much of anything.

He slides his hands through his hair, fisting the ends in a

white-knuckled grip as his chin drops to his chest. I am reminded that Harry is just a good kid raised by good people, who ended up here. "Just seems like we coulda' done away with the one guy. Think those people will make it to where they're going?"

"They have enough sailors to get them where they need to go. Captain Holt needed to make a show, you know?" I try to sound reassuring, but I feel much the same way he does. I was a part of that show. Nausea threatens. I force it down into the nothing.

Harry grows quiet again. Just as I begin to worry that he will not say anymore he squares his slim shoulders and his tough exterior is in place once more. "You're right. I'm not gonna' worry over it anymore."

He sounds decisive, but he stays in his seat among the coiled ropes.

I hesitate in my next offer, not wanting to offend him. "Want me to stay with you?"

Harry shakes his head. "Nah, I'll be up awhile. Thanks for askin'. Tomorrow's a new day and all that."

I cannot bring myself to move from my spot beside him when I know he is still hurting. Harry knocks his skinny shoulder into my side and chides, "Don't be such a mother hen, Dix. I'll get by fine."

Dismissed, I put a hand on his back before I turn from both Harry and the sea.

Captain Holt stands at the helm looking straight up as the stars begin to appear in the darkening sky, one by one. The plan is to turn back towards land and sell what we have taken, as a heavy pirate ship is a sunk pirate ship. We will not be returning to Azure Cove, thank goodness. Wherever we stop next must be better. I cannot imagine how it could be worse.

The town of Alouett is only a day or two of sailing from here and Hugh claims he can unload what we have there easily. The quartermaster is so confident that many of us newer sailors are wondering what Hugh knows about Alouett that we do not. Mickey Compton is especially thrilled to be heading that way.

I approach the captain and stand by him at the helm. "What day is it now? I have lost track."

My guess is that it has been close to a month since we left Azure Cove the first time despite being not terribly far from it. That means it has been a few weeks more than that since we left Grand Port.

Bennett is happy to have me finding him rather than the other way around, even if it was presumptive of me to do so. He smiles and answers with the assurance only a man who writes the date each morning could, "It is the second day of spring, though in this part of the seas it does not much matter what day of the year it is. It is always hot. Hurricanes come in summer. We will head further north, or maybe east, if I can convince the lot of 'em."

He seemed distracted before I came, and the roundabout way he answers my query confirms it. He has been drinking heavily, if I had to guess from how he sways.

"That is a relief." I search the sky and attempt to spot what he is looking for in the stars. I much prefer watching the sea. Staring upwards on deck makes me feel dizzy.

Captain Holt turns from the stars to me. "Why do you care what day it is?"

I find myself shrugging, but my voice cracks with emotion I was not expecting. "I have been a pirate a little less than two months, if your dating is true. I am still not used to it. I would cut off the ear of someone who came at me no problem. Just seems like a lot of those men did not do us any harm. Two months is a short amount of time. Maybe I will grow accustomed, yet."

He chuckles darkly and looks back at the stars. In their dim light I can see tears stand in his eyes, but they don't fall. Bennett swallows hard and they vanish as quickly as they came.

"I still can't move on so easily, so you may be waiting longer than you would like to grow accustomed. Those men's eyes will keep me awake tonight. Necessary suffering, but suffering, nonetheless. The stealing, the violence, the unfairness of it all, I don't know if I've ever gotten used to it."

I know full well how our crew demanded punishment and Captain Holt had to give them something. He is our leader, but he is absolutely held to the whims of his crew in such matters. He saved the innocent passengers with his order and struck a fearful story, which is the pirate's game. Still, the reasons will fall flat in my nightmares, and his nightmares, too.

"Your hands were tied. I know that, Bennett." I attempt to comfort him.

The use of his first name brings a smile to his lips.

"Ensure none of the rest hear you call me that or I'll never hear the end of it being called such by a ship's boy." He reprimands me, but his voice remains gentle. I notice that the locket is back around his neck, and I restrain myself from asking about it. Now is not the time with how haunted everyone feels.

"Will you be out all night?" I ask softly. Though I am in no position to be handing out advice to anyone, I offer to be a confidante for the second time tonight. "If there is a way for me to lighten your burden, you can tell me, and I will try."

His eyes smolder with familiar desire. I struggle between feeling like I should flee to the security I often feel on the ratlines and wanting to reveal everything I am to him. I try to remember myself as his eyes scan the deck, feeling relief for only a split second, thinking he had been distracted when truly he had been checking for anyone watching. When he turns back to me his lips are pressed to mine.

I should pull away. I should act scandalized and put-off like a man whose masculinity or sexuality or both has been brought into question. Instead, I kiss him back because I desperately want to know what he tastes like without the pipe smoke or the whiskey. I fool myself into thinking it is only a kiss and will not go further. I tell myself yet another lie: that we are both sating a curiosity that will soon be over. My breasts pebble beneath the linen that hides them, and desperate heat settles low in the core of my body seeking friction and embrace.

The truth rings in my mind clear as a bell every second I remain wrapped in him. I want him. I want him like I have wanted no other in my life. I want him to touch me and kiss me and *know* me.

His large, calloused hand lands on my arm and the other on my neck under my cropped, unwashed hair. I allow him to deepen the kiss because I want him to. I want this kiss to never end. Everything that is tied in knots inside of me feels unimportant when he kisses me.

Then his hand on my neck starts to slide lower towards my chest where he will certainly discover something he is not expecting. It takes all my willpower to force myself to pull away. When I manage, I make an unmasculine and mournful whine at the loss of him.

Breathless and flushed, I stand just out of his reach, unable to look at him. I spot Mickey watching us from across the ship where he plays a round of bones by lamplight. His expression is unreadable.

Bennett looks so shocked that I feel the need to explain. Fates, if I could just tell him the truth I would return to his arms in an instant. I stammer as I try to find my voice. "I am sorry. I have never—"

He snaps in a harsh whisper, "I'm not stupid, Dixon. You're not as innocent as you appear."

Bennett sounds hurt and I am uncertain what his words imply. I want to reveal my lies to him so loudly that it will wake the monsters lying at the bottom of the sea.

He is right. He only knows me as Dixon Ables, the sailor on his ship. I, Jane, am not so innocent. My body has been used in ways he cannot imagine. My body has been owned by a husband who used me as a tool for his own pleasure and nothing else. My body has torn itself apart to bring forth life only for cruel fate to tear apart my heart as well. My body has been invaded by countless men of all walks of life in shady alleyways while wearing borrowed skirts.

I am far from innocent, but I have still never done anything that feels the way kissing him does. I am torn. Kissing him feels right and then when we part, frightening.

My expression must give away more than I realized because when he speaks again it is with a softer tone, like he is afraid I will fly away in fright. "I'm sorry. That was the day speaking, not me."

With eyes locked on the distance, looking at nothing, I cannot bring myself to tear them away even knowing he is waiting for me to answer. I swallow hard and try again, but only manage to shut my eyes tightly which is hardly better than staring off.

"You have left my ship again, Dixon." He sighs so tenderly the wind almost carries his words away without my hearing them.

With great effort, I finally meet his hazel stare and part of me is surprised to find myself on the deck of *Sneaky Lass*. I could swear I had smelled the pine and crushed earth around my once-home.

I search a long time before finding words to answer him with. How much honesty can I gift him without giving too much away? Would giving too much away be a worse sin than keeping such a secret from a man who clearly cares for me? I am a wretch.

"I am nearly willing to bet everything on a chance to kiss you again." Finally, I manage to find some. My chest feels tight, like I have been running rather than fading from one place to the next in my head. "I asked you once not to tempt me. I told you before all the trouble lies with me. Do you wish so badly to prove me right? Do you want to risk me for it?"

I feel desperate. It feels like my soul, if we indeed have souls, is being torn in two. I am being unfair. He is not risking me anymore than I continue to risk myself.

He pinches the bridge of his nose, one of his many anxious habits. "No, I wish to prove you wrong. I cannot imagine any trouble lying with you. How could I risk you?"

Even in a whisper, his tone sounds like he is shouting an order. No man has ever wanted me, only what I could give him. Until I met Captain Holt, I thought perhaps that was how all men were and would always be with me. I do not think Bennett just wants me. I suspect Bennett likes me a great deal more than he should. Otherwise, my rebukes would not wound him as they clearly do.

My innate sense of self-preservation, which has grown strong over the months on the run, wrestles with the dangerous urge to lie with Bennett Holt and see if he makes good on his word. I like him a great deal more than I should, too.

"Would you share a drink with me, Bennett?" I offer a compromise, since I have started walking on this thin ice already.

The quick switch in subject jars him from his own thoughts and he nods in agreement, leaving the helm to Mickey, who gives me a knowing smile that makes my cheeks warm. Mickey thinks me to be more honest than I am if he thinks I will be sharing my secrets.

Unlike in times past, I lead the way to the captain's quarters. When I enter, Bennett goes to the liquor cabinet and brings out the now-familiar faceted glasses. He does not grab whiskey.

In each glass, he pours something clear that smells terrible before taking a seat. Holding the glass in one hand, he fiddles with the locket resting on his chest with the other. He stops when he notices my watching him.

His fingers are unsure where to go when not on the polished

oval frame and he picks it up again. Almost shyly, he explains, "Just a habit at this point."

"I keep wanting to ask you about it, but it never is the right time."

Bennett rubs the back of his neck and sips his drink. "It probably never will be a good time."

I cannot tell if that is an invitation to ask or a warning never to do so. I stay silent and drink. My entire body shivers up and down after each taste as though it is my spine that cannot stand the drink rather than my tongue.

He shakes his head again as if he cannot really believe I am here. "I considered myself a secretive man until I met you. I am an open book in comparison."

Guilt lies heavy on my shoulders at his admission, and it does not escape his notice. "Do I get one question answered?"

I nod, resolving that I will not lie to him, no matter what he asks.

"Who has hurt you so badly that you now cannot allow me close? Why can you not believe that I can hold you without crushing you?"

Truly, I pause only because his metaphor is so apt. I feel like a fragile thing in the hands of anyone but myself.

He takes his drink and must not expect me to answer because he sits straighter when I do. "I have been hurt by nearly everyone I have ever met."

"Am I being held at bay by the ghosts of past lovers?" His teasing smirk falls away when he looks at me.

Something in the terrible day has given me permission to speak and once the words start, I cannot stop them. "I have never had a lover."

Bennett's expression is a perfect mix of shock and disbelief. "You're joking, surely?"

"Lover implies something different than what I have had done to me. I have never loved anyone who has ever had me. None of them have ever loved me either. I do not know if I want to change that. A lover sounds like a dangerous, fearsome thing. Far more dangerous and fearsome than strangers or abusers. How would I know what to expect of a lover?"

He examines his glass, throws back the liquor, and pours another before answering. "I have never thought about it like that. It is just a word."

I knew he had not. Most free men have never had much reason to give it thought. "Being truly at the mercy of others turns honest people into liars. I sit before you completely changed by their cruelty. I am not certain who I am anymore." My hands rise to my collar, my cheeks, my hair. I have no idea what to do with my hands. I want to put them up and shield myself somehow. I settle on holding the back of my sunburned neck and mumbling at the sticky table. "They killed the person who used to live inside of this body and left me with something empty that I am trying to find the right way to fill."

Describing my new identity of Dixon Ables in that way appeases some demon inside of me. I have found the words to describe them and in speaking them, I find a modicum of peace. Jane had poured herself dry at the whims of others and now, Dixon has taken residence in her empty cup.

Bennett is confused and I can see why. "That is why you pull away? Because you don't feel you know yourself?"

I wish I could tell him that I am pulling away so that he does not discover my breasts. It would be simpler, but it would only be part of the story. Instead, I must share something with him that is much deeper than physical. "When you kiss me, I feel afraid. I want to keep kissing you and yet... I am afraid, too."

"Because you don't know what to expect?"

I do not answer his question. Instead, I just state facts. "Until I do not feel afraid, I cannot do more."

My skin crawls when I say it and my heart, which I had not known could still break into more pieces than it had, aches.

Somehow, I have managed to tell Captain Holt the truth without revealing my secret. With him, the words flow as easily as ink from a loaded quill.

I throw the remainder of my drink back in the same way he does. The drink tastes just as bad as it smells. Maybe worse. "When I kiss you, I almost forget how much everything hurts, but when I stop, the pain is still there. So, we should not do more."

For the second time in Bennett's quarters, I allow tears to fall before I sweep them away on my dirty sleeve. At least this time I have broken his heart more kindly than when I pushed him away in Azure Cove.

When I manage to look Bennett in the eyes again, his face holds a tenderness I was not anticipating. Not heartbreak or anger, but sympathy, maybe? Understanding.

Without me having to ask, he pours me another drink. "After a story like that and a day like today, I think we should make an exception to the rule of one drink."

I manage to choke out a laugh through my tears and tease, "You just want to ask two questions."

He leans back in his chair and smiles at my accusation. "One question apiece. The rules have not changed, only the amount of liquid courage to face the answers."

"Fine. I will ask mine quickly then because this second drink will put me to sleep."

He laughs heartily at my expense and the mood lifts considerably after my dark confession, but my question rests heavy on my heart. "Do you think less of me now? Even knowing I am broken and a tease?"

Bennett shakes his head. "I don't think anything about you could scare me away, Dixon Ables. It's a frightening feeling for me as well. I am unaccustomed to wanting someone as much as I want you. I am even less accustomed to having to work hard at having them."

I wish again that I could just tell him who I am. Would he kill me for it, though? Have I already taken this farce too far?

The corners of his lips tug up, a bemused sparkle lights his eyes as he shrugs and repeats something I have been told more than once in more than one way. "You're not usually my type."

I respond automatically, precisely the way I did the first time he said something similar to Jane Polk. "Not into blondes?"

As soon as the words leave my lips, I close my eyes like I can forget my own stupidity. Thankfully, Bennett does not have any awareness of having had this conversation once before.

"No—" He cuts himself off and I wait for the rest of his answer with dread. In Grand Port he had said *desperate*. It had been an accurate, but hurtful description. "—Honest. Man or woman, I don't spend much time around honest people. You have never shirked from telling me the truth. It is a welcome change."

His answer is a kick to my guts. I am probably the least honest person Bennett Holt has ever met. I want to apologize and beg for forgiveness. Instead, I lean forward and kiss him, knowing it is a teasing move that can go nowhere.

I am dishonest and selfish, and I will get off in Alouett and that will be the end of this deceitful tryst.

Kissing me back, he sighs at the loss when I pull away. I down my drink in one swift movement with only a shiver.

"You are becoming a master at that." He pushes hair from his brow. I can feel his heart pounding in the air between us, and I sense the time to return to my own bunk is approaching. He adds, "The drinking and the teasing, both."

I mumble into the empty glass in my hand, "You may make a pirate of me yet, Bennett Holt. Teaching me to steal kisses like that."

He puts a hand on my knee under the table. "I will wait as

long as I need to in order to prove to your heart that I will hold it carefully, Dixon."

I am still reeling from his new description of me... honest. I feel such dread over it. I far preferred desperate. At least desperate had been true.

I force words from my tight throat, "You speak of me the same way you would a quest for treasure."

He taps his fingers on my thigh, his grin vulpine. "Are you not one?"

Forcing myself to stand up, swaying from the drink. I hold my spinning head as I answer him. "Morning comes early."

He chuckles at my drunkenness. "It will come all the earlier for you tomorrow, I fear."

I step closer to him again and put a hand on his shoulder, not yet wanting to leave, but knowing I must. I speak as Jane, allowing myself the pleasure of pretending to be someone worthwhile for just a moment. "I hope for your success in your quest for my heart. Truly."

The heat of his gaze warm on my back, I leave.

When *Sneaky Lass* anchors, I will get off and not return. I have no business staying. If I remain, I am hurting more than just me. Worse, I will be causing heartache to a man who does not even know his heart is in danger. A man who thinks me honest.

I know gods and fates and luck are not real. If any powers existed at all, I would be struck down here and now.

CHAPTER 21

THE CELEBRATORY MOOD IS CONTAGIOUS FROM THE SEAMLESS TAKING OF A wealthy ship today. The men around me, even Harry, have had far more to drink than I have. Still, I am lightheaded, and everything is funnier now that I am three or four swigs deep from the bottle being passed about. Our holds are full of prizes that will be easy to sell, the barrels and bottles of liquor we are drinking from among them. It was voted that we should keep it for ourselves since it is of a fine make.

The celebration will likely go on long after I have left to find sleep. Typically, I would avoid so many drunk men at once, but everyone here feels like a friend. Dixon has enough friends on this deck that no one would be allowed to hurt me.

Captain Holt has long since retired, having drunk himself to stumbling far earlier than the rest of us. It would have been bad luck for him not to accept every toast made to him.

There is not an entirely sober person aboard save, perhaps, Hugh Digby. The quartermaster is sitting straight-backed with Mickey Compton's head in his lap. The second mate is attempting to make up raunchy lyrics to a common tune but is so far gone with drink that he keeps repeating himself and giggling, much to the amusement of everyone listening.

Coming up with the next line for Mickey, I shout it across the circle. "His balls were of different sizes, so strange they'd win no prizes."

The men shout approvingly of my addition and Mickey finishes it, his lips straining to work around the words. "His wife didn't mind since he gave kids to mind, one slight and one size of a titan."

Hoooo! The men pick back up on the chorus that was decided on earlier in the game. When the second mate whoops with excitement at having finally completed a rhyme, Hugh Digby leans down to kiss his lover's drink-warmed cheek, wearing a rare smile that is reserved for Mickey alone.

No one else notices their quiet moment, but I see it. Just as it always does, their clear care for one another holds my attention captive.

When the quartermaster locks eyes with me I look away, resting my heavy head against the mast.

I have found someone who looks at me with care, and I must leave him sooner rather than later. The captain does not look at me tenderly, but Dixon. The thought offers me no comfort.

The sound of men arguing to my right shakes me from my

tipsy musings. Even in my state, my nerves stand exposed by the noise.

Looking over, I find a man standing too close to the railing, flushed with too much drink, a fist raised. I would take my leave now if not for the involvement of young Harry, being held aloft by his thin arm and shaken in the massive man's free hand.

The man shouts at the boy, "You cheat!"

Only after the statement do I see they had been playing dice. Harry has too smart of a mouth and shouts back, all while struggling in the man's grasp. "Put me down. How would I fake ya' at bones, Finnick?"

I am already on my feet, rushing over to help reason with the man named Finnick, when Harry spits on his face. Finnick, enraged now, starts dragging the struggling boy towards the railing. Horror washes over me like waves on rocks as I realize the man's plan is to toss Harry overboard.

Without a thought about my actions or their repercussions, I throw myself onto Finnick's back and dig my teeth into his shoulder so viciously that blood fills my mouth. I gag, but do not release him.

Finnick howls beneath me. I hear Harry's retreating footsteps on the deck just as I am slung over Finnick's head like a horse throws a rider. I land on the deck several feet away, coughing on the man's blood.

He is nearly upon me when the quartermaster fires a pistol into the air and everyone goes still and silent, save Finnick, who is hurling obscenities upon realizing I tried to take a sizable chunk out of him with my teeth.

"Blood and thunder! Where do you all get off breaking code over bones!" The quartermaster's booming voice is far louder than Finnick's howling.

James defends me from nearby, "We all know who started that fight, Hugh."

Anything else James had to say is drowned out by Hugh Digby's continued furious bellowing, "I don't give a damn who started it. It's forty lashes on a bare back for fighting."

Though Harry and I have been thoroughly chastised, Finnick is not done with either of us yet and jumps at me again, barely held at bay by two of my shipmates. "I'd piss on your grave for being too cowardly to fight proper, Ables. All to safekeep some unlicked cub!"

Hugh pulls out his nine-tailed whip from his belt, its leather safekept and well-oiled by the quartermaster's hand, and lands it hard across Finnick's back with a snap that pierces the night. "Someone haul him from my sight before I kill him, vote or no. He can spend the night making his own cat below."

Finnick is wrestled away by several men, allowing the quartermaster's ire to land squarely on Harry and me. He growls at us both, "Tomorrow, I'll let the crew decide whether you two deserve lashes alongside him. I have ample time, a strong arm and I'm happy to count all the way to one-hundred and twenty."

When neither Harry or I move, Hugh Digby whips the mast to his left and shouts, "Blundering Fates. Git! Before I change my mind and hold a vote now with this drunk lot."

Harry yanks on my arm, pulling me from my stunned, silent stupor. I hardly have time to wipe the blood from my chin before he drags me to my feet. We move so fast that I barely notice Bennett who, even in his poor state, has climbed up near the helm to watch the drama.

Once the hatch closes behind us, Harry throws his arms around my neck and pounds my back with both of his hands excitedly, clearly unworried about any possible punishment.

"You, Dix! You're my hero! My best mate. Look atcha. Like a beast, you were. Where has that been, huh? The Dix who chews men up and spits them out like bad leaves. Damn. And all for my sake?"

My young friend releases me and pulls his winnings from his purse, handing the coins to me. "Take it. Have my dice, too. They're loaded and, gods above, I won't use them again."

Upon realizing that Finnick was right, that Harry had cheated him, I snatch both the purse and dice from Harry's hand, stuff them into my boots under my hammock, and land in my swinging bed steaming mad.

Damn this boy and this ship of villains!

In the darkness, Harry is more subdued now. "Don't be like that. He'd of cheated me had he any wit."

I spit more blood onto the floor beneath me and growl quietly at the dark above. "If I get punished tomorrow you know how I will land, Harry. And it will be for protecting you from just ends. I will haunt you until the end of your days after they leave me on a lonely beach."

Arrogant once more, Harry assures me, "Hugh's not gonna flog us, Dix. If he meant to, you think we'd be sent back down to our own canvas? Nah."

When I do not answer, Harry reaches out from his hammock that hangs only a finger's width from mine and touches my shoulder gently. "You wouldn't really have seen me tossed to the sea for the trick, wouldya?"

All his bluster spent, I cannot stay mad at him. I wrap my hand around his small, rough fingers. "I would have jumped in after you, little good it would have done us."

He leaves his fingers in mine and says no more, but I feel his body jump each time the hatch opens for one more of our number to trickle back in.

With the morning pipe comes a gruesome show. Hugh Digby is already on deck with Finnick's wrists tied to eyebolts on the railing. On Finnick's left stands Mickey, stern faced with arms crossed over his chest. At the sight, I begin stepping backwards towards the hatch. I can feel Harry's loaded bones pressing into the side of my heel in my boots. This all feels too close, too dangerous and, not that I condone Finnick's reaction, terribly unfair.

I am so caught up in my own thoughts, I back right into someone. Turning, I find the captain is my victim.

Captain Holt's eyes are hard, his face a mask of annoyance. I look down at my boots.

"Not trying to sneak off, I hope. Hugh wouldn't have it, and he'd be right to keep you on deck. It would seem reading the charter alone is not enough to teach you the consequences for fighting on my ship."

I open my mouth to make excuses and then close it. It is a fair assessment, considering the circumstances. What would the captain care that I was defending Harry? That even if this gets me properly torn apart and discovered in one fell swoop, I would bite Finnick again for the boy.

Stepping out of the captain's way, I say nothing. Captain Holt moves to stand on Finnick's right.

When most of the crew is up and watching, the quartermaster addresses the ship. "If any man steals from the company or strikes one another whilst these articles are in force, they shall suffer forty lashes to their bare back. That is the fifth line of our agreement."

Mickey passes Hugh Digby a nine-tailed whip made of tarred rope, thinner than the wooden handled one Hugh wears on his belt, but longer and knotted in a way that looks like it may hurt just as much as the carefully kept leather braids of Hugh's more ornamental instrument.

The quartermaster continues, "Based on what I have gathered from the many witnesses, Ables joined this brawl in defense of Harry Lewis. I ask for a show of hands on whether those gathered believe Dixon Ables should suffer punishment."

I close my eyes like not seeing the crew's decision will somehow protect me from it. I toe the three coins in my boot and pray they are as lucky now as they were getting us through the cays but a few days ago.

Lowering his voice, Hugh addresses me, though still loud enough for all nearby to hear, "Ables, I hope you better remember your oaths in the future. You get off this time."

Relief floods through every muscle in my body upon the realization that Harry was right, I will not be flogged. I wish I had kept my eyes open to see who voted which way.

Hugh Digby continues. "Now, I ask the same in the matter of Harry."

Before the vote can be called Harry steps forward from the rest of us and adds his piece so quietly only those closest to him would hear. "I cheated Finnick at dice."

Those who heard Harry share what was said through mumbles and whispers. Far worse than the thought that anyone should be hurt at all is the idea that Harry will be flogged before my very eyes. He is only just a kid.

Louder, Harry repeats himself, "Everyone should know I cheated 'im. I started it all."

The whispers continue as the crew waits for the quartermaster's judgment. Having admitted his piece, Harry's entire body is shaking. I find myself wishing he were not so good. I wish he had kept his mouth shut. I worry that he only admitted it to appease me in some way. Gods strike me if proving something to me is what has brought this on.

Finally, Hugh announces a decision. "Finnick will take twenty since he was robbed. Harry will take twenty with the lesser cat for being a damn lying trickster, and a poor one at that."

Mickey leans down by his feet and stands again to pass Hugh a red sack. I assume it holds whatever a lesser cat is.

To Harry's great credit, he squares his shoulders, takes off his shirt, and stands beside Finnick to receive his due. Mickey ties his small hands and legs in the same spread-eagled stance as Finnick. I feel sick and begin backing up again only to be held firmly in place by a shipmate's hand on my shoulder.

I lack Harry's bravery. I do not wish to see him harmed. The crest of Harry's spine stands out and the skin on his slight back is unmarked, having never faced such punishment before.

"A weaker hand than yours should punish that mutt if we're not to cane his behind like a boy. You'd tatter him beyond repair, Hugh, even with that flimsy cat. He told the truth. That counts for something." Someone to my right offers.

Affirmative shouts rise among the crew, myself included, but my relief for Harry is short-lived when Hugh Digby opens the sack and points to me with the rope pommel of the lesser cat. "Ables, serve your crew and remember well the lesson here."

Despite not being asked, I shake my head and step back only to be pushed forward once more. The decision has been made, and with the ebb and flow of punishment ever changing, I take the handle of the whip for fear that a worse action could be exacted against me if I do not.

I imagine the whip is lighter than the more wicked one that Hugh wears. It only has seven tails and is knotted in fewer places than the one made by Finnick. I wonder who made this one. I wonder if it was made last night or if it has been waiting for a long time to be used. It feels like an important distinction to me. Was this cat made for Harry specifically?

Harry has been tied in place on an upright grate, so he faces the high railing of the deck. Neither Mickey nor the captain look me in the eyes as I approach. My feet do not wish to obey me. Every step is against my mind shouting at me to flee.

I should thank the gods for small mercies. At least I did not have to see Finnick flogged first to know the worst of what I am about to do. Still, the task before me is impossible. Harry is little more than a child playing tricky games with the wrong people. He is my friend.

From beside Harry, Mickey Compton speaks instructions warningly, "You'll show no favor to the boy, Ables. Lest I tie you up next."

His warning snaps me out of my head. If I do not do this, I might not survive the day.

I raise my arm and bring the whip down on Harry's back.

Once.

Twice.

Twenty times.

CHAPTER 22

Moving gingerly throughout the day, Harry avoids me. I would probably avoid everyone, too, if our positions were reversed.

I have heard stories of the punishments handed out on other ships from the crew. They are unjust, often crippling, and decided on by the captain alone. That is why the punishments are laid out so clearly in our charter and are at the discretion of the crew. At least in this way everyone feels that the punishment fits the crime. Before today, all punishments aboard *Sneaky Lass* have been mild. I imagine the rest of the crew would consider today mild, too.

Still, there are always those that voted for the losing side.

I have spent my day vacillating wildly between numbness, fury, and nausea. Now, with nothing to occupy my mind, I find I can hardly sit with myself.

Taking off my boots, I put the damned loaded dice in my palm and climb to the very highest point on the ship. The wind whips about me wildly. At this height every inch the ship moves on the sea sends this point on the ship several feet. For a moment, I think about what it would mean to jump. It is not that I want to die. I just do not want to feel what I am feeling right now.

Cruelty is a part of life. Cruelty is certainly a part of piracy. Still, I had begun to grow comfortable on this ship. It was a fearful sort of contentment, but it was more content than I have ever known before. The type that could almost be mistaken for safety. Guilt for beating Harry is coupled with guilt for forgetting myself so badly that I was wrapped up in this at all.

I am always one small misstep from everything crashing down around me. One day, it inevitably will.

Today.

This dark pit of a terrible day.

I got lucky.

This crawl-out-of-my-skin feeling is what lucky is on *Sneaky Lass*. It means my secret is still mine. It means I can keep pretending I am safe. It means I am alive.

Sitting atop the topsail, so high that even I feel dizzy when I look down, I throw the loaded dice as hard as I can to the sea.

I remain above everything, swaying in the wind with my eyes closed until long after dark. Until my bones ache and my ears ring from the wind. Until that queasy, lucky feeling starts to pass.

When I climb down, the captain waves me over to where he stands, and I pretend not to see him.

Harry is in his hammock when I climb in beside him. He is not asleep. I do not know how he could be with what I did to his back today. The lesser cat did not break skin, but it left him bruised and red all over. He hisses when my body bumps into his.

"I am really sorry, Harry." I hope that he knows all that I am sorry for.

"You didn't get me whipped, Dix. I did. It's not the first or the last time it'll happen either... My ma said I'm made of trouble."

I cannot come up with a good argument against that. He is one of the most reckless people I have ever met. I have not spent much time around kids. Almost none, in fact. Perhaps they are all like that. Based on how women complain about their broods, I am willing to bet that is the case.

Finally deciding on something to say, I answer, "I think you will grow out of it."

"Or have it beaten out of me if Digby has his way." He grumbles. He meant it in jest, but the reminder of this morning's punishments makes us both flinch.

Knowing it may hurt his pride to answer, I whisper, "You okay?"

He nods again, his bobbing chin casting a shadow in the flickering light. "I will be. Mostly I'm just all ashamed. Breaking my ma's heart, and now everyone knows I'm a cheat."

I had not even thought about that, so caught up in my own grief from the day. Nervously, I ask, "You did not tell the crew to appease me, right?"

He punches my shoulder weakly. "Full o' yourself, eh? I did what Ma woulda' wanted. Honest is the least I can be for her sake."

It is a touching thing to hear. Not for the first time, I think Harry must have come from a kinder place than all this. "I do not know your mother, Harry, but I know her life's work and it is clear enough under the tar that she made you good."

Harry sniffles in the dim light and does not answer me.

I speak some of my worst thoughts from the day aloud. "It

was cowardly of me to take that cat. I should have told them all no."

Harry snorts, his nose runny from crying, the sound shocks me from the clouds I have lived in all day.

"And gotten yourself licked, too? No offense, Dix, but twenty swings from you is about the same as five from Digby. I should thank you for it."

I do not get a chance to sort out whether I should be relieved or insulted as the hatch to deck opens. I blow out the candle in a hurry and feign sleep in a silent agreement with Harry to avoid everyone but each other until morning.

I am not so lucky to get away with it.

Bennett tugs on my sleeve on his way in the dark. I do not want to follow him tonight. I would rather just let things lie until sunrise. It is often true that things look brighter after a night's rest.

Torn between being too tired to argue and too bitter not to, I follow only because he is the captain.

When the door shuts behind us, Bennett's shoulders slump and he sits down behind his desk rather than at the table. Unsure of what I should do, I stay by the door. I had not realized I was angry at him until now. I blame him, despite his having nothing to do with any of it.

Bennett looks nearly as defeated as I have felt all day, but it does nothing to still my raging blood.

"You risk yourself for nothing, Dixon?"

Struggling to find any decent thing to say, I realize I am too emotional for this discussion. I am uncertain where to even begin. Do I defend Harry's life as far more than nothing? Do I explain that, to me, there was no option not to risk myself? In the end, I bite my tongue and say nothing at all.

Frustrated from my silence, Bennett continues reprimanding me, but it is not Bennett at all. Captain Holt glowers at me in all his commanding glory. "Do you have any idea how close you were to sharing in that punishment? Three votes. For what? Harry Lewis?"

I can hear the concern behind his aggravation, but it does not do anything to soothe my own anger.

"If you believe that by having me beat Harry, I was not punished then you know less about me than your quartermaster does." I grind through clenched teeth.

Captain Holt's eyes widen, taken aback by my tone, and digs himself deeper. "Letting you lash Harry was a kindness. Far kinder than he'd get elsewhere for the same offense."

"I do not think flogging anyone is a kindness. Why have you brought me in here? If you are looking for gratitude for the opportunity to beat Harry Lewis, you will not receive it." My voice grows louder and louder, ending in a shout.

Deflated, Bennett sinks deeper into his seat. "I could see how disturbed you were all day. I brought you in here to explain why it must be this way. Were you not struck as a boy?"

"I was."

Jane was.

He smiles as though I have suddenly seen his side of things. "Then you know why he needed to be punished. It is how he will learn to be better."

Baffled by his reasoning, I shake my head and sit down in my usual seat at his table. "I must have been hit harder than you were."

Sighing, Bennett appears to give in and joins me at the table. "In this matter, we may forever disagree. I do not wish to fight with you, Dixon."

As eager as he seems to set this matter aside, I am not finished and struggle to reign in my hurt. "To think, you never would have known as much if you had left me to my hammock instead of bringing me in here assuming I do not know my own mind."

Bennett tilts his head towards the floor and then looks up at me like a child who knows he has done wrong. "Will you forgive me, then, for my incorrect notion that you needed guidance in this matter? Please understand... I only want you to be careful."

When I take too long to answer, Bennett fills the space again. "You are the strangest man I have ever met."

His words stop me in my tracks. Strange how? I have been working very hard to appear typical.

"I never knew how much time I spent accepting how things are until I met you and how you fight everything. Have you always been so contrary? It often feels like you spit in the face of the whole world for the sake of it."

Being described as contrary, well, I could grow to like that. I even know the answer to his question. "It is not for the sake of it. It is because the world and the people in it are unfair and cruel, and someone should resist unfair and cruel things. To have a voice to argue with is a privilege many lack."

A privilege I lacked until very recently.

Bennett raises a brow. "You could have argued when Hugh handed you that cat. I don't think fear of a whipping alone would stop you, reckless as you are."

I have been beaten before, though never with a nine-tailed whip. If it had been an option between taking a whipping beside Harry and whipping Harry, I like to think Bennett is right. As it stands, flogging is not an option I can choose without facing a worse fate.

I parrot Harry's words as an explanation. "Twenty hits from me are more like five from Hugh."

Bennett exhales with a nod, shrugging his acceptance and speaks in a tone somewhere between pleading and playful. "You still haven't forgiven me."

Taking a deep breath, I try to remember what he asked

forgiveness for and fail. "Ask for forgiveness again so that I can be certain of my answer."

"Forgive me for being one of the unfair and cruel things you wish to argue with."

His words trigger my still bleary memory and I remember enough of the first time he asked to know he has changed his apology. In truth, I would forgive the captain far greater offenses than coming to different conclusions in his life than I have.

"Are you sorry for it?"

Bennett levels his hazel eyes with mine and speaks earnestly, "I am sorry that, as captain, I sometimes must be cruel and unfair. Be it to strangers on a merchant ship or to your young friend. If I had my way, I would listen to your kind heart, always, even when I think a cheater should be beaten."

I feel the truth in his statement. He is trying to meet me half-way. He cannot change his thoughts and he cannot change his position. The fact that he would wish to for my sake is enough. "How could I not forgive you when you speak so?"

My answer brightens his eyes, but he sounds regretful when he tries to send me away. "You should return to your hammock. I won't keep you another moment since I dragged you away from rest."

I no longer wish to leave. Tomorrow, we will be in Alouett, and if I have any sense, I will stay behind there. I remain in my seat.

"Can we share drinks instead? Early mornings or not, I would rather stay."

Bennett's smile is all the answer that I need.

CHAPTER 23

FROM A DISTANCE, WHERE *SNEAKY LASS* IS ANCHORED, ALOUETT IS A nicer town than Grand Port and is miles beyond the likes of Azure Cove. Tucked on the far side of a small gulf, it is not a common stop for anyone. It does not seem like the type of place the Navy would come too often. It does not look to be the place that should see pirates ever. Yet here we are.

Mickey has looked thrilled beyond measure ever since we dropped anchor. The second mate rowed to shore alone before anything was sold or any coin was handed out, unable to wait for reasons unknown to me. No one questioned his leaving. In fact, many encouraged him.

The gunpowder, sugar, and other items of value that we stole are sold at great rates quickly by Hugh Digby alone. It would seem everyone in Alouett has a debt to pay to Hugh. No one I have asked has been able to tell me why.

Shares are handed out in due course and, though no one told me of the change, I receive a full share. I am no longer a ship's boy but a sailor, it seems. Hugh did not even look at me when he handed it to me. No words were exchanged between us. James did wink at me though, like he might have been the one to recommend this change.

Soon, I find myself on an empty ship with another purse of money and no idea what to spend it on besides a bath. Captain Holt and Harry left with the rest of the crew and neither has returned. It seems like as good of a time as any to leave the ship and see if I can find what I seek.

I roll a new set of clothing that I hope will fit nicely, stolen from a taken ship, under my arm. It may make me stand out among the other men, but I have been looking forward to getting out of the once recognizable clothing that have been rags for nearly as long as I have worn them. Tucking my new pistol into my worn belt and slipping my jackknife into my pocket, I am ready to go. The city may look nicer than Azure Cove, but I will not walk in it unarmed.

Unlike when we stopped in Azure Cove, I am thrilled to be on dry land this time. So long as I do not think about how I must remain behind when the *Lass* sets off again, I can almost keep it that way. Skipping the brothels, where I know many of our crew will be, I walk past the docks and nearby businesses towards a reputable looking inn. A wooden sign sporting a large fish, carved in relief, hangs above the door. Along the fish's length it reads, *The Leaping Jack*.

Inside, I discover a mostly empty inn, save the innkeeper and a few older men who look like regulars. When my eyes fall on two familiar figures seated at a corner table I almost run out. Hugh and Captain Holt are drinking from clay mugs. Hugh is grumbling about something to the captain, but Captain Holt's eyes are on me and do not leave.

Gods and fates I hope he does not believe I followed him here. What would he think of me, then?

Hugh, notices how Bennett's attention has glided away to me and kicks the captain beneath the table. The captain kicks him back and I try to pretend I have not noticed their presence. If it were just the captain, that would be different. Hugh Digby, on the other hand, still dislikes me, at least as much as he dislikes everyone but probably more. I will not be the one to disrupt our tense truce where I attempt to stay out of his way, and he pretends I do not exist.

The keeper is a fit looking man with curly, brown hair cut short. He raises his eyes to survey me, and then raises a skeptical brow before asking, "What are you looking for? Seems most of your folk are at the brothels down the road."

I approach the bar, purse in hand. "I am looking for a room, a bath, and a hot meal."

The keeper takes my purse and takes his price before returning it to me lighter. "You got it, lad. I'll have food and hot water brought. Easy enough."

He reaches below the bar and hands me a key attached by a chain to a red piece of painted wood. "Red door on the right is clean and ready for you. I can send a lady your way as well, if you would like?"

I answer too quickly and loudly to sound casual, "Absolutely not."

The barkeep arches an eyebrow at me and says nothing more. I hear Bennett stifle a laugh behind me. Whether it is at something Hugh has said or my predicament, I cannot know, but his timing is impeccable.

I turn away from the bar towards the hall, accidentally meeting the gaze of the captain in the process. He nods in my direction, a smile in place, and I nod back shyly as I head to the room in a hurry.

A large tub filled with water is brought first and a steaming kettle of more fresh water is put aside should I need it. The boy who brought the tub stands to leave after stoking a fire to life in the hearth and I stop him. I have never had so much money to spend before and I can afford a few comforts before I must try to sort out the rest of my life.

"Boy, if you can find me a vest in good shape in a close size, I will pay for the item plus extra for your trouble. Fair?"

The boy's face brightens considerably at the prospect of earning something extra and, with a quick nod, he runs off on my errand. I lock the door behind him, shed my filthy clothing, and unbind my chest.

My breasts feel strange and sore unbound, and I find myself massaging them in small circles in the hot water for relief. As my muscles begin to relax my thoughts stray to Bennett Holt just outside the door, thoughts which only become more sinful the longer that I remain in the bath.

I cannot recall the last time I felt any pleasure from my body. Sometimes my customers sought my pleasure even above their own, but no matter how kind they were, they were unknown to me with the coarse hands of strangers.

My own hands are hardly any better, but I have the time and solitude to change that for the first time in years. More importantly, I have the desire to change that right now.

The ghosts that live in my mind rent free tell me I am not worthy of kind touch even from myself. I will not be dictated to by such ghosts. Not today.

Alone, clean, and safe; I allow one hand to drift lower, leaving the other on my breast. My body feels foreign. My tanned, freckled skin beneath hard calloused hands... Am I someone I want to meet?

That distance between my mind and my body helps keep the many ghosts at bay. I settle into thoughts of Bennett Holt. I imagine myself in his arms, with his lips upon mine. *My lips.* Not Dixon's. What would *my* name sound like on Bennett's tongue?

I can almost hear it. Jane. His Jane. Wouldn't that be an impossible something? I have a better imagination than I gave myself credit for because I can hear it in my mind when I slide my fingers along my center.

Until this moment I had not realized how rarely I have felt like Jane in my weeks on *Sneaky Lass*.

I am me once more.

What would Bennett's strong body feel like astride mine? He is sturdy, like an oak. Not like most reedy sailors at all. Purposeful, maybe. I think Bennett's touch would be like allowing the earth itself to hold me. There would be no risk of losing myself in such a sure embrace.

Shuddering, I slide two fingers in circles around the knot of nerves at the apex of my cleft and arch towards my hands. Instinctively, I move them away when pleasure rolls through me. I do not think Bennett would do that. He would stay to lead me through such waves. I try again, willing my hand to be Bennett's and, sure enough, peak with pleasure and then sink once more.

I allow myself to rest until I have caught my breath. Then dunk my head beneath the water. To clear my head, I run the soap through my hair over and over without coming up for air.

Stupid.

Lustful imaginings of Bennett will not serve me well. My crush will get me killed if I am not careful.

I covet the sea and the freedom I have found, but not nearly as much as I crave Bennett's company. I could find a new ship easily enough, a reputable one even. One without a man who I lust after and who lusts after me. Worse than lusts, he cares for me.

Even after arriving here, certain of my plan to stay, and having become a grand liar, I am not convinced I will manage it.

Emerging with a gasp for air, I step out of the tub and dry myself with the towel. Curling naked under the covers of the soft bed, I wait for the boy to return with a vest that may serve to hide my small chest without having to bind it. It feels decadent to lounge about on a clean feather mattress after so long swinging in canvas. I allow the fresh sheets to help me drift to sleep. My weapons rest on the other side of the room, but I do not go to them. I feel safe enough as I am.

The boy returns with a knock, and I startle awake. I do not know how long I have been dozing, but by the placement of the sun it has been at least a few hours.

The key turns in the lock and the door swings open before I have time to cover myself in any meaningful way. The boy steps in holding a small package in one hand and a hot plate of food in the other. His eyes widen at the sight of me naked on the bed and I hide my embarrassment under a prideful smirk.

Clearing my throat, I open my purse. Perhaps my cause is not so lost. "Leave it on the table and tell the barkeep to put the vest on my tab."

I toss him a silver piece and he catches it deftly from the air.

I toss him a second coin and instruct, "For your trouble and silence."

He nods wordlessly, wearing a grin, and reassures me with his resolute answer. "Thank you, *sir*."

The boy darts from the room and I lock the door behind him once again. Adrenaline is flowing through my veins and I have nowhere to put the nervous energy buzzing inside of me. I jump up and down in place several times and wish that I could shout without drawing attention to myself.

I eventually approach the package and open the brown paper wrapped around the vest. It has been dyed a greenish blue color, almost like the pine trees that grew near Grand Port and appears to have been worn a good deal before, which is not a problem. I would prefer not to stand out overmuch. I wonder where the boy found such a thing. Perhaps he stole it or has an older brother who has outgrown it.

I pull on my plain shirt, brown trousers, and wool socks, which will likely see little wear since I so rarely don my boots on deck. I leave the vest uncinched in the back and am flooded with relief that I no longer have to bind anything so long as I wear it. Not for the first time, I have found reason to be grateful for lacking curves that men often seek out.

My belt is a bit worse for wear but serves its purpose. I put my pistol back on it. I pull back on my leather boots and toss my old clothes into the corner. Let the inn cut them apart for rags. They certainly wouldn't survive washing. My linen shirt was so worn from work and the salt air that I could pull the fibers apart with my fingers. I will keep an eye out for a spare set on the next ship we board, as always.

Dressed and clean, I turn my attention to the plate of food. Potatoes, onions, and mushrooms with bits of seared pork greet me. Everything is smothered in a brown sauce that tastes much more like what I would get back in Grand Port than anything I had in Azure Cove. Two bites in and I find myself shoveling it into my mouth. I almost regret ordering the meal. The food on the ship will be harder to return to after being reminded how good food can taste.

Except I am not returning.

Checking my reflection in the glass in the hall one last time before taking my leave, I would not guess I am a woman by looking at me. I look like a strong, young sailor. Tan, tall and, now, well dressed to boot. I consider finding a barber to shore up my hair, but decide against it, unwilling to part with what short locks I have grown.

When I re-enter the tavern Captain Holt is gone. I am relieved. I paid the servant boy well for silence, but for the captain to be gone is safest. The keeper is nowhere to be seen, and in his place, a woman with light brown eyes and long, dark hair braided to her waist scribbles in a book.

The part of me that had just been feeling confident in my appearance fizzles to nothing in her presence and envy takes me by surprise. Comparison was almost constant in Grand Port where my livelihood often relied on looking a certain way. Jane left that behind, and Dixon has had no use for such frivolous emotions. Still, there is a softness about her that climbing the lines and passing days in relentless sun have stolen from me and I can not help the pinch of longing seeing her brings.

The beautiful woman looks up and smiles brightly at me. Before I can ask what I owe, she waves me off in a friendly manner. "The captain paid for your clothes. Said he needed a well-dressed crew. Be safe on the seas. Come back if you're ever in Alouett."

Bennett thinking to dress me is almost enough to chase away the darkness I felt. I wonder if Bennett hoped for this reaction or only meant to be kind.

My heart, which has not ceased finding reasons to return to the *Lass,* clings to the captain's kindness. He wants a well-dressed crew. It would be terrible to repay him by not returning.

Outside the inn, I stop at a stall and buy some marzipan for Harry. The store owner wraps the sweets in paper and ties it off with a piece of twine. I slip the gift into my pocket with a grin. I know Harry will pretend he does not care one way or another whether I think of him, but he always smiles when I do. I feel I owe him after being made to whip him only yesterday. If I am to stay in Alouett, it might ease our parting, but the longer I think of remaining here, the more certain I am that I will not.

The sun is setting and casting a beautiful light as I walk past the brothels and whores on my way to the ship. The men and women in the streets are loud, drunk, and celebratory. I find myself looking into the lit windows of the taverns and watching the people inside. It is not until I see Captain Holt through a window with a beautiful, dark-haired woman on his lap that I pause.

She is rosy-cheeked and plump, her long hair curls loosely down her back. One of his hands is resting on her waist and the other holds a pint of some brew. Her lips are to his ear and he is smirking at whatever flirtations she whispers.

For the second time today, I find myself wishing to be a beautiful woman with long hair and colorful gowns. It is not as though I miss that life. I have worked among women just like the one in Bennett's lap. Most of them do not feel appealing at all. They feel used up and tired. They wish the men would just get on with it and pay them so they can pay the madam or the pimp. I do not envy her, but I do envy how Bennett is looking at her.

Captain Holt is interested enough in me at sea with no greater beauties available to distract him. He likes me enough to pay for my clothes. In the end, he only knows me as Dixon and must continue to. It is just a fleeting but painful thought that if I were a lovely, rosy-cheeked someone with long locks of blonde hair for men to run their fingers through...

I cut off the thoughts and force my eyes back onto the cobblestone path that leads to the docks, but I do not start walking. I am not like them. Even living as a woman, I was never someone anyone would envy the looks of. Being a woman only ever led to trouble, but jealousy and vanity have me getting lost in dreamy thoughts. I cannot afford to think about it. The furious tears that slide down my cheeks at seeing the captain with that whore only serves to remind me of my own idiocy.

I clear my eyes and mean to return to the ship, but I enter the brothel instead.

A woman is beside me in an instant to lead me to the bar. She is wearing her skirts tied high on her thighs with bright green ribbons that match her sea-foam colored dress. All of it is very seemly against pale, freckled skin and wavy, strawberry-blonde hair.

She is a beauty and I would feel flattered for her approaching me if it were not her job to do so. I force my eyes to stay on her and not wander to the captain a few seats away. Idiotic or not, I want him to see me here. I want him to feel as jealous as I did when I saw him.

The woman in green leans in close enough that I can smell the fragrant powder she uses on her face and neck. "What are you searching for, sailor?"

I put on my handsomest smile and look her up and down in the way many men have done to me in my past. *An actor on a stage.*

"Mostly a drink, but I will not turn down beautiful company."

I feel stupid saying it, but I must have done a fine job of acting because she simpers brightly and calls for drinks. A mug of ale is placed in front of me and I pay with copper coins from my purse.

Taking a heavy swallow of the ale, I steal a glance towards the captain. Captain Holt's eyes have strayed to me and I inwardly applaud at the victory. I return to watching the beauty sitting beside me and lean forward in my seat. Perhaps it is the boisterous atmosphere that spurs me on but I decide that if anyone could know how to charm a whore it is a woman in disguise.

She gets plenty of men who ask about what is between her legs. I study her looks and find something to ask about that she likely has not heard before.

"The lace on your sleeves is lovely. The repair is almost impossible to spot. Did you do it yourself?"

The tactic works and I manage to make a whore blush, a feat in itself.

Her laugh mixed with her lilting accent sounds like ringing bells. "A sailor who knows of lace? I am intrigued."

"I have many sisters. You must be very talented. You could open a shop with skills like that." I lie.

She waves me off shyly and I start to worry that I do not know what I am doing when she lays a hand on my upper thigh.

"I am talented in many things, sailor. I can do a lot with these fingertips."

This time her words clearly imply something different than tatting lace. I steer us clear again.

"I am certain they can. I used to be able to tat, not so well as you. Now, with my calloused fingertips, I would tear it apart as I went. I am Dixon. What is your name?"

She is shocked that I would care to ask. I drink more ale for the courage, and to sneak another glance at Captain Holt, only to discover he has moved from where I last saw him.

"I am Ellen." She slides her hand higher on my thigh. If I am not careful, she will discover all I lack under my disguise. "A sailor who tats lace. You are one of a kind, Dixon."

I force myself not to blush and persist. "Now I use that skill on sails instead."

Out of the corner of my eye I see Captain Holt being led back into the halls of the brothel by the same dark-haired woman who had been in his lap, but his eyes catch mine on his way. I finish my drink and then look back to my whore.

"Do you get paid to keep secrets, Ellen?"

Her eyes alight happily when I use her name. My wish to tell someone, anyone, about how badly it hurts to see Captain Holt leaving to sleep with someone other than me has me taking stupid risks.

The rouge on her lips makes her teeth shine like pearls when she smiles charmingly. "I get paid to do whatever it is you want, Dixon."

The other patrons are so loud that I do not fear anyone listening in. "The captain of our ship, who was sitting at the bar moments ago, is the reason I came in. I used you to make him jealous. I do not think it worked, but he seems to think he can have me at sea then forget me on land."

I do not know if it is because she knows I will be paying for her time or if it is because she has actual interest in my tale, but Ellen nods kindly and taps her fingers on the bar before responding to me. "Most men have this affliction, even with their wives. One stays true and the other pays no such courtesy."

I laugh at being compared to the captain's wife. She thinks me sinner and sod, but she is kind enough about it.

"It turns out he is right in his expectations though, because I want no other. I may be a passing fancy to him, but I am apparently too dim-witted and have fallen hard. So, if your time is better spent with a sailor who is going to use you for something that pays better than talk of lace, I will let you go."

"I do not believe you are dim. It is such a pity that you are by far the most charming man in the room and yet you want only for other men." Ellen moves her hand off my thigh but remains seated by my side. She dramatically sighs and then winks in my direction to assure me she is jesting. "That is often the case with you sailors."

Her frankness is refreshing and helps me feel brave enough to stand, leaving a few coins in her hand for her time. She pushes half of them back into my palm and keeps the rest, saying, "Thank you for noticing my lace."

Then her lips are on mine. She tastes like rum and the flowers she crushed to make her lip rouge, there is a slight metallic tang there, too, from the chemical that keeps the color so vibrant. Her kiss is passionate, deeper than she needs to go with any paying customer. Her hands roam across my chest and then down my back.

When she pulls away, I am breathless and confused. She whispers in my ear, "I made sure your captain saw that, dear sailor."

She leaves me for other patrons with a wink and sure enough, Bennett is watching me from across the hall, his expression unreadable from the shadows he stands in. Feeling foolish, I look away quickly and take my leave.

CHAPTER 24

I WAKE LATE AND GROGGY. MY MEMORIES OF THE NIGHT BEFORE COME back to me slowly and out of order, but what I remember is plenty to dampen my mood. Captain Holt did not return last night. No matter how much ale I had, he would not have been able to sneak past me. The passageway where Harry and I sleep is so tight no one can walk through it without jostling us both.

Harry's light snores, just a few inches from me, is comforting confirmation that he made it back fine last night. He is sleeping off his own ale by the smell of him. Before I head onto deck, I pull the wrapped marzipan from my pocket, now a little smushed, and place it on Harry's stomach while he sleeps. He does not stir.

On deck, my head starts pounding from the light, a parting gift from my single mug of ale last night. It is not the acute headache that comes after a night of rum or gin, but a soft, thudding in my skull with each beat of my heart. I am not built for drinking.

The captain does not want to give *Three Queens* time to catch up with us if he can help it, and so we are only staying until the tide returns on the third day. I think everyone would have preferred to stay longer. It would seem Alouett is a favorite stop. Even Bennett had been thrilled to be here.

I shake thoughts of Bennett from my mind again and get back to pretending I have work to do. To keep my mind from wandering, I start reciting a prayer aloud while I climb and shine brass. Having been married to a preacher means many are seared into my memory. Twelve gods, plus the Goddess of Luck sailors have invented, and each has their own long prayer. That doesn't go into the countless fates. Someone must know them all, but most pick a few favorites and stick to speaking only to that handful. Every time my mind trails off, I force myself to start at the beginning of the longest prayer I know by heart.

Having worked myself into a trance, I barely notice the men returning to the ship below me. I nearly jump out of my skin when James finds me.

"I need to keep you off the ship at port. You make me look like a bum every time."

I pause my restless fingers. "At some point you simply moved to a rank where you get to do what you please and have others work for you."

He throws his head back and laughs.

"Who would have thought a man born as lowly as me would one day have a servant of his own." He slaps me on the shoulder. In a more serious tone, James continues, "Make yourself rest.

Climb to your favorite perch an' watch the water or whatever it is you do when you stare as you do."

His jovial mood lightens my own, the tension in my muscles relaxing slightly. In fact, everyone seems to have had a nice time in Alouett.

Hugh Digby has returned and is assigning jobs to several new sailors on the main deck, and I shudder at the thought of even more bodies aboard. *Sneaky Lass* is building its crew back up slowly but surely. Each time we make port or take a ship, more desperate souls join ranks. *Thieves and beggars*, as Captain Holt would say.

I do as James asks and climb to my favorite place on the ratlines to stare at the town. Harry soon joins me and passes me a piece of marzipan from his pocket. "To wet your whistle. Thanks for the present."

I take his offering gladly. I forgot to eat all day and now that I have paused, I am ravenous. "I was just thinking about you."

He knocks me in the shoulder and teases. "Don't get all sweet on me, Dix."

Despite his nonchalance, I know he is as glad to have my friendship as I am to have his. Harry pops another morsel into his mouth. "It's my favorite. I don't usually get these because they don't keep."

"It was a lucky guess."

Harry chews thoughtfully on the sweets to savor them. "Good one, then."

We sit in amicable silence for a time but I can feel the question hanging in the air between us.

Eventually, Harry hands me another sweet and asks, "Will you be staying in Alouett?"

The question is made worse because he and I both know I should stay and neither of us like it. The list of pros and cons has grown muddy just as I knew it would. "I do not know."

Harry nods and leaves sticky residue on the ropes from his fingers as he climbs down, which is just as well since I have tracked tar in my own wake. My frustrations with Captain Holt feel further away and I am content to watch the activity below. I put the question of staying or going from my mind. I will avoid it as long as I can.

Just as with most times we make port, Captain Holt is one of the last aboard in the night. He whispers something to the second mate, who climbed up just before him looking dour, and suddenly preparations are being made to sail with the night's tide rather than waiting for tomorrow morning. We must be back to running. The captain makes a show of not looking at me. I know that I should be relieved to be back on the chilly side of his cold shoulder. If he means to give me a wide berth, then I can stay. I do not feel relieved though.

Just as my feet touch the deck Captain Holt's hand lands on my shoulder and my stomach does a wicked summersault. I was not relieved to be ignored by him, but I am not glad to have his attention either. Damn me.

"Come with me, Ables."

Bennett does not break stride as the cabin door closes behind us. He immediately walks to the small window at the back of his ship and looks out at the bay surrounding Alouett. I stand by the door with an uncomfortable feeling that I will not like what he has to say.

Bennett pinches the bridge of his nose and sighs, heading towards the cabinet where he keeps his liquor. "Let's have a drink and speak like rational men. I don't wish for there to be another rift between us."

I do not want there to be a rift either. Dixon might. I am not certain.

He motions to my usual seat, and I take it, arms crossed defensively in front of my chest. I did not realize until this moment how irrationally angry I still am with Bennett for being in that brothel. Between that anger and my uncertainty about him and my place in the world, this cabin feels too small.

Once I take my seat, he pours a drink in front of each of us. We are both silent. Then something like an apology surprises me again. "Last night in the brothel, I was just trying to get you out of my head. I should not have done so."

The jealous creature resting in my broken heart rattles its chains in response to his admission of guilt. I find myself in the undeserved role of accuser. "Then why did you?"

Who am I to ask such a thing?

Even so, Bennett appears to be trying hard to suppress a small smile at my possessive tone. "Is that your question for the night?"

I suddenly remember our typical game of an answer for a drink and nod, knowing I will not have the mind to think of anything more pressing under the circumstances. Deserving or not, I am possessive. "Yes. That is the question that I want answered tonight."

"I am sorry. I was taking something out on you that is not your fault. Last night I had the mind to bed a woman, as you probably know. When it came time for me to perform..." He looks away from me and anxiously rubs the back of his neck, releasing a frustrated groan before finishing his answer in a hurry. "I could not perform."

Bennett's face turns slightly pink, noticeable even through his suntanned skin. It colors the tips of his ears. He throws back half of his drink in one go and defends himself against his own thoughts. "They all bored me. I already knew what they would say before they said it. Then there you were, so easily flirting with that woman just to make me jealous."

I open my mouth to deny it and he holds up a hand to silence me. "Clearly, it worked just as you planned. When I got back to a private place with a woman of my own, all I could think about was your smile, your vague answers, the way you say my name. I was furious over it. How could I not be? You will not have me, and I can have no other!"

His honesty releases a flood of shame through my body, so much that my hands tremble in my lap. He has just repeated what I said to the whore last night almost word for word.

I have been laying claims to him that I do not have the right to, and they are affecting more than just me. I should run from this room and watch *Sneaky Lass* sail away without me on it. The mental list of reasons I had made, and lost, becomes clear once more. I pick up my drink and toss it back in one gulp, hissing in the aftermath.

Just as every time I have thoughts of giving all of this up, I remain where I am.

Bennett finishes the second half of his drink and walks to the drawer of his desk where he stores his silver locket in times of strife. I am surprised when he returns to me with a silk box. "I bought this for you. I noticed you were in need of a new one. I hope it is not too flamboyant."

His nervousness at having gotten me a gift is evident in the way his eyes flick from the box to my face, shyness staying my hands from reaching for it. "You already purchased the vest I am wearing. Did you think of me the entire venture?"

I meant to sound teasing, but instead I sound stunned. No one has ever shown me such care, yet he does so even when angry with me.

He motions for me to open it, so I do. I find a leather belt dyed a rich forest green. Tears spring to my eyes and I must stare at the floor to keep them at bay. I do not remember the last time I received a gift, and never one so fine. I do not deserve it. Dixon might, but Dixon is all false.

My anger and jealousy begin to melt away alongside my

shame even as I try to righteously hold onto it all. In the end, I find myself filled with understanding instead. "Thank you."

Bennett seems at once both terribly uncomfortable and pleased by my reaction. I undo my well-worn belt, put it aside, and buckle the new one. The stiff, new leather fits around my hips perfectly with a bit of extra length that I tuck back into a loop.

His face transforms instantly from nervousness to satisfaction. "I was worried it wouldn't fit. I've no eye for measurements, but it suits you well."

His eyes hold a now familiar lust.

I fiddle with the settings until they are right to avoid his gaze and put my pistol in its new place, while attempting to steer the conversation. "I fear it will not remain so beautiful for long."

Bennett shrugs. "Clothing is meant to be worn, and it will still work long after it has lost its shine."

"I believe it is your turn to ask a question, Bennett."

He eagerly asks without hesitation. "I want to know what you said to that whore last night that had her laughing and blushing like a virtuous maid. I feel as though you have some secret that you absolutely must share to tease us all around your finger as you do."

Perhaps it is the drink or the gift, but I am unable to keep back my laughter. The irony is too much. Bennett seems bemused but is clearly waiting for my reply.

Between giggles I finally manage, "We talked about tatting lace."

"Lace made a whore blush?" He shakes his head in disbelief.

"Her name was Ellen. She had repaired her lace sleeve beautifully and I complimented her on it." I recount to prove I am speaking in earnest before deciding I may as well keep explaining. "The rest of the conversation was about you."

I finally manage to get my laughter under control, but Bennett's grin only grows wider. "What was said about me?"

His lupine grin is contagious and, despite my reluctance to continue, I want to tell him the truth. He already has correctly guessed my plan to make him jealous, so there is little reason to not tell him the entire tale.

"I told her I would not be bedding her because I only came in to make you as jealous as I felt when I saw that woman in your lap. She talked of how it was a shame that the kindest sailors only had eyes for one another."

I study the floor and Bennett's eyes could sear holes in the top of my head with their intensity. I can hear his smirk long before I gain the courage to look up and see it. "Hmm, she failed to mention that it is also often the most beautiful sailors that prefer one another."

I blush, my mind immediately starts listing flaws like a prayer I have recited my whole life. I mumble towards the ground, "I would not describe myself as beautiful."

"Well, you're not stupid, Dixon. I will simply assume you have never looked in a mirror. Perhaps you would prefer handsome but it is the wrong word. It does not suit you at all."

It would not be right to toss his compliment aside by telling him I have looked in mirrors often and, until very recently, have always seen the plain girl with brown eyes that are too small and too far apart, and a nose that is too thin for her face.

He continues despite my obvious discomfort, "Beyond the reflection in the mirror, I think you have a beautiful soul."

My chest feels heavy. I wish again that I could just tell him and be through with this masquerade. If I once thought he would forgive me, it feels too late now. If I told him tonight he would feel like a fool. I have tricked him for too long. My dishonesty is too great to take back.

If gods and fates and the lucky lady on the coin above our heads were real, I would burst into flames for my crimes against Bennett Holt right this instant.

I curse my willful heart and try to leave. "I should go. We sail with the tide."

Before I can stand, he kisses my cheek like a boy would a young crush. The act is so innocent that, for a moment, my heavy, dirty soul feels lighter.

Back on deck, I keep looking at the docks and wondering if I should stay. It would be an easy thing. Everything I own is already on my back. It would be hard to leave the home I have found but I could forget it eventually.

"Alouett is a nice town." I jump at the sound of Mickey Compton's voice. He makes no comment on my reaction and follows my eyes to the lanterns of Alouett. "It'd be an easy place to stay behind. Maybe even an easy place to make a life in. There are lots of good people here."

Grumbling, I look to the nearby boat. It has not yet been brought up and stowed. "I do not like how you do that."

Mickey leans against the railing, looking troubled. "Do what?"

"You guess what I am thinking. You and the captain both do it."

He tosses a twig he has skinned of its bark into the water below. "You make it too easy. So, you're thinking of jumping ship, then?"

"It would be better for everyone if I did."

"Not better for you. Piracy suits you. You made a cheap whore in Grand Port. I fear you would stand out among the ladies here in a bad way." He speaks the truth, whether I like it or not.

The way the second mate speaks of me like he has known me all my life, despite not even knowing my true name makes me shiver. I close my eyes, knowing he is right. "Better for Bennett, then."

"He'd be all hurt and boring without you." Mickey leans closer beside me. "I keep meaning to give you an ultimatum. Tell him or

I will. Tell him or I'll kick you off this ship myself. But that doesn't seem fair to fates, so I just watch."

For the life of me, I cannot sort out how telling my secret would somehow offend the fates. Mickey explains himself without me having to ask.

"I've had a few secrets I was determined to keep. They tend to wash out at the right moment. Who am I to interfere with that?"

Oh. He wants to leave me to the cruel designs of the heavens. "When he finds out, I will be tossed overboard just so he can save face. Worse than death, he will hate me and—" Not love, but something like it, "—I care about him more than I should. I do not want him to hate me."

Mickey shakes his head, disappointed in me. "Is that the man Ben strikes you as, one who would toss you over for the truth?"

I let go of the breath I was holding in a huff, more frustrated than anything else. "No." My reply sounds as uncertain as I feel, and I add, "But it is the captain he strikes me as."

Mickey does not have any response to that. Instead, he makes up my troubled mind for me. "Don't stay in Alouett. We come here twice a year or more. If you want to get away from Bennett, and keep your secret, wait until we drop anchor elsewhere."

I speak to the lanterns of Alouett, "I do not want to leave."

Mickey purses his lips in thought and then snaps his fingers as though he has had the most brilliant idea. "You could tell him. If you told him in private, then he would not need to respond like the captain."

In truth, I am more fearful of Bennett's scorn than anything else, but I cannot bring myself to say it aloud again. I would rather be thrown into the sea to drown than face Bennett's hurt on my account. I would rather Bennett come to hate Dixon Ables for being an unwinnable prize than learn of Jane and hate me in truth.

Quietly to the sea, Mickey changes the subject to himself and why he watches Alouett so bereaved. "This is my last venture with *Sneaky Lass*. With some luck, I'll return to Alouett with the last of what I need to start anew. Six months more and I'll be a man of the land and trees."

I try to picture Mickey anywhere but on a ship and struggle. A greater struggle, still, I try to picture him without Hugh and cannot. Whatever Alouett holds for Mickey Compton, it must be great for him to be so willing to leave everything else behind.

"Why not stay now?"

Mickey chuckles to himself and wears a look like he has been asking himself that a lot. "I think I might yet convince Hugh to join me in retirement. Call me hopelessly romantic."

The last of what he needs to stop sailing is the surly quartermaster. Well, that answers my question of picturing them parted.

Like so many of my conversations with the second mate, it ends abruptly. He claps his hands together and stands up straight. "Come on. Kiss the coin. We've a tide to catch."

CHAPTER 25

My head hits the floor beneath my hammock seconds before my body slams down. My mouth fills with blood from where I bit my cheek.

"We have enough lazy know-nothings on this ship without you adding to their number, Ables."

The quartermaster is lording over me with a fist on each hip. I watch as Harry slips from his hammock and tiptoes by the quartermaster with a hunched back, like if he crawls Hugh Digby might not see him. He slips into the captain's quarters without knocking, rightfully assuming Captain Holt's ire will be nothing compared to Hugh's.

Hugh pulls back his boot to kick me and I roll out of the way just in time. I stumble to my feet and inch towards the ladder. The pipe only just sounded; I have nothing to apologize for. That does not stop me from trying to appease the terrifying man before he breaks me in half.

My voice comes out pitched higher than I would like. "I am sorry. It will not happen again, I swear it."

He practically growls in my direction but does not chase me or kick at me again. As soon as he turns his back to head onto the deck, I scramble towards friendlier company.

Mickey Compton is glaring at his lover's turned back. Since we left Alouett, we have been sailing under low, gray clouds. Rain and choppy seas have been nearly constant. Worse yet, anytime it is not storming, the air is as still as death with no wind for the sails. It has put us all in fouler moods, and Hugh's mood is foul to begin with.

I struggle to keep my opinion on the quartermaster to myself, too tired to keep hold of my tongue even about my friend's lover. "I do not know what you see in him. We are all soaked to the bone and miserable. No one else feels the need to take it out of everyone around him."

Mickey hides his glare behind a wink. "He doesn't kick at me."

Perhaps the miserable condition of sailing the past few days is getting to me more than I thought because I keep talking even knowing I should not. "Must be nice. Maybe if I sucked his—"

Mickey's harsh look stops my vulgar thoughts in their tracks, and I clench my teeth shut around the words. "Watch it, Dix. You slept through the pipe and it's his job to get on you about it."

Before I can apologize, Captain Holt steps into the small passage with Harry sulking in his shadow. Like all of us, the captain is still damp, wearing the same clothes that keep getting soaked on deck day after relentless day. We all smell of mildew and sweat. A ship in the rain might be more wretched than anywhere else...

Ghosts of my husband and his heavy fists, of the nameless stinking men in Grand Port swirl in the recesses of my mind. No, I would rather be here. Miserable or not.

Captain Holt is scowling, whether from the damp or Harry's sudden intrusion, it is hard to tell. He jumps on my back alongside his mates.

"Ables, you plan on being as useless as Harry this morning or are you going to get moving?"

Mickey is already climbing up the ladder and I follow the second mate in answer. At least we will all be equally miserable, the lot of us on deck.

I collapse into my hammock after another long day. Harry joins me soon after. flopping into his canvas so dramatically that it flips him out and he lands on his bottom beneath it.

His riotous laughter is enough to pull me from the edge of sleep enough for conversation, but his joyful tone does not last longer than it takes for him to climb back into his bed.

"The captain has been in a mood since the weather turned. I need this rain to let up so we can be searchin' for the next prize. Maybe that will sort him straight. I'm sick of his shit. He acts like the rain is my fault!" He whispers, but my eyes still dart nervously at the captain's door just a few feet away by my feet.

"Better you than me." I whisper back, "No one is much fun to speak to in this weather."

By nightfall I am so exhausted that no amount of warming drink, or even Captain Holt's company, could keep me from my hammock. As much as I miss seeing him, I am glad that we haven't been alone together. It will help me keep my secrets close until I can get off at our next port. It is no longer a question. I must leave *Sneaky Lass*.

Harry scoffs and grumbles towards the ceiling. "Yeah, you're lucky. He only speaks to you when he's in high spirits. I get him the rest of the time. Thanks to you, though, I have a way out from my position. You can teach me the ropes once you're able. Then maybe I can get a full share, too. Better not get yourself killed before then. I'm countin' on you."

Guilt rests heavily on my chest. I will miss him when I leave and, though he'd never say as much, he will miss me, too.

I put on my best grin before answering, "I like the way that future sounds, Harry. The same goes for you, then. No dying on me until I can teach you the rig. Hopefully, it will be in better weather."

He crosses his heart with a finger and wrestles off his sodden shirt and trousers, both landing on the wood beneath him with a wet smack. Despite the rain, it is not cold. With spring coming and us being so far south, it is steamy and miserable below decks. I wish I could join Harry in tossing my wet clothing aside, but I do not have a spare set to change into so it is my miserable lot to remain fully clothed and drenched night and day. Harry flips onto his side to look at me the way he usually does before drifting off. Then he reaches into the blankets bundled beneath his head and pulls out a honey-colored sweet wrapped in waxy paper.

"You want one. I know how you don't like comin' to port. Maybe next time I can convince ya' to come with me."

I almost tear up at the gesture and pop the candy into my mouth to suck on. After over a week of terrible weather and sour beer the sweet tastes heavenly.

"I will come to land next time with you and buy your toffees from my own coin."

At least that is not a lie. I will not vanish on Harry. I will have to say goodbye.

He smiles widely and shuts his eyes. "I'll hold you to that. Maybe the skies'll clear in the night and the wind'll blow better tomorrow."

He yawns, a loud punctuation to the hopeful thought. Within a few seconds he is snoring just as I knew he would be. His optimism comforts me.

Counting Harry's soft snores has me drifting on the cusp of sleep, even wet and hot as I am.

The brass bell splits the night. I spring up so suddenly that I collide with the beam above my head. Harry rouses, rubbing his eyes and cursing the man on deck as though it is the lookout's fault there was something to see.

Captain Holt opens the hatch above us in his typical weather-worn attire and shouts down into the darkness where we all rest. "Hugh! Put away your prick. All hands, on deck."

Before shutting the hatch once more, Bennett's eyes meet mine in the gloom and there is fear in them.

He adds softly, "Dixon, put this where it lives."

To my great surprise Captain Holt pulls his locket over his damp hair and tosses it to me. I catch it, more on instinct than skill, but I find myself only able to stare at the captain's most prized possession resting in my palm.

When I look up again Bennett is watching me expectantly, his voice holds all the authority of the captain he is. "Now, Ables."

Mickey and Hugh emerge, dressed and disheveled in the light spilling from the quarter behind them. Not sparing a breath for them, I jump to my feet and rush in the opposite direction to the captain's quarters.

Walking over to Bennett's desk, I slip the locket inside the drawer among the loose notes, golden rings, and journals that fill the space. I wish I could scour the rest of the items there, including the locket which I have never seen the inside of. Against every curious thought screaming in my mind, I close the desk with willpower to rival the gods themselves.

Cannons boom, my feet leaving the floor at the proximity, and the ship rocks as I try to steady myself enough to pull the cabin door shut. When the ship steadies, I rush towards the main deck, pausing when I notice Harry still in his hammock, clothes still in a pile on the floor beneath him.

"Harry, why are you not already with them? Digby will have your hide."

His usual boisterous optimism is gone along with any color in his face. Pale and trembling, terror is wild in his eyes. Fear is thick in his voice. "I don't wanna fight them again, Dixon. It's the Navy. Last time..."

Last time they ended up in Grand Port making repairs for weeks and lost what must have been over half their crew.

Fighting every instinct that I have to keep him below deck and protect him, I try the only thing I can think of to get him moving. "We need you at the guns, Harry. No one moves faster than you."

At the mention of the cannons, Harry's eyes focus back on me and then harden.

"All hands, on deck." He says and slides out of his hammock to pick up his clothes.

Slipping my jackknife into my pocket, I load and place the pistol the captain gave me into my belt and follow close behind Harry as he climbs up. In the wet, the gun might not even fire.

The deck is chaos. Men are everywhere preparing cannons, powder, guns and more for what is certain to be a fight. The wind is so fast that it whistles by my ears, blowing the next storm towards us. At least it is not raining at this moment. Perhaps some of the powder will be kept dry enough for use.

James grabs me within seconds and sends me up the ropes

with quick instructions. "Stay on your toes. When they get close enough to board, use this."

He hands me a cutlass in a sheath. At my troubled look he shrugs, tears standing in his eyes. "A dead friend would want to see it used. Now strap it on and no wasting time. It's gonna be a trying night."

I slip the blade into my belt and start climbing the slippery ratlines. In the dark and the clouds, a naval ship snuck up on us. From what I can gather from the men around me, it was very purposely done but this is not *Three Queens*. I am glad for that. I am not certain I would have the guts to draw a weapon against men with such a fearsome reputation as those of *Three Queens*. The men of *Sneaky Lass* never so much as speak of them for fear of cruel fates overhearing.

The captain is barking orders to those at the guns while James is snapping at us on the rigs to get the ship moving as quickly as she possibly can. The realization that we have turned towards the enemy ship rather than away dawns on me with a wave of nausea. The navy sloop-of-war is high in the water, carrying nothing but men looking to sink us.

The sailor beside me on the yard, a young man named Phillip, greets me with a humorless grin. "If they told me this ship had a vendetta against it, I would have stayed in Alouett."

Like most sailors, he is young. He has freckles across his tan face and wet, brown curls that hang in his eyes.

I do not get the chance to answer him as the captain yells orders at the same moment. The wind carries away the words before I can catch them. Thankfully, the crew echoes the call loud and often to ensure everyone gets the notice. We are to prepare for a fight. There is no outpacing this one.

The ship is rocked again by cannons, leaving me desperately clutching the ropes alongside my shipmates until the *Lass* steadies in the water once more, and we begin the crawl back down to the deck

Hugh Digby's booming voice rises above the others. "Any man fleeing from the fight will face a worse death than these navy oafs could give you, I promise you that!"

With a cutlass in each hand, he strikes a fearsome image, one that no part of my entire being doubts. It is enough to stay my feet and keep me from running below.

The two ships are flying across the sea at one another like horses in a joust. In the darkness it is hard to make out any more details than that. Our only hope is that we can fight harder than they can before our ship is blasted to pieces.

I feel a hand slap my shoulder and turn to find Captain Holt, still in his working clothes. There is no time for any grand displays tonight.

"Get ropes and hooks ready. The more men we get on their ship the better. The crew of *Maiden's Musket* will give us a good fight."

The look of anxiety in his eyes, aimed at me, makes me want to reassure him in some way. I can still imagine the weight of his locket in my palm. "Yes, Captain. After this is over, let's meet for a drink. I have something to tell you."

The fear painted into his expression eases further away at the reminder that there will be an *after this*. At the very least, we are speaking as though there will be.

He is already jogging away when he answers. "Deal. I have thought of a few questions since last time."

Harry is shoving chain shot into the largest cannon on the main deck. Once fired, the sound of chain shot hitting the quickly approaching ship is not unlike the sound of a tree crashing to earth after being weakened with an axe.

He hollers excitedly and every sailor around me pauses to

watch as one of the masts of *Maiden's Musket,* falls sideways into the sea taking the men who had been upon it down to the depths.

The odds of the chain shot working had been slim to none and the men of *Sneaky Lass* cheer alongside the boisterous boy, suddenly feeling like Luck may be on our side.

The navy vessel fires back, and the jubilant mood quickly changes back to one of anxiety. More cannons blast. I hear the explosion of wood from our railing at the same moment I am pulled bodily to the deck by the muscled arms of our carpenter.

Landing on my stomach, I cover my head with my hands, like a startled tortoise. I would stay like that all night if I thought it would do me any good. When I look up from the wood of the deck, the young man from Alouett, Phillip, who had spoken with me on the rig lies dead inches from my face. Splintered wood from the railing has ripped him to pieces.

I lean over the remains of the railing and wretch the sour contents of my stomach into the sea. From somewhere beyond the din of men, in the stillness between cannons firing, I can hear the second mate shouting at me for it. "Pull yourself together, Dix. Grab that dead man's weapons and put them on. They will serve you better."

Somehow, digging up mental fortitude I did not know I possessed, I push away any humanizing thoughts of the dead young man on the deck and take his two dirks, his loaded pistol and shot, and quickly find spaces for each among the ties of my green belt and the pockets of my jacket.

Pax steps up behind me and, with no time for ceremony, throws Phillip's body into the sea to get him off the deck. I whisper a short prayer, just in case gods or fates exist.

With their mainmast gone, *Maiden's Musket* is crippled. I take a deep breath, entirely unprepared for a battle. I have never even fired a pistol and now I have weapons circled on my belt like a gruesome halo, only made more lurid by the knowledge that all but one of the weapons is borrowed from dead men.

Cannon fire continues to tear away at our ship, and we have no more lucky hits as we did with the chain shot.

I take note of where my friends are. Harry is running powder and shot between cannons. Mickey is at the helm beside Hugh, steering the ship dangerously close to the other. The captain is near me, watching *Maiden's Musket* approach with an axe in each hand and a snarl on his face.

None of them will remain where they are for much longer but knowing they are safe right now gives me courage.

James grabs me and pulls me towards the head. "You follow my lead."

CHAPTER 26

Maiden's Musket is now so close that I can hear the men on her deck shouting, just as the cry is carried out on our own ship. It is a resounding echo that gets more succinct with each repetition.

"Borders, away!"

"Cutlasses, lads!"

"Brave faces!"

All the calls mean the same thing. The first wave of our men jump from the bow of *Sneaky Lass* onto the crippled vessel. *Maiden's Musket* skirts the side as more men leap from one ship to another. Their hooks and axes land on the hull and deck. Pirates climb up like an army of insects picking over a dead kitten. Pirates are far more skilled at jumping between ships than naval men but the clang and clatter of fights resound behind me on the deck of *Sneaky Lass.*

"Save your pistols for when you're in a tight spot. You won't have time to reload." James shouts over the wind beside me. When I don't move, he catches my eyes, making sure they are locked on his before he asks, "You hear me?"

I nod and he returns it while ordering, "Don't die. I've put a lot of time into your teaching."

With that, James vaults to *Maiden's Musket,* which now sails so close to us that I could reach out and touch it. The hulls barely kept from scraping together and causing damage only by Mickey's careful guidance.

Taking a deep breath, I follow James. I miss the railing of the *Maiden's Musket* completely and land on my hands and knees on the opposing deck. Three silver coins that *are* lucky slide out of my boot and roll into a puddle of blood. There is no time to retrieve them. We will see if I am lucky anyway.

Stumbling to my feet in a sea of danger, I find the only thing differentiating my company from the enemy is the navy blue worn by most of the rival crew.

Stupidly, it is not until a man tries slashing me in half with his blade that I realize being a part of the fight means fighting back.

I barely dodge the blow. I do not think the man in blue expected my ineptitude, which is why he did not attempt to evade me when I threw my entire body onto his, stabbing one of the daggers I took from Phillip's body into his neck and sliding it down like I would a pig on my father's farm. The noise he makes is not unlike that of a pig, either.

Blood is everywhere, all over me and my victim and the sand that has been spread over the deck to keep us all from slipping. I do not have time to wretch over it. More men in uniform are all around me and soon they will spot me as the easy prey that I am.

Pulling my dirk out of the dead man with a sickening sucking noise—not unlike pulling a stuck boot from the mud—I attempt to get a part of the ship behind me so that I do not have to be so concerned with those at my back.

I do not bother unsheathing the cutlass from my belt; I have no idea how to use a weapon like that with any skill. The daggers, on the other hand, are a lot like farm work. There is no elegance or glory in it, but when I stab another man in the back while he fights with one of my shipmates, he dies, glory or no.

I have read accounts of battles before, and heard countless stories of grand deeds from my shipmates. Battle is a very different picture than the one they painted. The men around me are all terrified and I am terrified with them.

Screams, the blasts of gunshots, the clash of swords meeting, they are all so loud it is hard to process. The sand laid in preparation for this fight falls woefully short compared to the volume of blood being spilled. There is no grit beneath my boots. Just endless pools of blood. Everything smells like gore. It smells of hot, raw red meat with a metallic tang. The sting of black powder wafts in the salty air, lending a sickening spice. In truth, battle is a lot of people wrestling on bloody decks covered in dead men, both whole and in pieces.

If I stopped moving for even a second I am certain I would piss myself, vomit, and then someone would kill me and I would never have to move again.

My system of stabbing unsuspecting sailors in the back is working as well as any other. A few of my shipmates have taken notice and purposely try to get the men they are fighting to turn their backs towards me.

Why have we even joined this fight? We took out their mast. We could have fled. Nothing but male egos have landed me in this mess.

One man in blue comes right for me, having caught wise to

the game, and I pull out one of the flintlock pistols and fire. The man's jaw is ripped off by my poorly aimed, but lucky, shot and he lands on the deck with a thud. His eyes grow dim as his body stills.

In any other circumstance I would be horrified but I do not feel like I am in my own body. None of the enemy men around me look like human beings. I have become a spectator to the entire bloody scene. Corpses lie all over the deck. There are only so many men who can be present for a battle on a ship, and there seems to be more dead than there are combatants.

These navy men were unprepared for *Sneaky Lass*. They are a small crew on a small ship who probably thought a brig full of pirates would be an easy prize to take. They are paying for it now. I sail amongst men who murder for fun. When given a reason to do it, they grow even more dangerous.

The tide seems to be turning in our favor when I spot Harry, surrounded by danger. He looks so small compared to the men around him. The man he is fighting is twice his size and is pushing him back quickly.

Without another thought, I begin running towards him to help, shouldering past enemy and friend alike. Harry is only here at all because I convinced him to leave his hammock, that we needed him in this fight. And he listened to words I never should have offered.

I feel a sharp pain on my right side and ignore it, running over the blood-soaked deck towards my friend. No one else is watching out for the cabin boy. Knowing Harry, he has been goading the man who is now bent on killing him. There is no way to reach Harry before the sailor manages.

Two pistols are fired one right after another and Captain Holt shouts over the fading clamor. "Your captain is dead! Surrender and I may let you swear into my crew!"

I hear several swords hit the deck and the battle quiets

further. Harry is distracted by our captain's announcement, but the man has not ceased the assault. The man grabs at Harry's shirt with one hand, and I see a hint of blood-coated silver lifted in his other.

I pull the last of my loaded pistols out of my belt, and stretching my pistol arm between a gap in the bodies around me, I point it at the man towering above Harry, and fire my last shot into his back.

The enemy sailor drops to his knees at the same moment Harry Lewis does.

Harry is holding his guts in his hands, his skin white as a sheet. My young friend collapses to the deck, his face splashing in the puddle of blood we all stand in like the remains of some macabre rainstorm.

I force my way through the surrendering soldiers and my shipmates, heart breaking even as my mind tries to reassure me that all must be well. It *must* be. What sort of world would allow anything to happen to Harry?

Kneeling, I pull Harry's head into my lap. He is still breathing, but only in quick bursts. Panic grips me when I realize I cannot save him. I was not fast enough. Harry will die on the dark, windy deck in a pool of stranger's blood.

"No, no, no. Harry, you promised me. You cannot die here. I have not taught you the rigging." Tears spring to my eyes and my mouth begins talking before my mind can catch up to the words.

My calloused fingers catch on matted blood as I run them through his dark hair. His eyes meet mine, but he is not looking at me. He is looking through me to somewhere or someone I cannot see. My spine shivers as my heart shreds apart. I had not known it was still possible for it to break even more after it was so thoroughly destroyed in the past.

I press my hands against his stomach to staunch the bleeding, only for the blood to flow through my fingers. It is like trying to hold back a river with only my palms.

Harry's voice is so quiet, and the rest of the ship is so loud, that if I were not inches from his lips, I would not be able to hear him.

"I'm gonna meet you there, Ma." Harry's words come between gasps, more air than sound. His eyelids are bruised and fluttering like the wings of a bird. In a moment of clarity his brown eyes lock onto mine. They tell me he is leaving me without any words spoken.

Harry's last breath leaves him in a quaking sigh. His eyes stare at nothing and no one. I do not realize I am screaming until something is wrapped around my shoulders. It takes me several heartbeats to realize it is arms that hold me.

"Easy, Ables. He's gone. Not a thing you can do."

Hugh Digby, of all people, attempts to comfort me, but his words mean nothing. My mind is fixated on the dead boy in my lap. The thought of moving from this spot and leaving Harry alone here is too much. Impossible.

I twist out of the quartermaster's arms to look at the man who killed Harry. I meet the cold, dying stare of the young tar in blue trousers who I shot in the back. His dirty curls are matted with blood. He is breathing in gasps and, like Harry in his final moments, does not see me.

He could have been anyone. He looks like my neighbors, brothers, shipmates. I do not care. He could never have been so good as Harry.

Pulling a dagger from my belt, I rush forward and slit the murderer's throat. Part of me realizes that the young man had a mother, but I hope he never meets her again. I hope his soul, if we have souls at all, burns somewhere alone.

Irrationally, I shout at the dead man. "He was just a kid! A boy!"

I do not care what the men think of me as I weep for Harry, whose snores lulled me to sleep each night. A kid who spent the money he earned from piracy on pipe tobacco and sweets. A boy who was raised for something kinder and better than this.

The quartermaster's arms are around me again and this time I collapse against his chest and sob. "I am the reason he was up here. Gods strike me!"

Hugh Digby pets the back of my head, the way my mother used to when I was small, and speaks gently into my hair. "You have to pull yourself together, Ables."

I know he is right, but how can I?

With shaking fingers, I look up and wipe my eyes. Captain Holt is watching my scene. The sun is just beginning to brighten the cloudy sky behind him, illuminating the terrible battlefield in the middle of the sea. There is work to be done and comforting a member of his crew is not part of his job, but his pained expression tells me he wishes he could do just that.

Mickey stands frozen with wide eyes but a few feet from me, like he might have been too late to save Harry just as I was.

Somehow, I clear my throat enough to croak, "I can't leave him here."

Like an answer to a prayer I never said, James comes and scoops Harry up from the blood on the deck with his long, dark arms.

"Come on, Dix." James motions with his head toward the boats that are already being prepared to return to *Sneaky Lass* with our crew and any prizes worth taking. The two ships having drifted apart during the fighting.

"I..." I do not know what I want to say to him. No words feel adequate to express what I feel, so I return to silence as I so often do.

James just nods at me and uses his chin to motion me to follow him again. All my rage and sorrow spent; the sting in my side intensifies to something deeper. It is a pain unlike any I have experienced before, and I know without looking that I am wounded in a bad way. I sway on my feet but manage to steady myself. With the waning shock comes the realization that I am badly hurt, but as I press my hand tightly to my side to try and hide it, my thoughts drift to the three lucky coins I lost.

I wonder if my luck has run out.

CHAPTER 27

On *Sneaky Lass* it is fairly easy to disappear amongst the shuffle. James does not try to stop me when he sees me vanish below deck. I head to my hammock and gingerly unbutton my vest and lift my bloody shirt to reveal a straight, deep gash stretching several inches along my right side. I am not even certain when it happened, and it does not hurt much. It grows shallower towards my back, but I cannot see the wound's end even as I crane my neck as far as it will go. I can only feel it when I press with tentative fingers. It is bleeding and will need to be stitched.

Lowering myself onto the floor, I slide beneath my hammock and dig through my few possessions. The curved needle I pull through the canvas sails seems impossibly thick, as does the strong, silk thread. It will be like sewing my flesh closed with a nail. I could find someone to help. Mickey already knows, he might help me. But if I take him from whatever work he is doing, he will be missed. Someone might come looking.

I could tell Bennett, but he might just as soon leave me to die than help me.

My hands are shaking, and tears blur my vision, but I know I must do this myself. I want to tell Bennett the truth, but I do not want him to find out like this. I need to survive first.

Forcing my hands steady, I thread the needle and then hold it for a long time over the gash. It is so deep I can see my slick white ribs and it bleeds more with each move I make, each breath I take, each beat of my heart. In a strange way, the wound seems to say *you are alive*. Harry's wound had not been like this one. His was surrender, where mine is begging to be healed.

With a deep breath I push the needle through one side of the fissure and into the other as quickly as I can manage. I bite hard on the insides of my cheeks to keep from crying out, tasting blood.

I had initially planned to sew my wound like I would a sail or a sock, but soon realize that doing so would make the wound crooked and full of too much thread. I cut the line and tie it in a knot, pulling my skin closed like a roast with twine. Another deep breath and I plunge the needle in next to my first stitch. This time is worse because I know exactly what is coming.

Each time the needle pierces my skin it relights a fire in the wound. My bloody hands grow used to the pressure it takes to force it through, but the pain only grows with each stitch I tie.

Blood is everywhere and I move with sticky, trembling fingers. At any moment someone could come down the hatch and find me. The only thing keeping me upright is sheer force of will. I *will* get this wound closed and I *will* survive this.

Sweat drips into my eyes and I wipe it away with my filthy

shirtsleeve. Halfway through closing the wound, for reasons I do not truly understand, I think of my father—Jane's father.

The things that happened to Jane are like a terrible story I once read about someone else.

I think of Jane's brother in a boat full of blue coats, just a boy himself waving goodbye with tears in his eyes. His last words to her were, "*Be good*". I tie another stitch.

I think of how her father would smell of whiskey and throw her mother around the house like a rag doll. I push the needle through again and tie a knot.

I think of Jane's husband's cruel hands and push the thick sail-mending needle through my flesh.

Jane almost wretched on her wedding night. She slit her wrists the same week and woke up in a pool of blood. I push the needle in and back out, tie another knot.

I think of the boy she bore with beautiful blonde hair. She named him Bryce. I tie another stitch.

I choke on a sob and bite my lip until it bleeds to quiet myself.

I am Jane again, kissing the cold earth where my son was buried before running away with nothing because I had nothing worth taking with me.

In and out.

Discovering that the only reliable work I could find was selling myself. My brother's words echoed in my mind with each thrust of my first customers.

Be good. Be good. Be good.

I slide the needle through the other side.

Luring that poor, drunk boy into the alley and leaving him naked in the cold. He belonged to someone, and I took him for scraps.

Three stitches left.

Arriving on *Sneaky Lass* and wrapping my blisters each night feeling a sense of pride in myself for the first time.

Just a little more.

The captain stared at me while I worked, wanted me, wanted Dixon. Called me honest. Called me beautiful. Called my heavy soul beautiful.

One to go.

Contorted at an awkward angle to even reach the back end of the wound, I push the needle in with a groan and then out for the last time with a strangled sigh of relief. I cannot see how it looks.

With the wound closed, I am Dixon again. A sailor, drenched in sweat and blood, both his own and that of others.

The daunting job finally complete, I settle my shirt down over the wound and put away my bloody tools, making a note to remember to clean them later. Then I lean my head back against the side of the ship, too heavy to move anymore. My head is swimming from blood loss and exhaustion.

At the same moment I begin regretting my determination to remain living, the hatch to the deck opens and Hugh Digby pokes his head in and spots me. "It's time to send 'em off. Collect Harry's hammock."

He pauses at the bloody scene before him. I can only imagine what I must look like. White as a sheet, covered in blood, and shaking like a leaf. I imagine I must look like the walking dead. Hugh manages to dig up something resembling concern for me for a second time in one day.

"You okay, Ables?"

The quartermaster motions to everything around, disgusted by the look of me and all the blood around me, but his concern is genuine.

I answer mechanically, "Yes, sir."

Torturously, I stand and untie the hammock and collect the few meager belongings of my young friend. Despite everything I have done today, touching Harry's things with filthy, blood-soaked hands feels like the worst sin of them all; his hammock, his pipe, and a small stone taken from his home's garden that he often held at night. There is a fraying red ribbon I do not know the story to, and a miniature portrait of a woman with the same dark curls as Harry. I place them all in the hammock, grab my bloody set of tools, and try to lift it, only to end up a shuddering mess on the ground from pain.

This is not the bruised eyes or twisted ankles I have suffered through before. This... I have no idea how I am going to get through this.

I painstakingly rise once more and try again, carefully moving one item at a time up the ladder and onto the deck. Last, I climb up and perform the same procedure again to get everything to where Harry lies. No one appears to notice me or my strange means to an end, occupied by their own work or grief.

Harry's body is lined up with the rest of our dead. He appears so small in comparison to the rest. Appallingly small. The sun has risen in full now and the clouds have dispersed. It is hard to believe that last night the wind had howled so hard that cries and screams were stolen from the mouths that made them before anyone could hear. It is difficult to fathom that for days on end rain pressed us into the sea like the thumb of a god. The fine day Harry wished for us last night has come and he is not here to see it.

As soon as everyone is gathered the men will be wrapped in their hammocks like a shroud, a cannon round with them, and overboard they will all go, buried at sea.

Men work on friends and strangers, a duty and honor to stitch the bodies into their makeshift shrouds. The last stitch pushed through the upper lip and nose of the dead, a courtesy to ensure they are truly gone.

The thought of Harry being tossed away so far from wherever his home had been seems especially cruel. Resolve sets into the depths of my ailing body that no one else will touch him. Friendly hands are the last gift I can give him.

Setting Harry's hammock beside him, I maneuver his small body carefully onto the fabric. Working in careful stitches from the bottom, he starts to become cocooned in his bed. I wrap his right hand gently around the portrait and ribbon, while slipping his tobacco-filled pipe into his left. Last, my fingers place the garden stone into his pocket, safe and hidden away just as he kept it in life.

Managing stitches with a steady calm is simple until I reach his face. My hand rests on his cold, pale cheek and a sob escapes me. My vision swims and agony flares within me when I release a shuddering sigh. For a moment, my grief is forgotten, replaced by fear that I might never draw breath again for how terribly it hurts to do so. I am uncertain if the gods are cruel or kind that I manage the task.

Harry is dead beyond a shadow of any doubt. Tradition be damned, I cannot push the needle through him as the others do. Carefully, I tuck his curls away from his face and close the shroud.

Only then do I allow myself to weep.

Tears fall for the boy before me and his suffering, for the entire world that led him to this ship and this life. I sob because the gods, if they exist at all, chose such an unkind fate for Harry. I lament for the woman I left on the docks of Grand Port, for her pain, for Dixon's pain, both of which I suffer in silence. I mourn because the world is unfair and cruel, and I do not have the strength left to fight against it anymore. I cry because I am not the only man crying on deck, and I do not fear judgment for it.

A hand comes to rest on my shoulder. I think it must be Bennett, but when I look, I find Mickey. He is not looking at me, but at Harry's body, sewn into its shroud before me. The second mate kneels beside me and puts a hand on Harry's brow atop the canvas covering it. "I am sorry. I…"

Mickey's eyes fill with tears and his chin quivers. With a long, shuddering exhale, a tear tracks down his cheek. "I had meant to keep you breathing, little villain."

Then the second mate stands and leaves me again as quickly as he came.

By midday, the fallen are committed to the depths with few words and little fanfare. I stay and watch until Harry sinks too deep to see and, even though I do not have any profound words to say, I find something because Harry would smile to know I did.

"Harry Lewis was all marbled with trouble, but he was good in all the ways that mattered."

Men around me nod solemnly, bandanas and caps in hand. Harry was the first body brought back to the ship and was the last to leave it.

Familiar footsteps approach. I cannot muster the energy to stop myself from staring off as Captain Holt speaks softly by my shoulder. "I found these on the other ship. I know you don't have a spare set to change into."

Forcing my eyes from the distant nothing, I find Bennett clean of blood and in fresh clothes, as if the terrible night had not happened. He is holding a new set of clothing out to me like a peace offering.

I take them and allow my fingers to linger on his hands, yearning to fall into his strong embrace and sob, longing for him to comfort me.

But it cannot be.

"Thank you. I had not even thought of it." Looking down at

myself, I realize I probably should have. The sun is setting, the day went by quickly, and I forgot to wash.

"The basin in my cabin is full if you want to wash up."

That he thought of me, found clothing for me, and now offers me respite in privacy makes my worn heart jump a little back to life. He gave me his locket to put safely away. He trusts me and I keep betraying him. I must tell him my secret, but I do not know if I can tonight. I do not have it in me to defend myself, and I know that once he is informed a defense will be necessary.

Excuses, always.

Captain Holt speaks quietly as he leaves so others will not hear. "It has been a long day, and a fight like that is as hard to see the hundredth time as it is the first."

I have nothing to say back to him.

I grab a rag and soap and climb cautiously below deck without drawing any attention to myself. Each movement causes me agony so intense that black dots dance in my vision. I am hauling an anchor, and the eyebolt where its chain meets me is set between my stitches.

In Bennett's quarters, I peel away the ruined clothing from my skin, being especially careful when trying to pry my dried, blood-soaked shirt from my wound. Gingerly, I run sudsy water over the gash on my side and every other inch of me. The wound is angry and swollen, though whether from festering or just the nature of such a wound, I have no way to tell. I have almost no medical knowledge.

Despite the pain, both in my heart and on my person, washing makes me feel human again. The act of sliding new clothing into place over clean skin and buckling the now-stained green belt into place on my hips helps me feel more like myself.

Dropping my old clothes to the floor, I use my feet to mop up the mess to save myself from having to get down on my hands and knees. Scrubbed clean of the gore, I now wear a navy officer's daily wear and it is so clean and pressed that it appears to have never been worn. Already, some blood has stained the shirt from my side.

I drop the blue jacket out the back window, not wanting to ever see one like it again.

Searching Bennett's cabin for anything to bind my chest with, I find nothing. I just have to hope that my waistcoat does a good enough job of hiding all I wish to hide. It also serves to keep me from bending and moving in ways that may pull out any of my hard-won stitches. I will already face enough trouble on the rigs starting first thing tomorrow morning.

Exhaustion coupled with grief is too much. I lean my head against the wall of Captain Holt's cabin and fall asleep.

CHAPTER 28

THE SOUND OF THE CABIN DOOR SQUEAKING ON ITS HINGES STARTLES ME from a heavy sleep. Forgetting my injury, I attempt to jump to my feet, but the poorly stitched wound on my side tears my muscles like a scythe.

My sight goes white and red, and I end up doubled over on the floor panting but taking in no air. I am so focused on my own breathing that I do not see Bennett's reaction. When I finally manage to clear my eyes, he is on the ground beside me, but he looks afraid to touch me.

"What has happened to you?"

I shake my head and gingerly move myself upright once more.

This time, I only see stars. When was the last time I ate or drank anything?

Instead of waiting for him to pour a drink or to offer me a seat, I lower myself to my usual spot at his table and put my head in my hands. I am more drained than ever before in my life. It could be that I am feverish. It has been a long time since I was last ill, but the realization that I am unwell dawns on me as absolute truth.

When Bennett lights several candles to illuminate the space, I watch the shadows skitter away like roaches. The chain around his neck reflects the light and I am relieved to see he returned his locket to its rightful place. If he is wearing the locket, then all must be well.

Bennett clears his throat and pours two drinks.

"James covered for you on deck. You're not the only sailor aboard that needed a moment of respite. We'd have fared better with a surgeon, though. *Maiden's Musket* didn't even have a surgeon to take with us." He pushes a drink towards me when I cannot even muster a nod for him. "Have it, it will help."

I take it all back at once in the hopes that it helps both the mental and physical pain, putting my glass out for him to pour me another. Tonight, the taste and burn do not bother me. I just want to be drunk.

Bennett pours more into my glass and sits down across from me. I take my second drink back immediately, hissing from the pain in my right side the movement brings. Memories of Harry, holding his own insides in his hands, threaten to bring the drink right back up. I clutch my ribs under the table like doing so will hold me together.

Once, my father threw me and I hit the bone above my eye on the leg of the table. It bruised terribly and for days afterwards each time I touched it the world would careen dangerously one way and the other. The same thing happens when I touch my side now. The pain makes me feel dizzy.

Bennett speaks and I am brought from my trance like one being lifted from water. Slow and heavy and dripping.

"My questions are different now than they were before the fight. How badly hurt are you?"

Concern still paints his features. I hesitate and run my finger over the edge of the empty crystal glass. It takes more time than I would like to remember how to speak. "Is that the question you wish to exchange the drinks for?"

"So, it's worse than you would like to let on? Yes, it is the question I am asking."

I cannot show him the wound without giving myself away but I am tired of lying. Never before have I been so close to telling Bennett everything. He trusted me with his locket. It had felt like holding his heart.

The liquor pushes my mouth ahead of my thoughts and I immediately say more than I intended. "I already did the stitching, and they are straight enough. I can sew better than Pax at any rate."

At the mention of stitching Bennett's eyes widen.

"I am certain I will heal, and I will be back to myself in no time at all." I start to backtrack, but it is too little too late.

My mouth feels full of cotton, dry and thick in a way no amount of drink can cure. I do not know if it is from the fever or the lie.

I avert my eyes from his severe stare. He shakes his head, releasing a frustrated huff. "No, it will not be fine. Those navy men rub shit on their swords to kill as many of us as possible. I know it because I have done it. Let me see."

He starts to approach to get a closer look. I nearly fall out of my chair to get further away from him and then a searing burst of white-hot pain wracks my body, everything spinning around me as I am back on the floor again. Bennett takes a startled step back.

I feel like a frightened deer stuck in a trap, and Bennett recognizes that, in this scenario, he is the hunter.

"I will not hurt you, Dixon." There is a panicked edge to his voice and I try to steady my racing heart.

"I know you will not hurt me, Bennett, but I do not want you to see it."

"What will keep you from dying if you will accept no help? It is not shameful to accept help freely given." Speaking through clenched teeth, he struggles to control his frustration.

I almost laugh that Bennett thinks my fatal flaw is pride and not being a wicked liar. It benefits me more than I deserve. Pride is at least something a man can understand.

"You must let me do this my own way, Bennett. I am too stubborn to die. I still have too much to prove."

He is unconvinced and I fear if I do not appease him somehow, he will pin me down and inspect me, consequences be damned. "I cleaned it well enough, I promise. It just smarts because of location, is all."

More lies. They stack up behind me like dominoes ready to topple.

Bennett watches my eyes and movements studiously and nods, returning to his seat. I return to mine as well and I let him pour me another glass even though I already feel sleepy from the first two.

Guilt from keeping so much from him leads me to ask, "Would you like to have another question? I feel I have slighted you with your first."

Bennett smirks in his typical crooked way but it does not reach his eyes, which are still scanning me up and down. "That would break the rules of our game."

I try to find a good enough reason for him to accept my offer. It would be easier for me to let it rest, but I want to be fair to him.

As fair as I can be. "Then you can have my question for tonight because I cannot think of anything."

He takes precious little convincing. "That is gracious of you. I have so many."

I fiddle with my glass and try to keep my eyes focused under my impossibly heavy eyelids.

"Do you remember when you asked me about killing men? I now levy the same to you. You killed men today. Do you feel the weight of them?"

I sip at my drink and cough at the taste, wincing at the pain the motion brings. Bennett stays still. I guess I rebuked him enough times that he has learned not to try to come to my aid.

Once I catch my breath, I look at my glass then meet Bennett's hazel eyes. "I feel the weight of all but two men I have killed in my life."

Bennett gives me a quizzical look. I suppose I never told him that I have killed prior to last night.

"The man who killed Harry and—" I almost said *my husband*. I am too sick and drunk to be safely answering questions. I swallow hard and evade, hopeful that he will not push me further. "Well, and one other. I would kill them both over and over again in slower and more painful ways if I could. I hope they are still suffering wherever it is they have gone."

It suddenly strikes me that both men for whom I feel no remorse earned my wrath by killing innocents.

Bennett does not try to quell my anger with platitudes and, as I hoped, he does not pry for any more detail. He just nods and sips his drink. "I know you were protective of the boy. I'm sorry he is gone."

In my slowed mind it takes me a moment to sort out that he is speaking of Harry and not the baby I buried under the pines of my old home. "I tried to be something safe for Harry."

The image of Harry's shrouded body sinking into the depths

returns to me in full force and I physically shake it away, this time, too drunk to notice whether it hurts my side to do so or not. "He cried at night for his dead mother and carried sweets and seashells in his pockets. He behaved like a man, fought like a man, worked on this ship like a man. Everyone seemed to forget that he was only a kid."

Bennett hesitates before responding. I am too far gone to even begin sorting out why, but he seems uncomfortable with the topic of Harry. "Kids grow up fast at sea. It is a dangerous place. While I offer some shelter to my crew, I would have done him no service by being soft on him."

Pausing for a moment, he changes the subject. "If you have thought of a question, you can still ask one. You have had enough drinks to earn one."

I have had three glasses. I do not think Bennett has taken a single sip.

I can only come up with one question. My thoughts are muddling together and my tongue feels swollen when I speak, but the third rule on the ship's charter is clear to me like a ringing bell. As clear as it has been every day since I signed my name to it.

I could recite it now from memory. *If any man runs away or keeps any secret from this company, he will be marooned with one bottle of powder, one bottle of water, a small arm, and shot.*

Instead of a recitation, I ask, "Have you ever marooned anyone for keeping secrets?"

From the way his brows rise, I have surprised Bennett again. His eyes narrow, not out of suspicion, but to look at me carefully like I may be delirious. Perhaps, I am.

I stand on unsteady legs. Bennett stands as well. I meant to return to my hammock but there is a pull in my chest that makes me take a step towards him instead. The small part of me that knows the truth of things, that realizes I am very much doomed, reminds me that there may not be another chance.

245

Wrapping my arms around his neck, I press my body against his and kiss him with the honest passion I have been suppressing these long months beside him. I can feel the depth of his desire in the heat of his kiss while his tentative arms tell me he does not want to take advantage of my drunken, grieving state. In this moment, I do not let fear rule me. There is plenty of time for fear and precious little time for kissing someone who wants to kiss me back.

His arms circle me, his hands grasping my back and pulling me closer to him. My body alights, the liquor doing a fine job of easing my painful wound just enough that his embrace is tolerable. I can feel him growing harder against me. He is sober. I expect it will not be long before he realizes the physical manifestation of my own arousal does not rise in the same obvious way as his own.

Still, I deepen the kiss and he moans against my lips. Even in my poor state, the sound makes a small, prideful smile tug at the corner of my mouth.

I must stop. Slowly, I move my hands away from the back of his neck, down his shoulders, his arms...

When he releases me from his embrace, I trace my fingers along his palms and watch his face like I might memorize it.

One day soon, when I am dead, perhaps I will remember the planes of his face. Maybe I will remember the way he is looking at me now like he wishes nothing more than to kiss me again. Lust clouds his eyes alongside something I have only ever seen from him: Care. Maybe it is even love. I will tell myself it is love because I might not wake up tomorrow and it is such a nice thought, to die being loved by someone. Even if Bennett only loves a carefully crafted lie.

I step back towards the door and speak as close to the truth as I dare so that if I die in the night, he will know it. "I really care about you, Bennett. Love is a game I do not play, but it is something like love."

There is an unspoken apology in the words: I am sorry I cannot love you. I am sorry it has all gone so far. I am sorry I lied.

He nods, still stunned by my sudden kiss. His fingers dance lightly over his bottom lip like he cannot believe they were truly on mine seconds ago. He opens his mouth to say something back but I leave before I can hear them.

I meant to tell him about Jane. I should have told him. I am too weak to reach my reason for honesty in the whirlpool of reasons to lie.

It feels like the pipe sounds after just moments of rest. Thankfully, the quartermaster is moving even slower than I am, having spent much of the night with Mickey on deck.

Peeling back my shirt, everything is crusted to my wound with yellow, sticky puss. I may have little knowledge of medicine, but I know plenty to be certain this wound is not healing as it should. Uncovering it releases a reek as if something has died and is rotting inside. It is so swollen and red that my angry skin puckers around my stitches. I do not know if it is a good or a bad thing that it no longer hurts.

Up on deck, a new layer of work has been added to the load. Over half the crew is trying to make repairs with wood scavenged from *Maiden's Musket*. James has noticed my slower movements and has been understanding to a point, but he cannot keep me from work altogether with so much to be done.

Captain Holt, among others, watches me through a series of worried glances. No one has time to stop. My limbs feel as though they weigh more than a barrel of water. My will has grown strong on the deck of *Sneaky Lass,* and I dig into those depths to find the fortitude to carry my own weight.

Unfortunately, the world begins crushing me with its weight, too.

James is shouting from above me, but his words come slow and slurred together to my ears. I clench my teeth, moving towards the ratlines to follow him up, before stopping again. I can still hear James' voice but nothing he is saying makes sense. I am so tired that I just want to float in the muffled, weightless place I have traveled to. My eyelids close without my permission.

I have been running for so long. Lies, like monsters, always chasing me. This must be where they catch up.

When I open my eyes, I see Bennett above me. He is shouting over his shoulder. I want to say his name. I want to tell him the truth because I am going to die anyway. All I manage is that unspoken apology from last night. "I am sorry, Bennett."

He smiles, maybe because I am aware enough to speak, and he talks to me like my mother used to when I was a child. "Shush. Try to stay awake, Dixon."

I shake my head and my entire body aches with the effort. "I am sorry I lied."

Someone begins struggling with the buttons on my coat. Then my own hands are pinned to the deck at my sides. They were struggling because I was fighting them. When did I start to do that?

Bennett's eyes do not leave mine even when my shirt is untucked. He keeps reminding me to stay awake, but everything feels so heavy. It is as though the air itself is trying to crush me.

"I have kept secrets."

Am I even speaking? Can he hear me?

I feel someone take the jackknife from my pocket and slice open the bloody canvas I have wrapped around my wound.

Bennett's eyes slide away from mine and down. I close my eyes again and speak the only words I can find one more time. "I am sorry."

There are several shouts of surprise. Gasps. An exclamation, "All the gods and fates together!"

Then I cannot hear anything but ringing in my ears. Then I cannot hear that either.

CHAPTER 29

CRYING.

I hear it crying. A high-pitched wail, full of pain and fear.

There is a baby somewhere in these woods. I search under bushes and piles of firewood to no avail. The crying keeps growing louder and more frantic. I run towards the sound like an animal, desperate to soothe the hidden babe.

My body lurches forward, sending my splayed to the ground.

The crying stops.

I turn around and find I have tripped over a dead lamb, it's fleece bloody from the teeth of some foul beast.

I wake from the nightmare, but I cannot get my eyes to open. I can hear a voice comforting me, I think it is Mickey.

Then, louder, the second mate asks, "Who's Bryce?"

My captain responds from further away. "I've no idea."

Wind blows against my face. Everything has been hot for so many months. Now, I am cold. I am so cold that my teeth are chattering. I open my eyes to see only sky. I hear oars in the water. What lake do we row on? There are a few near the farm.

The sky above me is so blue it is almost like the sea.

Then Hugh Digby is looking down at me. He looks relieved. I cannot muster enough energy to speak.

I struggle against the panic gripping my heart as something holds me down.

People's hands pin me against a table. The wood above me is not that of *Sneaky Lass*. I want to be home.

A familiar voice urges me kindly, "It's okay, but you must stay still."

I cannot find the source of the words. The edges of my vision are spotted with dancing dots, and my head is held straight. Searing pain, the smell of burning flesh. I scream again. I did not know I was capable of such a noise.

Another familiar voice warns that I will wake all of Trinity. Where was Trinity? Have I ever seen it on a map?

A leather belt is pressed between my teeth as they continue their work. I am being torn apart.

Why can I not get away?

Hands.

All over me, there are hands. Someone presses a damp rag to my temple. I open my eyes and see Mickey Compton. He smiles and reassures me softly, "I'm still here, Dix. I'm right here."

I am comforted by his words. If he is here then I am still alive. Why is he here but not Bennett?

Someone in the room says, "It is done. We can only hope she's strong enough to survive it."

She. I do not remember why that word frightens me.

I now seem to live somewhere between sleep and awake. I catch James' voice mid-sentence, "—us all fooled, Dix. Some are right mad. Don't worry, most are just impressed. Even Digby's a little impressed."

Opening my eyes, I find a plain room. I still feel so cold. I do not know why we would sail anywhere so cold.

James notices my eyes are open and gifts me a smile before speaking again. "At least landing on deck didn't strike you dumb. Are you able to hear me?"

I think I manage to nod, and his smile brightens. He holds a cup to my lips, and I swallow every drop of the freshwater, grateful for his help. He nods his head and I close my eyes again, glad to have a friendly voice to listen to.

James chuckles softly. "Too stubborn to die. Told him so."

I said something like that once. Opening my parched mouth, I add in a hoarse whisper, "Too much to prove."

"We are setting sail in the morning."

Bennett.

I open my eyes and see Bennett spinning his locket on its chain in his hand. He has several days of stubble on his jaw. How many days has it been? Where am I?

Trinity. Someone said that.

I cannot make my mouth form any words. Even if I could, I have no drinks to trade for answers. He might not even want to answer me at all.

He meets my open eyes and shakes his head before looking away again. "The surgeon said you will likely live. Your fever has broken. I paid for the room through the week for you."

My mouth feels like I have been eating sand.

I watch how the silver catches the fading sunlight from the window as Bennett continues to toy with the locket.

"We cannot dawdle. You know what chases us. Even if we could wait..." He shakes his head again. The motion fills in any possible ending he had to his statement. Even if they could wait, I cannot come.

He puts his hands down on the end of my bed and the silver light from the locket vanishes. "Your clothing and belongings are under the bed. Your share has been added to your purse."

I choke on my words, but manage to stammer, "My knife?"

He genuinely smiles, like he cannot fathom why I would care. "Yeah, it's there."

For reasons I cannot fully understand, that brings me some peace.

Memories are flooding back. Harry died, I was injured, and we were still days from any land. I fell to the deck, and my secrets have been laid bare to all now.

Trying to sit up, I only manage to lift my head a few inches before I land back on the pillow beneath me. "How long has it been?"

"It's been eight days since you were injured. Five since we got you to Trinity." Bennett is no longer looking at me. The locket is not in his hands anymore, but I did not see him put it around his neck.

There is a mug of water by my bedside. I reach for it and drink with shaking hands. Bennett reaches out to help me hold it steady and, as much as I want to swat him away, I let him. He looks uncomfortable. More uncomfortable than I have ever seen him.

I clear my throat and speak more clearly than before, "You are leaving in the morning?"

He nods and waits for me to continue. If it is decided that I cannot come, then it is decided. I do not want to be told no outright and I will not beg. Pride is the wrong word for what stops me. It is more like fear.

The silence in the room is suffocating.

Bennett releases the pressure by asking the question I am the least prepared to answer. "Why did you not tell me?"

I want to motion to our surroundings, but my arms feel too heavy to lift. I would rather save my strength. Instead, I just state the obvious. "Others were injured. Where are they?"

Bennett cannot argue with the truth. The other men who were injured are still on the ship. They will recover or die there. As soon as it was discovered that I was a woman, I was brought here. I will not be allowed back. It does not matter how good I proved to be at sailing, or how valuable I was to the crew, or even how much Bennett liked kissing me. I am a woman, and I will be left on land. Kinder than marooned, I think.

Still, my answer is only a half-truth and I owe Bennett some explanation. "I never meant to become such a liar."

His hazel eyes return to mine. He does not look angry, but I cannot pin down his emotions. He might be as frightened as I am.

"Was fear the only thing keeping you from telling me? Even with my feelings for you on full display?" He sounds so hurt that I struggle to find my voice.

I whisper to the ceiling, struggling past my rusty throat, "I found myself wanting you close."

Speaking any of these thoughts aloud feels dangerous, but I am already damaged, and I will not likely see Bennett Holt again. He is the only man who has ever maybe loved me, even if it was not me that he loved. He deserves more than lies.

Swallowing hard, I continue, "How many times did I want to just tell you and let the consequences be damned? Countless."

I hate the tears that sting my eyes, but I do not wipe them away. A hollow feeling settles inside my chest when I speak what I have feared far more than anything else. "I thought if you knew you would hate me just like everyone else always has hated me. I thought you would like me better if you knew as little about me as possible."

I find myself wondering if my circling response has answered his question. Whether it does or not matters little at this point. I have said my piece.

He is watching me with disbelief. "You came aboard my ship, and I found myself..."

He pauses to find the right word. I watch as he surrenders to his anger with me. The precise moment when he gives up on trying to understand me is etched onto his features. He growls, "I have been made a fool."

Bennett slips his hat onto his head, his expression hard. He walks away to the door. "Trinity is a good town, Jane."

The way he says my old name feels practiced, careful, and yet clumsy on his lips. He must have found my wanted poster among my things to know it at all.

I would shake my head if it were not so heavy. Even moving my lips to speak feels like a large task, but I manage. "Jane can find work in any port in the world, but it is not the work I want."

The statement is the closest I will come to asking for a place among his crew.

Bennett's eyes shine when he looks back at me from the doorway. If his words were not so cold, I would think he was close to tears.

"What you do is not my business."

I close my eyes, unwilling to watch him go.

Bennett once told me nothing about me could scare him away. I knew at the time that he was wrong, but it still hurts to know I am right. Then, the heartbreak turns to anger. If he does not mean to understand me or to care a moment longer, then I will not give him the benefit of seeing my anguish.

I open my eyes and force myself upright in bed, groaning at the effort. Panting and covered in sweat, I lean against the headboard. My glare lands on Captain Holt, who is lingering in the doorway watching me but refusing to meet my eyes.

Men have come and gone and hurt me all my life. This is no different. "You best go then. Morning comes early." I throw it at him in a tone that I can only hope injures him as he has injured me.

His eyes turn liquid once more and then to stone so quickly I might have imagined it. I want to beg him to stay. I want to apologize for lying again and again. I want him to carry me back to the ship if that is what it takes to get to my seat at his table.

Instead, I set my jaw. "You have already dawdled with me too long."

The captain tips his hat, shuts the door, and leaves without another glance. If I were not so weak and furious, I would cry.

Instead, I shiver and rest against the cool, wooden headboard. I have the room for a week. I will take time to rest and regain my strength. There are other ships that need riggers, and Dixon is skilled enough to get a job on one of them.

Settling back down into bed, a metallic *thunk* sounds through the empty room as something falls from the mattress. I scan the floor and spot Bennett's silver locket forsaken on the hardwood.

FEATHERS AT SEA, THE SILVER LOCKET BOOK 2 IS AVAILABLE FOR PRE-ORDER NOW

Her ruse uncovered, Jane finds herself in exile from the home and family she found aboard *Sneaky Lass,* marooned on the island of Trinity.

What little money she had now gone, Jane's options are to find a livelihood or starve.

The pirate sloop *Deceit* is anchored off the coast. Helmed by a notoriously mad captain. His lethal crew is leaving their mark across Trinity's many brothels.

Left with no other options, Jane dusts off Dixon Ables, the boyish disguise that got her kicked off *Sneaky Lass,* and desperately prays for a different outcome.

Deceit's first mate, Tom Heath, suspects Dixon is more than he seems. Realizing too late that there is no honor among these thieves and murderers, Jane finds her position aboard *Deceit* to be more captive than crew.

Opportunities for escape buckle under Tom's scrutiny. Jane resorts to leaving desperate missives in her wake with the hope they cool the ire of *Sneaky Lass* captain, Bennett Holt, enough for him to reconsider her position on his ship... And in his life.

Captain Holt, reeling from heartache brought on by Jane's deception, has sailed away. The sour feeling in his stomach over leaving Jane behind intensifies when he finds her notes, each more dire than the last, scattered throughout brothels and docks where the infamous vessel, *Deceit,* has anchored.

The irony of Dixon-turn-Jane being on *Deceit* is not lost on him, but is her violation of his trust worthy of being caught in the hands of a crew feared, even among pirates, for their ruthless cruelty?

Is it worth risking his loyal crew for someone who deceived them all and broke his heart?

About Kennedy Sutton

Kennedy Sutton is an emerging author of period romance. *The Sneaky Lass* is her first published work as part of a rapid release of a series she has spent the better part of the last two years writing.

She grew up in a small town in Wyoming and spent her youth wishing she was somewhere big and full of people. She now lives in one of the largest cities in the United States and is seeking an opportunity to find a small town again.

She has always been full of stories, but it was not until she became a mother that she started writing them down. She is thrilled to now share them with the world.